To Christine
Enjoy and God bless!
DC Nelson

AT DOBSON'S CROSSROADS

Book One In The Bethany Series
DG NELSON

AT DOBSON'S CROSSROADS

TATE PUBLISHING
AND ENTERPRISES, LLC

At Dobson's Crossroads
Copyright © 2014 by DG Nelson. All rights reserved.

No part of this publication may be reproduced, stored in a retrieval system or transmitted in any way by any means, electronic, mechanical, photocopy, recording or otherwise without the prior permission of the author except as provided by USA copyright law.

This novel is a work of fiction. Names, descriptions, entities, and incidents included in the story are products of the author's imagination. Any resemblance to actual persons, events, and entities is entirely coincidental.

The opinions expressed by the author are not necessarily those of Tate Publishing, LLC.

Published by Tate Publishing & Enterprises, LLC
127 E. Trade Center Terrace | Mustang, Oklahoma 73064 USA
1.888.361.9473 | www.tatepublishing.com

Tate Publishing is committed to excellence in the publishing industry. The company reflects the philosophy established by the founders, based on Psalm 68:11,
"The Lord gave the word and great was the company of those who published it."

Book design copyright © 2014 by Tate Publishing, LLC. All rights reserved.
Cover design by Junriel Boquecosa
Interior design by Gram Telen

Published in the United States of America

ISBN: 978-1-63122-601-4
1. Fiction / Romance / Historical / 20th Century
2. Fiction / Romance / General
14.05.14

In the bleakness of the Second World War, there was a family that bound together. When all else failed, they met together at the crossroads.

—DG Nelson

To those individuals, like Bethany, who sacrificed of themselves for a better world for us all, and to those soldiers and families who still sacrifice today.

ACKNOWLEDGMENTS

First and foremost, I'd like to thank my children, Ashley and Zack, who continue to be my support during my quest to reach my dreams. To Amber, Danny, Maggie, and Mike—the best siblings anyone could ask for. For my niece Ashlee, the other author in the family. Love you, Mommy. Miss you, 303! Thanks for always being there, Heather. Much thanks to Windsor Square Retirement Center for their tremendous support and guidance in collecting valuable information from those who were there. Special thanks to Donna Chumley for having faith in me. Joseph and Patti, I couldn't have done it without you. Lastly, thank you to my God, for the patience to reach the last chapter and the humility to let it be read.

PROLOGUE

LONDON, 1939 (PREWAR)

Scotland Anthony Jenkins raced to the door of the family manor with backpack tightly strung over his right shoulder. He considered himself a master at multitasking and his mother watched in horror from the kitchen doorway as Scott attempted a one-foot hop, left shoe tie, hair combing - head dive over the marble floor. He reached the front door and felt that, in all honesty, he'd have managed all the way to the door without injury if not for tripping on the floor covering with that final hop. Placing his right hand against the wall for support, Scott made one last attempt to pull his left sneaker up without any more mishaps, giving the shoelace another tug for good measures.

"If you're late for school again, I'll tan your hide," Scott heard his grandfather growl from the library. "Being a Jenkins means succeeding in everything we do. I will not accept but the best from you at all times. Do not disappoint me again, you little bounder!"

Scott mumbled something under his breath and placed his left foot on the floor. The young man was stubborn in his thinking, even at seventeen, and his mother often told him he was more like his grandfather than he would ever admit. However, Scott didn't believe he was anything like the man he grew up with. Bradley Jenkins was ruthless and without scruple—a man who would conspire against anyone if in his way of success. Naomi was very closed-minded when it came to his grandfather, or so he thought anyway. Scott believed he only inherited Bradley's bullheadedness. When the mind was set, there was no changing it—for either of them.

He noticed his mother's movement out of the corner of his eye and sighed. After one last brush through his dark hair, he replaced the comb in his back pocket, sighed, and turned to his mother. There were many features Scott shared with his mother, including dark hair and an athletic build. Both also shared a unique tenderness toward others and a deep desire to please. But there was a dark side to Scott as well. He found himself in trouble many times during the course of his teen years while running with the wrong crowd, and even managed to break the law a few times. If it wasn't for his best friend, William Hill, Scott knew he would still be walking down a path of self destruction.

Naomi, without words, held up a brown paper bag and gave a soft smile. Scott grinned and realized he had, once again, almost suffered starvation over the course of the day if not for his mum. Naomi met Scott halfway and her frail fingers offered the bag to her son.

"I have another doctor's visit so I may not be here when you return from school." Her voice sounded tired and drained with the slow recovery from her recent battle with pneumonia. "Your grandfather is right, Scotland. You have been late almost every day this week."

"Not so loud, Mum. The last thing I want is for Grandfather to hear either of us admit he's right on anything." It was silent for a moment. "Mum, being part of the council does not give him benefit of being right on everything."

"No, my love, he is not always right. However, he is your grandfather and deserves a little respect…even from his seventeen-year-old grandson."

"Is it disrespectful to have an opinion?" Scott took a few steps back. "Mum, this war isn't going to end in a room with a number of political patrons flapping their gums. One day the Nazi party will find their way to England—and then what?"

"How does a conflict between you and your grandfather have anything to do with the Nazis?"

Scott chose his words very carefully. "Because, Grandfather's interest is only in something that has a pound or two attached. His decisions are based on financial gain and that is what contributed to the start of this war. It's coming, Mum, whether it's financially logical or not. And, to be perfectly honest, sometimes I feel as if he and I are on the wrong sides in just about everything, I suppose." Scott tucked in his shirt and glanced at her again. "It's like Churchill says, we need to step out of our ignorance and prepare to meet the enemy on our terms."

Naomi studied her determined young man. "I wish you spent as much energy on your grades as you seem to do on politics."

"You don't see what I see. Sometimes I feel you spend too much time defending him."

She looked down at her hand towel. "I simply try to be the peacekeeper."

"Will you ever come out of his grip and think for yourself?" Scott sighed. "I guess the moment you let him drive my father away you answered that question, aye then?"

Her son's words cut deep. "There is a lot you do not know and could never understand, Scotland."

Scott opened the door forcefully. "I don't mean to disrespect anyone. But, yes, there is a lot I cannot understand. Not because I haven't tried, but because this family has an overwhelming knack for keeping secrets."

"I don't wish to have this conversation with you, Scotland. Perhaps one day, but not now."

"Why? Because you are afraid it will lead to questions about my father again?" He noticed the hurt present on his mum's face. This was only one of many conversations they shared about his father that went nowhere. As he got older, he realized that, perhaps, his questions would remain unanswered forever. He could see the hurt in her eyes each time he brought the topic to the table. Scott sighed aloud and pulled the door open.

Naomi stood silent as her son disappeared behind the solid mahogany doors into the central courtyard. She gazed at the white and discoloring marble floor, sadly shaking her head. With her hand trembling uncontrollably, Naomi reached to her left brow. The manor was still, with only the sounds of her father's shuffling drifting into the empty lobby from his study. She stood alone and knew her son was right. Bradley Jenkins, her father, had always been a selfish man. His actions, even before Scotland was born, sealed her fate to a life of loneliness. Scotland had a right to his answers. Yet, her own fears prevented the honesty she knew her son deserved. He was becoming a man, and Naomi knew this conflict between Scotland and his grandfather was only beginning. The forty-five-room manor made her feel small, insignificant, and very much alone. She sighed again and moved up the long hallway. The swinging doors bounced wildly as she returned to the deafness of the silent kitchen.

Scott reached the enormous cast iron gates that protected the manor. There were, of course, many more well off than the Jenkins family. But, from the street, passersby would consider him very fortunate indeed. The courtyard, although extremely neglected with the loss of the groundskeeper recently, remained beautiful with blooms and ground coverings. The sound of a roaring trolley filled the streets as Scott stepped onto the sidewalk that led away from the family manor. Scott was startled by the grasp of a hand to his arm, and felt his heart skip a beat as he met the eyes of an older man dressed in a top hat and a long overcoat. The Englishman was obviously very high classed and educated by first impressions. Scott's arm became numb.

"Might you be Scotland Jenkins? Please do not be alarmed." The man was in his mid-forties with a mustache that seemed to curl with his smile.

Scott stared annoyingly at the hand still gripping his arm. The man pulled away. "Forgive me."

"I'm Scott Jenkins. What can I do for you?" Scott asked suspiciously with slight annoyance.

The man placed his hands in the pockets of his overcoat. "I only require a moment of your time—that is, if you can spare?" The man gained no response from Scott and so continued. "I do not wish to be intrusive, but merely to give you a special invitation."

"Might I ask, invitation from whom?"

The man snickered. "Why, Sir Winston Churchill, of course," he said quickly.

"Churchill has sent you to speak with me? To what end would he have any interest at all in me?"

"I can understand your suspicion. Scotland, Churchill spent these last months, since Poland fell, trying to derive a plan to form a sort of resistance, if you will. Your name came highly recommended."

Scott folded his arms and considered the man's words very carefully.

"Mr. Jenkins, we feel it is only a matter of time before Britain is invaded. Before that day comes, Churchill intends to develop a resistance under the radar to work inside the perimeters. I cannot give much detail, only to say that members of the auxiliary unit will be an important weapon in fighting this war. But it will also be very risky. I can also tell you that this resistance is one of many established in various locations throughout Britain already," he said, throwing his head outward.

Scott watched as the man extended his arm to offer him something.

"If you're interested, then take this card to the Highworth Post Office in Wiltshire. The postmaster will know what to do."

Scott intercepted the card, still eyeballing the man. "How do you know I can be trusted?"

The man chuckled, nodded, and returned his hands to his overcoat. "I have been watching you, Master Jenkins. You have a dedication to what you perceive as right, a sort of personal obligation to play the hero, if you will. I saw you the other day, the way you came to the aid of that homeless man in the city. People can rely on you to get the job done. Your worth is being wasted where it can do some good for your country. Scotland, there are about three thousand people—men, women, even children, some very close to you, already a part of the Auxiliary Unit. All like you, with strong will and persistence, attributes needed to make this unit work."

"Who are these people close to me?" Scott demanded.

"We all have a part to play in what's coming, Scotland. It is time you found where your place is in this war. We want to simply offer you a few choices. If you choose not to go, well then, I wish you my best. Men like you are needed to save Britain, my lad." The man paused, turned, and moved up the street only to vanish as he reached the corner.

Scott noticed that the card in his hand contained the address and name of the postmaster in Highworth. Scott's name and the initials WLSC were written on the back in light pencil. Scott gazed at the initials for a long moment only to be interrupted by a loud voice echoing across the street.

"Come on, mate, or we'll be late again. I thought you were meeting me at my flat?" William Hill called and raced across the street toward Scott.

Scott looked over the empty street again, confused, and placed the card in his pocket. "Sorry, mate."

William pushed his dangling blond curls from his eyes. "What is up with you these days?"

NORTH CAROLINA, 1943 (POSTWAR)

"Scott…Scott, will you wake up!" Jeffrey Davies shook him again. Scott opened his eyes, stared at the bus ceiling a moment, and finally remembered where they were. His head came off the headrest and glanced at the soldier sitting next to him.

Jeffrey pointed out the window. "Look at all that snow!" His excitement elevated as the miles and miles of farmland passed by. "Oh man, I can taste Mama's home-baked biscuits now." He looked back at Scott. "What was going on with you anyway? That must have been some dream."

Scott grinned and sat up, feeling a sharp pain in his lower back from the vast hours of sitting. "Everyone dreams." He pulled an apple out of his bag with a look of disappointment, examining the unappetizing thing. "Are we stopping soon? I need to get out of this bus for a while." He grinned again and threw the apple back in his bag.

Jeffrey gazed out the window again. "We haven't even reached Forsyth County yet. I'm sure we'll be stopping for a break soon." He hit Scott on the arm. "Look, buddy, I'm really glad you changed your mind and came along. You're going to love my family." Jeffrey sighed and sat back in his seat. "I imagine Taylor is ready to have that niece or nephew of mine any day. And my little brothers are probably driving Papa absolutely crazy as always. I've been mostly thinking about my sister Bethany. Things have been hard for her this last year. Fair warning, Bethany can be very outspoken. She has a big mind of her own."

Scott groaned, attempting to massage the knot in his neck. "Sounds like every woman I have ever come across, mate."

"She has a stubborn streak a mile wide. In fact, I'm a little nervous about getting the two of you together because you're both so much alike."

Scott stared at the floor as the other half dozen passengers talked amongst themselves. A woman with her two children sat across the aisle from Scott and the boy watched him with great interest. With a smile, Scott took an apple out of his bag and held it up to the boy's mother questionably. The woman nodded with a smile, and Scott handed the apple to the boy. He retrieved two additional apples from his bag and handed them to the boy as well. He turned to Jeffrey. "I still don't know why I let you talk me into this, mate."

"It's not like you had anything better to do for the next few weeks. It'll be good for you to spend some time with a real family. I think you've become quite a recluse."

"And you think staying on a farm is going to help build my social life?" Scott laughed. "You have been smoking what the Krauts are dishing out, bloke."

"I've been worried about you. Since England, you've seemed very uptight. You need to relax, stop taking things so seriously, and forget about the war for a while."

Scott shifted positions and grinned. "Mate, take a look around, all I see is passing cows. We're as far from the war as you can possibly get. You really are a farm boy, aren't you?"

"I would be very careful not to make comments like that in front of Bethany. Let's just try to relax and enjoy this visit, okay? Who knows how long it'll be before I earn enough points to come home again." Jeffrey's voice became soft and sad.

Scott nodded, noticing the concern in his friend's voice. "Sure, mate," he said, studying him closely. "Jeffrey, you okay?"

"Just going to be good to be home, that's all. It's been almost a year and I'm looking forward to being a civilian for a while." Jeffrey placed his head against the window and gazed out at the countryside. "I've lived on this land my whole life. But it took going to war to realize how good it is to have a home to go to." Jeffrey looked over his shoulder at Scott. "It must be hard knowing what London looks like since the Blitz."

Scott brought his boot up and slammed it over the spider that had, only seconds earlier, started for cover under the seat. "London hasn't been home for a long time. Besides, home is where you hang your hat, right?" He smeared the bug deeper into the floor and looked up at Jeffrey.

Scott protected himself emotionally, but Jeffrey knew deep down who his friend was. Jeffrey met Lieutenant Scott Anthony Jenkins under awkward circumstances the year before. Although an extremely disciplined soldier, Jeffrey admitted he could get bored very quickly. One particular evening, following a nice bowl of rice and beans, Jeffrey and a few of his friends saw fit to place an explosive in the latrine. Logically, the latrine would be visited many times following a meal like that. The 101st had landed after a secret military operation with their intentions on using the facility. In all fairness, Jeffrey had no idea Scott would be the first caught with his pants down.

Other soldiers questioned what to make of Scott, the arrogant English-born twenty-two-year-old who, somewhere, had an American father. Many thought him to be a reckless paratrooper that volunteered for every assignment no one else wanted. He was, by all rights, suicidal and careless in his own safety. Everyone learned soon that if a job needed to be done, Scott was the man to make it happen, and he earned as much respect as he gave. Although that didn't keep Jeffrey from starting the night off with a black eye, by any means. But Jeffrey knew he had it coming to him and it became the beginning of a great friendship.

The more Jeffrey got to know him, the more he wondered what events in life had turned Scott into the hard shell man he was, and couldn't imagine Scott to always have been that way. Although the topic was brought up many times, Scott never seemed comfortable speaking of his life before Germany invaded Britain—or the past at all, for that matter.

Jeffrey only knew that, over time, Scott had become the best friend he ever had. He knew that, no matter what, Scott was someone he could trust, respect, and ultimately count on under even the most extreme situations. Scott had become his brother and always had his back. For that, Jeffrey felt very fortunate, but wished that he could do as much for his friend as Scott unselfishly did for others. Jeffrey knew he would have never made it through the year without his friend and told his parents that very thing in a recent letter announcing his homecoming.

Jeffrey looked down at the dead spider with sympathy and turned toward the window again. "Hard to believe a war is going on when I look out the window. Maybe if the enemy could see this place, they'd change their mind about war. Do you think there's a chance it'll end before we're sent back to Europe?"

Scott stared at the rivets in the floorboards. "Only way the war will end is if we go over there and end it," he said in a whisper, looking up at his friend. "Hitler still thinks he's superior. Until we change his mind, or he's dead, this war will never be over."

Jeffrey looked over his shoulder shockingly. "How can you be so sure?"

Scott stared at the back of the seat in front of him. "Hitler's not the only man in the world with the belief he's entitled to whatever he can dream up. No way to change the mind of a man like that except to just end him. I hope I'm there when it happens."

Jeffrey paused, a little taken off guard, and replaced his head against the window. "Don't talk much about the war in front of Mama and my sisters, okay? That kind of talk will only upset them."

"What else do you expect me to talk to them about, mate?" Scott crossed his arms and looked around the bus with the look of boredom.

"You're right. We should work on your social skills while we're here," Jeffrey said, covering himself with his jacket. He placed the back of his head against the seat and closed his eyes. "Might as well relax, we still have a ways to go."

Scott picked up the magazine he must have looked at ten times over the course of their travel. "That's just wonderful to hear." Scott's sarcasm very apparent. "Your sister, Bethany, is she pretty?"

Jeffrey laughed. "Very, but I suggest you just stay far away from Bethany, for your own safety! If you take another nap, let's try to keep the dreaming down to a low level, all right?"

Scott nudged him and Jeffrey laughed again.

CHAPTER 1

DOBSON'S CROSSROADS, NORTH CAROLINA, 1943

"Move it, you stupid cow!" Joshua Davies tugged as hard as a nine-year-old could on the rope of Old Gracie's mouthpiece. Gracie had gone from the Davies's first milking cow to a member of the family, and as the years passed, the farm had expanded from one Jersey to over fifty. But Gracie had maintained the position as their first and so was special. However, for some reason, Gracie had been on her own schedule all morning, and the twins had lost all patience.

"Oh, this is taking forever!" Joshua shouted as he tugged on Gracie's rope, stretching it as far as it could possibly go.

Gracie managed a few steps ahead before stopping to take a moment to enjoy a bite of sweet grass peeking from under the fresh fallen snow. Her eyes widened and she lifted her head with a loud bellow as Jacob slammed his body against her backside.

"Move, you silly beast!" Jacob slammed against her again. Gracie looked at the boy's and simply took another bite of grass.

Jacob continued slamming himself against Gracie's hiney, grinding his teeth, with no luck. "What are you doing up there? Pull, for pity's sakes!"

"I am pulling, dummy!" Joshua tugged harder and stomped his foot. "Move your hiney, Gracie!"

The two nine-year-olds looked toward the farmhouse at their older sister who was mocking them from the top of the wraparound porch. "You know what they say about the blind leading the blind?" Bethany Jean Davies smirked loudly, her beautiful smile grinning from ear to ear as she threw her long chestnut hair over her shoulder and shook her head. She pushed a small paper bag under her arm and pulled her gloves tightly around her wrists, then moved down the steps toward her twin brothers. "Didn't Mama send you two out here to milk that old cow over an hour ago?"

Joshua sneered and pulled harder on the rope of Gracie's mouthpiece. "She won't budge dang nabbit!"

Jacob's heels dug deep into the dirt as he pushed his body against Gracie's hiney. Jacob and Joshua Davies, identical twins, shared their older sister's chestnut hair and blue eyes, but many times could surpass her stubbornness without any difficulty. Mischief seemed to locate the brothers without much effort on their part. Although very mature at the age of nineteen, and seldom stooped to childish games, Bethany felt it would be a shame to lose an opportunity to annoy the twins when the situation allowed. Her laughter echoed down the dirt drive when Jacob began making screeching noises.

Jacob pushed with a grunt. "Joshua, will you pull already!"

"I am!" Joshua tugged harder. "She won't budge an inch!" Joshua moaned with teeth clenched and gave a hard tug on the rope to no avail.

Bethany laughed hysterically as she made her way up the long driveway. "What good are nine-year-olds if you can't even get a cow into a barn?" Shaking her head in disbelief, Bethany continued up the drive as she sent a fleeting look back at her brothers. "I'm off to town. Am I to assume I'll find you here, still working your way to the barn by the time I return?"

Joshua loosened his grip on the rope and gave his sister a mean glare. "You think you're so clever. Why don't you get this fat cow into the barn yourself?"

Bethany tossed the brown bag in the air and the sound of bottle caps jiggling echoed over the street as she ignored her younger brother's comment. "If the two of you could only see how silly you look!"

"Yeah, well…you should have been here earlier." Jacob's snotty tone emerged, as it always did, when perturbed. "David Carson came by looking for you." He stuck his tongue out. "Na-Na, Bethany has a boyfriend." The cow took a few steps forward and suddenly stopped again. Jacob found himself face down with a mouthful of snow, pulling Joshua down with him.

Bethany laughed and shook her head. "Good grief!"

Still laughing, she moved up the long stretch of fence that ran along the driveway. Bethany could still hear her brothers' ranting as she reached the old tree house, located at the end of the drive and high above the old oak tree. Joshua and Jacob became even more persistent as they, once again, were forced to push Gracie along. Bethany did notice, after evaluating the distance between her brothers and the location of the barn door, they most surely would have the cow inside by the time she finally returned. Bethany laughed again, wishing she could witness their attempt to milk the moody animal.

The old tree house took a beating over the years, but this winter had been brutal. She and Jeffrey erected the tree house with fragments of wood she talked her papa out of when she was seven. The small scrappy-looking thing dangled ten feet high in the branches of the oak tree and was no more than a shell now, with fragments of wood missing or relocated at the trunk of the tree. Deer prints covered the snow around the tree, vanishing into the heavily wooded area leading away from the farm.

The tree house was the first place Bethany ever communicated to her cousin, Whitney, her desire to be a teacher. Only a few years earlier, she had also told Whitney of her first kiss with David Carson. Although Bethany didn't find the kiss impressive, she really had nothing to compare it to, and was sure his talents in that particular area wouldn't improve much no matter how hard he tried.

Once, she and her older brother Jeffrey shared a long heart-to-heart discussion in the solace of the oak tree. She was confused about her feelings for David. However, it was difficult taking a conversation like that seriously with your older brother. In the end, she felt perhaps her relationship with David shouldn't be measured by simple pleasures, like knowing where to put your lips, or even the understanding in how the tongue fit into the scheme of things. So she decided to give David a second chance. His misconceptions found his hands all over her, and that was that.

It was days following the slap upon his left cheek before David Carson had any desire to speak to her again. Bethany never had anyone grab her in such a manner and wondered if she had truly loved him, would her reaction to his touch been different. Her belief was in sacraments between a man and a woman, how some things were shared only in marriage. Yet, she couldn't help but wonder where that day would have taken them had she not been so firm in her beliefs. As it turned out, slapping him was the best decision she ever made in that relationship.

She decided to take a shortcut through Grand and Grams' pasture which led her past the old hosiery factory just outside of town. The factory was one of the largest distributions of jobs in Dobson's Crossroads. However, as the war came to be a reality, the large facility ceased to distribute garments and became a booming parachute factory. Now, most of the work done in the facility was completed by women and men too old to lend their hand as a soldier in the war.

When her grandparents first came to Dobson's Crossroads, they claimed five hundred acres of the best farm land in Dobson. Over the course of time, their four sons split four hundred acres to begin their own homesteads. The shortcut came in handy when Bethany needed a quick trip to town.

Kip Gardner, or "Mr. Late As Usual," as most called him, waved in her direction as he headed to his shift at the factory. "Good morning, Bethany! How is that father of yours?" His wrinkly fingers were discolored by the cold.

"He's very well, Mr. Gardner," she hollered back.

"Will you be singing in church services this Sunday? Sure do enjoy that beautiful voice of yours!" Gardner had a deep tone that came in particularly handy when trying to speak over the whistle of the horn coming from the mill, sadly announcing the man's late arrival once again.

"Thank you. Yes, sir, same time as usual!" She waved again. "Have a good day, Mr. Gardner."

Gardner sent her a final wave as he moved toward the factory swinging his lunchbox and whistling a happy tune, with no apparent concern over his punctuality. Reaching down to pull his britches up over his meatless body, Gardner began to whistle again and twirled his lunchbox in time to what sounded like his own version of "Dashing Through the Snow." Hitting himself in the head with the metal lunchbox during a miscalculated twirl, he quickly looked Bethany's way to discover he had, in fact, been awkwardly seen by her. With a chuckle, Gardner waved again. He ran his fingers through his stringy, greasy, and graying hair, his pace quickening once he realized the front of the factory had been cleared and all others had gone inside without him. Gardner nearly tripped over his own feet picking up his pace.

Bethany covered her mouth, giggling as she headed up the trail that led to the back of the doctor's office. Dr. Conrad Malone had been around almost as long as Dobson's Crossroads. Her mama often said Doc must have slapped the behinds of nearly every butt in town assisting their arrival into the world. When she spotted Mayor Hicks standing in front of city hall, she couldn't help but giggle aloud. Some of the town's folks would have been more work for Doc Malone to bring into the world than others, if her mama was right.

The mayor's belly wobbled when he spoke, and by the looks of his jiggling torso, he seemed to be having a very intense conversation with Myrtle and Molly, the old spinster Bryant sisters. Mayor Hicks had a habit of holding his enormous belly when he laughed and his short legs seemed to disappear somewhere underneath him. When the man wasn't giving long-winded speeches or gossiping around town, he could be found at the café giving his advice on a newfound recipe the sisters had discovered.

The Bryant sisters shared bowl-shaped faces and pea-shaped eyes, and both carried an enormously pointed nose. Bethany had never seen anything like it and always had a chuckle or two whenever she came across the ladies. Molly was tall and thin as a stick while Myrtle was as wide as she was tall. Ironically, Molly was the cook between the two and owned the local café across the street. Both had half ownership in Myrtle's Bed-and-Breakfast, which was connected to the café. If town's folk had a liking for the most recent gossip, those were the ladies to see.

The shops were connected by a long boardwalk on either side, with city hall situated at the very end of Main Street, between the doctor's office and the library. The two-level building stood high and its shadow fell over the rest of the town. City hall was the oldest building in Dobson next to Korner's Folly and was the grandest of all buildings with its high-rises, chandeliers, and solid oak door panels. The building had been recently whitewashed with the help of donations from a special church fund. The beatification included flowers of assortment as one approached the building, but goes unnoticed now as snow spilled over the flower beds, drowning the annuals and perennials.

The group conversation consisted of the most recent happenings in Europe—not that Bethany had to eavesdrop in any way with their voices echoing into the street. She hurried along in hopes of preventing any long-winded conversations with the trio that would hinder accomplishing the morning mission in a speedy manor. Managing to sneak past nearly undetected, she stopped at the scrap metal collection site located in front of city hall. Bethany added the brown bag of pop caps to the collection and made her way up the boardwalk in the direction of the library.

If there was any place that Bethany could feel content, it was at Dobson's library. Although not as large as the one in Durham, it suited her thirst for literature. She rarely left without collecting a handful of reading materials. Bethany spent an hour reviewing the new release section and then brought her book choices to the checkout counter where Kristina Keegan was working at the printing press just inside the next room. Kristina cleaned the ink blots off her hands and began the task of checking out Bethany's books for her.

"Here you are, Bethany." Kristina pushed her glasses up and placed the books in a nice pile for Bethany, scooting them over the counter toward her. "How has your family been holding up with Jeffrey and Patrick so far away?" The library, as small as it was, contained the newest updated versions of literature by the most popular authors of the time. On any given day, however, the library was seldom utilized by many people.

Bethany pulled her books tightly into her chest and attempted to ignore the obvious snoring coming from Mike McCain's table in the far corner. The man had a history of coming to the library for, as he called it, a moment of rest. Apparently, Mrs. McCain's badgering over his continued laziness sent the man seeking refuge at the library nearly every other day.

"Not as often as I'd like, I'm afraid. Usually by the time a letter reaches us, it's a month or so old. Taylor received a letter from Patrick a few days ago, and he was still in Hawaii. She's upset, of course, that Patrick won't make it for the birth of the baby. Jeffrey has been stationed somewhere in England the last we heard."

Bethany noticed Kristina's gloomy stare. It was no secret the librarian and owner of the *Crossroads Chronicle* had a huge crush on her older brother. "Have you heard from Jeffrey since he left?" Bethany asked, attempting to take Kristina out of her trance.

Kristina moved her wavy blond hair behind her ear and softly nodded. "I've received a few letters. But they're so few and far between. I guess he sounds fine—I don't know, folks say sometimes soldiers make things sound better than they really are. You know, protecting their family from worry and all." She smiled, moving her eyes back to the counter. "He sent me a picture a few weeks ago. He sure is handsome in his uniform, isn't he?"

The honking sound of a man immensely deep in sleep echoed throughout the library and, after a few pauses between hoots, the old man became silent again with his face pointed upward.

"Jeffrey said in Mama's last letter he was hoping to come home for a visit soon." There was an awkward silence and Bethany decided to change the subject. "I read your article on people in the city cheating on the rationing. It's a shame. After all, it's our soldiers who really suffer. It's our job to make sure they get everything they need."

Kristina nodded and pushed her glasses up again. "Oh, my goodness, did you hear about the POW's at Camp Butner and Fort Briggs?" Kristina threw her head in the air. "I was beside myself when Penny Henderson told me."

"No, I didn't hear anything." Bethany seemed confused. "What do you mean?"

"Our men are being killed by the Germans and we're feeding them like they're part of the community, that's what I mean!" Kristina placed her hands on her hips. "You know, of course, that Derek Carson is one of the largest sponsors of the POW camps, I'm sure? Why, just yesterday, I saw him in town getting some supplies and he had two of those POWs in the back of his truck."

Bethany shook her head in disgust. "Our boys are sleeping in mud and rain without a hot meal and we're housing Germans?"

Kristina nodded her head angrily. "We most certainly are. And that's not all by any means. Carson is supporting the

Germans while our own town folk are fighting to keep what we have." Kristina placed the daily newspaper on the counter. "See here, Frank Madison came in yesterday. He's putting an ad in the paper to sell the land around Dobson's Pond." Kristina nodded vigorously as Bethany's eyes widened. "He was heartbroken, but the bank is calling on his mortgage, and he can't pay. Isn't that just like Carson—to help the Germans, but turn his back on his own community?"

Bethany nabbed up the paper and read a few lines of the article. "That land has been in the Madison family for generations! Leave it to Derek Carson to take advantage of making a buck at someone else's expense."

Kristina squeezed her hand. "Sadly, Derek is a very powerful man in this town, and his son David is just as greedy. You and David Carson—difference between night and day if you ask me. I was genuinely worried the whole year the two of you were together. I could never understand what you ever saw in him. Granted, he's very charming with as much money as arrogance, but I don't believe he ever treated you properly, not once. Did you know that Jeffrey wanted to beat the tar out of that boy the way he mistreated you? Then, when Jeffrey found out what David did to you that night, oh, my goodness. Why, David's lucky Jeffrey didn't just let him have it!" Kristina took off her printer's apron and smoothed the front of her pink floral dress, joining Bethany on the other side of the counter.

Bethany shrugged. "I'm just glad I saw the poor choice I made before it was too late. I best get going. It sounds like a storm out there." She turned toward the door and Kristina hurried behind her.

"Bethany, if you hear from your brother, will you tell him I asked over him?" Kristina asked eagerly. Bethany turned to her friend and Kristina looked at the floor. "I was very unhappy when he joined." She whispered and then moved her eyes back to

Bethany. "I know why he did," she said, looking down again, "but I wished he hadn't."

Bethany smiled sympathetically. "Have you ever told him how you feel?"

Kristina shook her head in terror. "Oh, good heavens, no! Jeffrey and I were always just classmates. Even when we went out those few times, I never really knew if he could look past the friendship to anything more. Lord knows there's much better looking than me within a million miles of here."

"That's not true." Bethany gave her an understandable smile and squeezed her arm. "I think Jeffrey has a lot of interest in you." She could remember many times Jeffrey coming home and all he could talk about over dinner was Kristina this and Kristina that. Her older brother was nothing close to a romantic, but she could tell that he was genuinely interested.

Kristina beamed. "Do you really think so?"

"He talked about you nonstop when he was home, especially when you started up your own paper. Jeffrey admired how you did it all on your own. Even after your papa died you kept on. He was very proud of you—still is." McCain sent out a snort and then a long whistle, nearly shaking over the book case next to him. Bethany and Kristina burst into laughter.

Shaking her head, Bethany's smile slowly faded. "I live for the day when this war's over. In the beginning, the war seemed so far away, like maybe it was a different world in another time. But now, with the Germans just in the next county and tragic news constantly on the radio, there is nowhere to hide from it anymore, is there?" Bethany sighed. "Some days, I wake and dread what is to come in the condition our world is in."

"At least we have the satisfaction that our guys are fighting to put an end to the horror over there."

Bethany's attention moved to the loud snoring. "Now, if we could only work on some of the daily horrors here on the home front. You may want to wake that one before he takes down the place." They shared in a long giggle as Bethany approached the door, feeling the bitter cold once again with the first step onto the walkway. She sent Kristina another friendly smile and waved, shutting the door behind her as she moved up the slippery boardwalk.

It began to snow, and within seconds of entering the street, the powder had covered all traces of Bethany's visit to the library. She shuffled Fitzgerald, Alcott, and O'Conner only to watch Steinbeck fall gracefully into the snow. She quickly collected *The Grapes of Wrath* and wiped the snow from its front cover before placing it atop *The Great Gatsby*.

Taking a moment to gather her thoughts, she looked around the near empty streets. Dobson's Crossroads seemed somewhat barren for a town of a reasonably average population. There were a few stragglers enjoying the winter wonderland, but she felt the mercantile and local shops would unfortunately have a very low profit for a Saturday morning.

Headed up Main Street past the mercantile, Bethany noticed Penny Henderson waving a feather duster inside the display window. Sending her a friendly wave, Mrs. Henderson simply nodded. Considered to be the wealthiest family in Dobson next to Derek Carson, Penny Henderson normally had no patience with the less fortunate, unless of course it was directly related to business deals at her mercantile. Therefore, knowing to receive any acknowledgment from Penny Henderson was an overall accomplishment, she considered it a very successful morning so far.

Bethany threw her hair over her shoulder and wrapped the scarf tighter around her neck. Occasionally, she'd stop to brush the snow off the legs of her blue jeans and stomp the packed snow from her cowboy boots. With all this, she still managed to juggle the books in her arms without any further difficulty. In her nineteen winters, this had to be the coldest she could remember.

Moving swiftly up the street, and pulling her jacket further into her face, she felt anxious to be snuggling over a roaring fire.

With the passing of Myrtle's Bed-and-Breakfast, Bethany made her way up Main Street toward the cut off at the edge of town. She could see Molly's regulars inside the café. Bethany knew, though very reluctant to admit, that Molly's apple pie was even better than her own mama's. In passing, Bethany could hear Monty Macpherson's voice carry over the streets from Greer's Bar. By the tone of his slurred voice, Macpherson seemed right on schedule with his contributions to the Greer family income.

Bethany approached the middle of town with hesitation as the church drew near. She took an uneasy breath and wished she had chosen to take the shortcut home as well. But the snow had come down so fast that it would prove very difficult to walk off the path of the street. As early as it was, the sky became black very quickly, yet the reflection of the snow lit up the town. Smoke arose out of nearly every chimney, and Bethany imagined she could feel the heat herself in passing.

She gazed ahead with her focus on the cutoff toward her farm. *Don't look toward the church*, she thought. Still, her eyes drifted to the oval headstone just to the left of the church grounds. Her heart ached with the same familiar pain that seemed to cling to her very soul, a pain that never gave her rest.

An assortment of wildflowers hugged the erected headstone and drooped with the weight of the snow. Bethany knew that a fresh batch of flowers would appear at Whitney's grave site in the morning following church services just like a weekly ritual. Uncle Robert and Aunt Page had taken the loss very hard. Deep in thought, Bethany failed to notice how close she had come to the church grounds. Now, standing over the four-foot fence that separated herself and Whitney's final resting place, Bethany felt a chill up her spine that was only too familiar to her.

Only a white picket fence separated the cemetery from church services. Bethany often wondered if some of the tenants from the cemetery hadn't stopped in, on occasion, to enjoy Sunday services with the rest of the congregation. Remnants of last winter's tragedy haunted her and left a dulling aftermath. Time hibernated emotion inside her—until the first signs of winter emerged, that is. And when the first drop of snowflakes appeared…well, it stirred something within her.

Now, memories of Whitney's death were all around her and everything reminded Bethany of her cousin. She became impassive over the course of the year and, in all honesty, couldn't remember the last hug she'd shared, with even her parents, that wasn't originally initiated by them. The past year made her insensitive toward some, even withdrawn toward others. It was hard to know how to feel most days, so usually she chose to separate her feelings all together.

Suddenly, she flinched, almost dropping Flannery O'Connor over the fence. She was able to intercept the book with a rapid twist of the wrist. Bethany's attention was suddenly drawn to a persistent voice coming from Dobson's schoolhouse which was located just up the road and across the street.

"Bethany, I'm over here!" the voice echoed from the steps of the large porch. Irene Maples was waving vigorously with both arms and hopping in place. The teacher reminded Bethany of a chicken, with her long slim legs and chubby torso bobbing up and down. Tint of gray, her hair bounced awkwardly in a bun.

"Please come see me for a moment," her voice echoed. "Oh, please do!"

Bethany gave a wave in reply and glanced at the grave one last time. With a brush of the back of her hand over her right cheek, she captured the tear before it fell. Leaving her thoughts behind, Bethany moved away from the cemetery and across the street to the one-room schoolhouse. The distance seemed endless until, at last, she arrived at the steps where Ms. Maples met her.

The teacher's long fingers waved her up the steps. "Come, warm yourself by the fire while we chat."

Bethany could smell the familiar fragrance of lemon verbena. She wasn't completely sure how old Ms. Maples was, but she knew from much talk in and about the town that she was one of the oldest spinsters in these parts, next to the Bryant sisters, that is. Bethany moved into the coatroom and waited for Ms. Maples to join her.

"If I'm late for breakfast, Mama is going to be awfully upset."

Ms. Maples closed the door behind her and took a moment to let the chill of the last few moments leave her. "It'll only take a moment." Squeezing her hair bun until satisfied, Irene passed Bethany, intercepting her hand along the way. "Come, let's move inside where it's warmer."

Bethany followed Irene, sat her books on the desk nearest the exit, and looked out into the large classroom as she had so many times before over the course of her childhood. Nothing had changed, yet everything seemed different. Fixing her eyes on her old desk, Bethany reminisced over the twelve years it had been her domain. Jeb Atkinson had occupied the desk just to the left of her. She remembered the huge crush she had on him at one time in third grade—until it was discovered he picked his nose and had a collection under the hood of his desk.

On the other side of her desk was Owen Stanford, the most callous boy in class. Her papa had told her that Owen Senior was just as mean, especially when he had taken to the bottle. From what Bethany understood, her old classmate was walking down the same intoxicating path as his daddy. Owen joined the navy soon after graduation and in no time was married to some city girl after knowing her only a weekend, making him an instant daddy to her two young children. He hadn't been heard from since.

Only small aisles allowed for movement about the one-room schoolhouse. It suddenly seemed smaller than Bethany remembered only a year earlier. She and Whitney spent many hours working alongside Ms. Maples and Bethany knew the building very well—the spots to avoid during a big rain, the draftiest areas on a cold winter day, and the creak of every floorboard. Bethany looked down nostalgically when her eyes drifted to Whitney's old desk. Irene Maples took a step toward her with slight skepticism and grasped Bethany's hand, pulling the nineteen-year-old away from her thoughts.

Her mentor led Bethany to the wood stove just left of the teacher's desk and squeezed her hand. "Here now, you stand and warm a bit while I do the talking." Bethany watched inquisitively. "Well, where do I begin?" Irene smiled and put her palms together, holding her hands to her lips as if in prayer. When she seemed to have organized her thoughts, Irene let her arms fall to her side. "I wanted to say first that I've missed working with you this past year."

Bethany shook off the cold that still remained. "I'm sorry, I've been very busy with choir and Sunday school. Lately, there have been lots of chores, getting ready for winter and all."

Ms. Maples slowly nodded understandingly and took a step toward her. "I know how much you always wanted to be a teacher. When you and Whitney would assist me—" Ms. Maples' tone got very soft. "I could see what a wonderful teacher you would be. I wonder where your thoughts are on the matter. Is it a vocation you still intend to pursue?"

The color in Bethany's hands slowly came back as she rubbed them in front of the stove with the numbness gradually subsiding. Although happy, in some form, to be out of the weather, Bethany almost wished she hadn't heard Ms. Maples call and just continued walking down Main Street. She is, in all fairness, the best teacher that Dobson's Crossroads ever had. It was her teaching that guided Bethany to find interest in teaching herself. But this was not a topic she had been prepared for when beginning her day. Bethany remained silent, and Ms. Maples sat herself in one of the desks nearest the fire. The room became chillingly silent.

"Bethany, there comes a time when one must think about life and the direction it is going," Ms. Maples suddenly said as she moved her hand up to the hair bun again. "What I mean is...well, Steven Geyser has asked for my hand, and I have accepted. We will be wed in the spring."

Bethany didn't mean to, but was sure the expression on her face wasn't at all what Irene Maples expected. "You're getting married...really!" Bethany quickly tightened her lips, realizing how rude she must have sounded. "I mean..."

Ms. Maples smiled and nodded. "It came as a whirlwind to me as well." She clasped her hands together over the back of the bench and went on. "We, Steven and I, will be leaving following the wedding. Steven will continue his mission work, and I will, of course, be assisting him as his wife. I've yet to post my resignation because my immediate thought was of you. In the past, we've worked side by side right here in this very classroom. I find you to be a very acceptable replacement for this community."

Bethany shifted her position, confusion coming over her. "Me—" She took a deep breath. "I'm not so sure what the future holds. I've been reading a lot, learning about new management techniques and assessments. But to be perfectly honest, I never thought a position would come available so quickly."

"Yes," Ms. Maples said, her tone becoming stagnant, "I've so loved teaching. But I find that being a new wife, and a mother one day, will fill my every waking hour." She seemed to pull out of her reflections. "Well, the moment is here and it is time you evaluated your thoughts on the subject." Irene Maples stood and held Bethany at arm's length. "Bethany, you were born for this. How many times have I heard you say how much you wanted to be a teacher? I'm offering this to you." Ms. Maples studied Bethany in a moment of silence. "You still want to teach, don't you, Bethany?"

Bethany contemplated the question for a length of time, and then looked at the floor as a sudden wave of emotions came over her. "To be honest, Ms. Maples, I haven't really thought much about it since—" She looked at Irene, unable to say her cousin's name. Bethany shook her head, frustrated over the whole conversation.

"Since Whitney…was that what you were going to say?" Ms. Maples waited for an answer that never came. "Bethany, you can't give up your dream of being a teacher. It's always been so important to you."

Suddenly, Irene Maples' words were lost in the air. Bethany's mind drifted back to that cold winter day only a year earlier, the day her whole world went wrong. Bethany moved her hands over the fire again and glanced up at Ms. Maples, suddenly coming back to reality. "Becoming a teacher was always a dream that she and I shared. Somehow wanting to be a teacher now seems selfish and unimportant."

Irene nodded silently, moved to the teacher's desk, and clasped her hands together. "There's time to think it over, Bethany, but not much. By the end of winter, I'll be leaving and, if you accept, you'll need to have passed the teaching exam." She watched Bethany in brief silence. "Think it over a few days and let me know what you decide. The exam is only administered twice a year at the university and the last chance is coming in only a few short weeks. Once you pass the exam, it's just a matter of applying for the position." She gave a warm smile. "I can name numerous recommendations here in town alone. It would be a treat for everyone to have you teach their children. After all, you are a native of the Crossroads." Irene sent Bethany a sad, almost sympathetic smile. "Whitney would want this for you," she added.

"I'll think about it, I promise." She moved toward the exit and lifted her books from the nearby desk. "I best head home."

Irene stood behind her desk. "Now, you mind what I said, Bethany Davies. Think long and hard on this. It's a big decision, and big decisions deserve time to ponder." Irene placed her palms on the desk and leaned forward. "Be sure to get back with me in a few days so we may plan accordingly."

"Yes, ma'am. I'll see you at morning services."

Bethany entered the coatroom that led to the front door. Now out of view of Ms. Maples, she slammed herself against the wall, closing her eyes tightly to gain composure. Bethany vowed she would never find herself in such an uncomfortable situation again. Still unable to speak of her cousin without trembling, Bethany felt the guilt of that day suddenly consume her. Irene Maples meant well, but could never understand. There were things she didn't know, things no one knew, about the day Whitney died.

Quickly pulling her gloves on and fastening the buttons on her jacket, Bethany moved onto the porch of the schoolhouse. Sending a wave to Reverend Michaels who suddenly appeared on the porch of the church, Bethany moved to the end of Main Street and turned right, moving in the direction of the baseball field. It was going to be a long walk in the snow before she reached the farm, but Bethany was almost relieved to be alone in her own thoughts. Things suddenly became very complicated.

CHAPTER 2

LONDON, ENGLAND, 1943

Bradley Jenkins, a large Brit both in height and stature, stood behind his desk and held the telephone tightly to his ear. "What does it take to get a little cooperation around here?" His stern English accent echoed in the remnants of what once was a lavishing manor before the Luftwaffe bombed the city. "I don't care if you have to look under every rock in London. I need those documents and I need them now!"

Jenkins noticed Tyson, the family butler, enter the room. With eyes still peeled on the dark man waiting at the door, the member of the British Parliament continued his telephone conversation. "I realize the city is in shambles, Mr. Flannery! I wonder if *you* realize how far down the toilet my assets are going without those bank statements. Of course, you don't!" Jenkins said without waiting for a response. "Because, Flannery, *you* work for a paycheck regardless of how much money I lose in the process!"

Wilson Tyson, a black man of sixty, held tightly to a silver platter that contained the daily mail. He found himself part of the Jenkins house many years prior to Bradley's success into power. As the room echoed, Tyson felt very fortunate it was not he on the other end of Bradley's fury, although there were numerous occasions of verbal abuse he himself had to endure over the course of his employment with the politician.

"No, I don't care what you have to do!" Jenkins continued, "I have a meeting in two hours, and I want those papers on my desk well before that." Jenkins looked sternly at Tyson. "If you want to continue your position as my personal assistant, you'll get it done!" He shouted into the phone. "Fifteen minutes, do you understand me?"

Tyson watched as Bradley slammed the phone down with a bang, and for a moment, his large hand continued to cover the receiver. Shaking his head in anger, he walked around his oak desk and took the path toward his liquor cabinet.

"What is it, Tyson?" Jenkins looked across the room at the man. "If you brought me more bad news, I've had my fill for the day!" He released the latch to the cabinet. "Why do people refuse to see my position? I am a man of means and my entire existence is based on building my empire. I refuse to be slowed because of lack of funds or the lack of competence of those around me!"

Jenkins lifted the bottle of bourbon, pouring it into his glass, and then took a swig before staring at his drink. "Churchill once said," Jenkins seemed to speak to the air, "'always remember that I have taken more out of alcohol than alcohol has taken out of me.'" Jenkins chuckled. "Course, in my own philosophy, drunkenness is one's own voluntary insanity." He raised his glass as if to toast himself and loosened his tie. Staring sternly at the butler, he took another big swallow. "Well, say it or belt up!"

"Sir Jenkins," Tyson said, holding up the platter, "I have your afternoon mail, sir."

Jenkins took another drink of his glass and threw his arm in the air. "Well, place it on the desk, and be off with you then, man!" Tyson waited with his chin dropped. The words were there, but Tyson feared them. Jenkins stared at him as if the man had gone plum loony. "Was there something else?"

"It's just—" Tyson mumbled. "Well, Sir Jenkins, a letter has arrived from your grandson."

Jenkins gave him a surprised look. Turning, he filled his glass to the rim again and took another long gulp. "You mean that little bugger hasn't gotten himself killed?"

"Sir, perhaps a letter back to Master Scotland this time would—"

"Tyson, I am tired of the way you stick up for my grandson. Have you seen the botch job he left me to clean up?"

Taking a deep breath, Tyson moved to the desk and placed the mail over a stack of papers in plain sight. He had hoped that Sir Jenkins would take the time to open this letter and not add it to the stack deep inside his desk drawer.

"With all due respect, Sir Jenkins, Master Scotland joined the American paratroopers. It doesn't mean he abandoned his country," Tyson said in fear of finding eye contact. He quickly tightened his lips, feeling the burning glare from the other side of the room. Tyson slowly backed around the desk as Jenkins came in from the other side. The man watched from the security of the double doors as Jenkins glanced down at the letter for the slightest moment. Tyson knew he would never see his employer open it.

Bradley turned to the large windowpane behind his desk, looking over the rubble of the streets below, and took another mouthful from his glass. "Scotland's only problem is the American blood he shares with that father of his. I tried, Tyson. Lord knows I tried to save him from the reckless choices he made. He certainly showed me whose side of the fence he's on. He left me to pick up the pieces of this blimey war." Jenkins chuckled. "That boy always had an uncanny knack for finding trouble, that's for sure." Jenkins turned his attention to the streets below once more. "Maybe I chose the wrong grandson back then."

Tyson looked down sadly with horrific thought of that day many years ago.

"Maybe it wasn't Scotland this family needed, but the other one." He took another gulp as if comforting his thoughts with alcohol. "I imagine that's the price we pay for gambling." He looked over his shoulder at Tyson. "What was the return address?"

"He appeared to be somewhere in Berkshire, England, sir. The letter is weeks old." Tyson placed the platter behind his back, holding it there. "Sir Jenkins, if there won't be anything else?" The tone in Tyson's voice was that of a defeated man. There was no sense continuing the conversation, one which he had lost so many times in the past. Jenkins had made up his mind, Tyson knew that, and the topic was no longer open for discussion.

Bradley raised his arm in the air. "Go then!" Jenkins finished off his glass and then suddenly looked up. "Wait a minute, Tyson."

Stopping at the door, the servant turned to him. Bradley sat his glass down on the desk. "Have the driver prepare the car. I'll be leaving in an hour." Bradley looked at the man. "Tyson, make sure you remember next time who you work for," he said sternly.

Tyson nodded, yet still avoiding eye contact. "I will, yes, sir." The man disappeared down the long dark hallway, glancing back only once with the look of defeat.

Bradley placed an arm against the wall to support his heavy weight. He shook his head in aggravation at the chaos in the streets below and let his head fall. "I'm so blimey sick and tired of this pear-shaped country," Bradley said aloud. Taking a deep breath, he kicked the wall with his heel and turned, yanking the chair out from under the desk, and slammed himself into it.

The letter seemed to stare up at him. With a long gaze, he reached for it, studying the inscription on the front. *First Lieutenant? Well, I find that very impressive—for an American!* Bradley thought to himself.

He dropped the letter and glanced up at the door. "Well, I see the moment you hear your position is in jeopardy, you get on the stick." Bradley came around the desk. "Well, speak, did you get them?"

Jameson Flannery, thin and aged, was wearing an expensive business suit covered in grunge from the flying debris on his walk over. The man took a step closer and held a beige folder out to Jenkins with the look of immense protest. "Sir Jenkins, this is not only illegal and catastrophic, but morally wrong!"

Bradley grabbed the file from his hand. "Don't go developing a conscience, Flannery. My grandson never wanted any part of the family money anyway."

Flannery shook his head in disapproval. "His mother left him those accounts when she died. Regardless of if or when he uses it…that money belongs to Scotland."

"What are you getting on about? If this isn't your cup of tea, there's always the door." Bradley's mouth fell open as he stared at the first page. "Blimey!" He quickly looked at Flannery. "Are you sure this is right?"

Flannery sighed in despair and dropped his body into the overstuffed chair next to the liquor cabinet. "What were you expecting? Those accounts have gone untouched for years and just sitting there collecting interest."

Bradley laughed in hysterics and hit the palm of his hand with the folder. "Flannery, remind me to apologize for rambling on about your piss-poor performance. You did well this time… very well, indeed!" He turned to Flannery with a sinfully pleased smile. "When I go into that meeting today, they'll see I'm not just some pissed-up Brit. I worked long and hard to get where I am. I won't let anything break me, not even this sod war!"

Flannery shook his head. "Bradley, you're trying to repair the damage the war caused before the war is even over."

Bradley lunged toward him and flung the file in his face. "I worked too hard!" He threw the file out with his arm. "Have you seen the streets, filled with gentlemen of the past?" Bradley returned to his desk and slammed the file down. "Chums I shared rum with at the local pub…washed up…broke." He leaned into his desk and stared in Flannery's direction. "Not me, not this Brit, not ever!" Shaking his head wildly, he straightened his posture and turned to the window. "My grandson never wanted what I built. I gave my sweat and blood over the years and made many sacrifices to get where the Jenkins name is today. He never appreciated what this family stands for…what I stand for! The first chance Scotland had, he joined Churchill's faction, and abandoned his family. Then, when it all went sour, he took off and ran to the Americas. He doesn't deserve it, and obviously doesn't want it, so let's put it where it can do some bloody good!"

Flannery shook his head and stood. "You are delusional. No bank is going to let you touch that money, not without a signature from Scotland."

Bradley laughed and lifted the letter from his desk. "The need for a signature, you say?" Bradley held the letter out to him. "Whatever it takes, Flannery, whatever the cost." Jenkins' lips curled when he noticed the defiant look on Flannery's face. "You let me down and betray me, and it'll be the last thing you ever do, I promise you that!" Jenkins flung the letter in the man's face again. "Go on, then."

Flannery looked at the letter. "Do you realize what you're saying? Forgery is a jail sentence I won't serve for you!"

"Whatever it takes, Flannery!" His voice became stern and demanding.

Flannery knew Jenkins wasn't giving him a choice and took the letter with the look of extreme protest. He watched Bradley, the man's smile of victory. Throwing his palms on the desk again, Bradley looked at him sternly. "Do not forget, my friend, you are in as deep as I. It was not I who drove his father and brother out of this country. I have your back so long as you have mine, you remember that!" Bradley laughed. "Someday, Flannery, I'm going to take it right to the top." The room echoed with Bradley's laughter. "Well, get on with it then, man! We don't have time to lose."

Bradley's lips curled again as he walked back to his glass. There would be no stopping him this time. With that kind of money, his prosperity and power would be endless. Jenkins filled his glass again and raised it to toast himself. With a large grin, he chuckled as Flannery left the room. Bradley emptied his glass with one swallow and, with a pause, stared deep into the firepit. He ran his glass over his lips and then pulled his arm back. Throwing the glass as hard as he could, it shattered into the fireplace. The sound of broken glass filled the room and in an instant it became silent again. "Nothing empty is worth having," he said to the air.

CHAPTER 3

DOBSON'S CROSSROADS, NORTH CAROLINA, 1943

Katherine placed the platter of freshly baked cinnamon rolls in the center of the kitchen table. Tossing her dark hair back, her eyes moved to the front door. Bethany closed the door, placed the books on the coffee table, and moved promptly over the living room floor toward the roaring fire.

"Just in time, breakfast is about ready." She examined the table one last time until satisfied and looked Bethany's way again. "Did you see your brothers outside?"

The scent of fresh baked goods, burning hickory, and Christmas tree pine drifted into the living room from throughout the house. Bethany could almost taste those fruit cakes baking in the oven. She warmed her hands by the fire, gazing up at the pictures on the mantel.

"Yes, ma'am, I heard them making a commotion in the barn." She blew on her numb fingers, moving her eyes over the picture of Jeffrey and Patrick together in their uniforms. It was only after Patrick left that Taylor found she was expecting their first child. "It's snowing again," she yelled toward the kitchen. "It was a real chore making it in from town. The trip to church in the morning could prove very difficult if the snow doesn't stop soon."

"Where were you off to so early this morning? You were up with the roosters." Katherine threw the hand towel over her shoulder and stirred the scrambled eggs.

"I wanted to get some books from the library." Bethany stared at the picture of herself on the mantel. It had been taken a few years earlier, just before graduation. She remembered how naive and trusting she was back then. Now, turning twenty in only a few months, she felt like an old woman. She moved her eyes back to her mother. "I saw Kristina and she is extremely worried about Jeffrey."

"Well, her worries are about over." Katherine beamed up at her daughter from the stove. "We received word that Jeffrey is coming home."

Bethany took a moment for the news to sink in. "He's coming home, for sure, really?" she gasped.

Katherine sent her a big smile. "He sure is! Uncle Robert brought a letter from him just this morning. It came all the way from England. Can you imagine? London, England!" Bethany began to clap, and Katherine admired the joy in Bethany, for to see a smile from her daughter was extremely rare. Katherine transferred the scrambled eggs into a large bowl and placed it on the table. "I ran into Kristina during Taylor's last visit with Doc Malone a few days ago. I do hope Jeffrey and Kristina finally get together when he comes home. I always liked that girl!"

Bethany nodded in agreement. "Where's Papa?"

"There was some disturbance in the far pasture last night." Katherine wiped her palms over the apron that covered her slender figure. Moving the pitcher of fresh orange juice from the counter, Katherine placed it next to the bowl of eggs on the table, and intercepted the coffee cup from the stove to take a sip. "He went to investigate."

Bethany removed her jacket and placed it on the coat rack near the front door. "There's so much to do before Jeffrey gets here. We need fresh linens on his bed, Papa will have to get us a big turkey, and—oh, no!" She suddenly gasped and looked at her mother in panic. "Jeffrey's going to want to see Sampson. What do we tell him?"

Katherine focused her attention a moment on a little girl with her fingers around a cinnamon roll. "Sara Sue, please wait for the rest of the family to join us."

"But Mama, I'm starving!" Sara Sue whined, licking her fingers one by one, with a long ponytail dangling over her plate.

"We'll just have to tell him the truth," Katherine continued, still giving a scolding look to Sara Sue. "Jeffrey knew that old dog was on his last leg. Jacob and Joshua will have to share a bed. Your brother's bringing a friend. His name is Scott and he's from London. According to Jeffrey's letter, Scott has no family so he'll be staying with us during their leave." Katherine pulled the letter out of her apron, tapped it on persistent Sara Sue's head, and held it out for Bethany.

Bethany quickly intercepted the letter. The sudden moment of silence was interrupted by a loud "Ouch!" that echoed the kitchen. Bethany looked up from the letter to see Sara Sue rubbing the hand that, only a moment earlier, was smacked by their mother. "He could be here anytime. This letter has to be at least two weeks old."

Katherine wiped her hands on her apron and nodded. "I do pray he makes it for Christmas!" Katherine paused sadly. "Taylor has yet to receive a letter from Patrick this month." She shook her head in despair. "It's not right to have him so far away with her this close to her time. Patrick Henry Langley is going to be a sight for Taylor's sore eyes, that's for sure."

Bethany folded Jeffrey's letter and returned it to the envelope. "Mail is moving slowly these days, Mama," Bethany said, sitting at the table. "I couldn't imagine how Taylor could do it, with child or not."

"Well, love has a way of getting you through when you feel the world has you beaten. Someday, when you find the right man, you'll see what I mean."

Bethany shook her head. "That's a long ways from now."

Katherine giggled. "Once, when you were just a little girl, you told me you'd only marry a rich man so you didn't have to haul another hay bale or clean another horse stall." Bethany smiled, remembering that conversation. "What are you going to do when one day you fall in love with a poor man?"

Bethany thought a moment. "I guess if he has my love, he's not exactly poor, is he?" she said, glancing up at her mama.

Katherine gave her a big smile. "Bethany, that is the best answer I would have ever expected from you." Katherine giggled with a nod and turned back to the stove.

Bethany smiled proudly in spite of herself.

Eyes fixed on the door when Joseph suddenly appeared with an armful of firewood. Balancing on one foot, he kicked the door closed. The room echoed with a thud as a few logs missed the wood box and rolled onto the hardwood floor. He replaced them atop the pile and pulled off his gloves.

"Boys are on their way in. It took them half the morning to get Gracie inside to be milked. The old girl isn't faring well with this weather, and we've been getting very little milk. Poor old girl just doesn't have it in her anymore." He scratched his graying overgrown beard. "I want everyone to be on guard. There were wolf tracks in the snow up the pasture a ways. Weren't fresh, but something was stirring late last night. I reckon it's a pack from the hills looking for food in the flat lands." He looked at the table. "Sara Sue, let that roll alone now."

Sara Sue dropped the cinnamon roll that, by this time, had her signature all over it. Katherine gave her a stern look. The six-year-old licked her fingers, quickly moving her hands to her lap and out of her mother's reach.

"Well." Joseph looked about the room as if talking to himself, which he did quite frequently. "I suppose there's a lot to be done if we're to have houseguests." He stomped the remaining snow off his boots and began the task of peeling his layers of clothing. "Who's this friend he's dragging along?"

"The letter says he's a paratrooper." Katherine poured her husband a fresh cup of coffee and replaced the pot on the stove. "His name is Scott and he's from London."

Joseph scratched his chin again in deep thought and started his conversation as he always did—with a noisy exhale and nod of the head. "London, you say? Not much left of London from what I hear. I can understand why he's coming our way instead." He took another deep sigh. "Well, guess they have big plans for them both, coming home for the holidays like they are." An uneasy silence filled the room.

Bethany had been watching her little sister cunningly move the platter of pastries an inch or two closer to her side of the table. The two had always been close, perhaps because when Sara Sue was a baby Bethany carried her about, pretending she was her dolly. Then again, Sara Sue was the last of the Davies's brood, and that just made her special anyway. That's not to say, however, that her little sister lacked a million ways to be a pest when the mind was set on doing so. Sara Sue also had days when it seemed her ultimate goal was simply to get on Bethany's nerves.

As quickly as it came, the silence was broken with the front door bouncing against the wall as the twins stormed in at full speed.

"Papa, Joshua locked me in the barn!" Jacob gave his brother a push.

"I did not! Only stupid folks get themselves stuck in a stupid barn!"

"I'm not stupid, you take that back!" Jacob clobbered his brother on the back of the head.

Joshua took a dive toward his brother in retaliation.

"Enough! Find your seat before breakfast gets cold," Katherine demanded. "Has anyone seen Katie Anne?"

"Here I am, Mama," Katie Anne hollered as she ran down the stairs to take her spot next to Sara Sue.

"Bethany, will you say prayer, please?" Katherine took her husband's hand. Bethany gave thanks over the food and asked for a loving watch over those struggling in the war, and then Joseph passed the eggs and cinnamon rolls around the table.

After a long pause, Katie Anne stared down at her plate. "Mama…Papa, Mrs. Henderson is looking for help in their store." Before her parents could protest, the fourteen-year-old intervened. "Can I please? I'd really love to have some Christmas money this year! I'll get all my chores done before school and finish my homework the second I get home. Oh please say yes!" Katherine and Joseph looked at each other questionably as Katie Anne waited anxiously for a response.

Sara Sue had been watching the plate of savoring homemade cinnamon rolls continuously pass her by. When the plate was finally returned to the center of the table in front of her, only bits and pieces remained. The girl held her head in her hands, pouted, and kicked the bottom of her chair repeatedly.

"Well, I don't see any harm in your working, so long as your responsibilities are taken care of here at home." Joseph took a sip of his coffee and then pointed a finger at his daughter. "But before I say yes, I want to speak to Penny Henderson and set a few ground rules."

Katie Anne clapped her hands. "Oh, thank you, Papa!"

Sara Sue pouted as she stared down at the empty platter. "I wish I was an only child," the girl mumbled. "Then maybe I wouldn't just sit here and just starve!"

Katherine gave her daughter a soft smile "Don't fret, child, there's plenty more." Her mama replenished the platter and placed a large cinnamon roll on the center of her daughter's plate, giving her a quick peck on the head.

"Bethany, you hardly put anything on your plate. Aren't you feeling well?" Katherine said, returning to her seat.

"I'm fine, Mama, just not very hungry," she said in a near whisper.

Over the course of the year, Bethany had filled out into a beautiful young woman, and without an ounce of fat, had curves that Katherine grew to miss following childbearing. It worried Katherine how little her daughter would eat. Although Katherine considered all her children beautiful, Bethany was exceptionally radiant—when she wasn't frowning that is.

Joseph reached over the table and placed a palm on Bethany's forehead. "Don't seem to have a fever." He caressed his daughter's face worriedly.

"Well, do your best to put something in your stomach." Katherine stared down at her own plate. "When Uncle Robert brought Jeffrey's letter by, he asked for you. Said he saw you in town yesterday and waved, but you walked right by him."

Bethany pushed her food around with her fork. "I guess I didn't see him, Mama," she said before taking a quick bite of her scrambled eggs in an attempt to avoid any further attention. Unfortunately, her plans had failed miserably.

"Robert was wondering if you'd like to sit with Chester and Marty. Your cousins always enjoy having you babysit when Uncle Robert and Aunt Page go out."

Bethany sent her mama a frown. "Is this more of that getting-back-on-the-horse stuff you're always talking about?"

Katherine placed her fork on her plate. "Perhaps getting back on *that horse* is just what you need," she said sternly.

Joseph studied his daughter for a moment. "I think it would be good for you to go. You can't avoid them forever, honey. It's time we all put the past where it belongs and move on." Joseph paused. "Honey, do understand what I'm saying?"

Bethany glared down at her plate. "I understand that it's the one-year anniversary of probably the worst day of my life, and you want me to pretend that nothing happened."

"That isn't what we're asking you to do at all. We simply want you to let yourself heal. We all loved Whitney, and we sure don't want you to ever forget. Your aunt and uncle, they don't blame you, why must you blame yourself?" Joseph tapped his finger on the table, a sign that he was concentrating on something very deeply. "Just think about it. If you want to visit, I know your cousins would love it, and I'd be happy to go with you." Bethany stared at her plate again and the room became uncomfortably silent. Joseph continued to watch his daughter as she took another bite of her eggs. The immediate silence was broken by Katie Anne, who took full advantage of it.

"Guess who came by the house looking for Bethany today?" Before anyone could answer, Katie Anne spoke up jumping in her chair. "David Carson! He was asking about *you*, Bethany."

Bethany dropped the fork on her plate and stared angrily at her younger sister.

"He's still crazy about you. I can tell!" Katie Anne bounced excitedly in her chair. "He wants to take you to a movie!"

Bethany grinned, shifted positions, and pushed her plate to the side. "When Gracie can fly around the moon!" she said, grinding her teeth.

"I like David." Sara Sue's eggs shot out of her mouth and went flying over the length of the table.

"Sara Sue!" Katherine gasped. "Have you lost all sense of manners?"

Sara Sue swallowed the remainder of her eggs and looked at her mama. "I'm sorry, Mama." She quickly looked back at Bethany. "But I do. I think he is so dreamy!"

Bethany squeezed the edge of the table in frustration. "Then why don't you go to a movie with him!" she shouted back at her sister.

"Bethany Jean Davies, what has gotten into you today?" Joseph scolded and looked around the table. "I think we all need to just settle down and eat our breakfast!"

Bethany stared at her glass of milk and the table became suddenly silent.

"Well, I wonder what other exciting turn of events will happen today? I must say it's been quite a festive morning so far." Katherine broke the awkward silence.

"I ran into Ms. Maples at the school on the way home this morning." Bethany mustered the courage with a few deep breaths. "She's getting married." Her announcement came as if sharing the prospect of Dobson's upcoming weather.

Katherine placed her cup down on the table, raised her eyebrows, and gave a happy gesture as she cupped her hands together in an almost prayer stance. "Oh, thank the heavenly Lord!"

Joseph chuckled and sat back in his chair with a nod. "Well, sounds like Steven Geyser finally developed a backbone."

"They're moving after the wedding," Bethany nearly whispered, staring at the table. She noticed the sudden stillness, and out of curiosity, looked up. The family was staring at her as if she had just told a sinful joke. The shock on their faces seemed priceless. A bolt of lightning could have come down and struck Bethany right between her beautiful blue eyes and still the look of surprise couldn't have been more incalculable.

Joshua threw his napkin on the table with a grumble of opposition. "Great! Wonder who'll be our teacher now?"

Jacob placed his head in his hands, giving a pitiful sigh. "Probably some fat lady who hits you with a ruler and smells like farts!"

Katherine placed her palms on the table and gave her son a stern look. "Jacob Michael!" Katherine gasped.

Jacob ginned, sat up, and looked at her. "Well, geez, Louise, Mama! Why do we have to have a new teacher?"

"Yeah, Mama, why do we need to have a new one?" Joshua said, shoving a slice of bread in its entirety into his mouth. "That is so stupid!"

"Joshua Marshall, you know better than to talk with your mouth full." Katherine looked at Bethany. "Did Irene give you any idea who might be taking over for her?"

Bethany fixed her eyes on her mama and then glanced at her papa. The entire table was waiting for an answer she wasn't ready to give. "I reckon it's still being discussed." She didn't want to lie entirely. Bethany pushed her chair back and stood. "May I be excused?"

Joseph nodded and watched his daughter disappear upstairs.

Bethany could still hear the protests from her siblings as she closed her bedroom door and looked around the room with a desperate sigh. Running her fingers through her hair, Bethany moved to the window. The snow was falling slightly again, and she could feel the coldness seeping in through the windowpane. Folding her arms, she leaned against the wall and browsed over the hillside as far as she could see. It was hard for her to believe there was so much going on in the world when simply gazing upon the hills and snow banks of Dobson's Crossroads.

Her attention was suddenly broken by a large thud behind her. She moved around the foot of her bed and noticed the picture of her and Whitney face up on the floor. For the last year, the picture had been face down on her nightstand and covered by an assortment of odds and ends. Bethany's heart began to race. She looked at the table. Perhaps without realizing it, she had bumped the table coming in. With the picture facing up at her, it was a simple reminder of the pain she had been feeling all day. She retrieved the picture, still taken off guard as to how it made its way to the floor.

Besides the difference in hair color and the few inches in Bethany's favor, she and Whitney could have passed for sisters. Both had elegant singing voices, but many have said Bethany's was much more defined, soft, and mesmerizing. But she found that nearly unbelievable because, to her, Whitney was always much better at simply everything. Bethany knew, had she died instead of Whitney, that her cousin would have handled the pain much better. Whitney had always been so much stronger than Bethany.

She ran her finger over her cousin's image. Whitney's smile was so trusting. Her long black hair was always perfectly held back by hair clips, and Whitney was always dressed in her very best. As for Bethany, she would wear blue jeans and cowboy boots to church if she could sneak it past her mama undetected. Whitney often called her a tomboy, but it didn't seem to bother Bethany one bit. She would much rather work the farm alongside her papa and get dirty, rather than be obsessed with looks all the time.

Bethany took a deep breath to control her tears and remembered the day the picture was taken. It was the day before their high school graduation and they had so much fun. They spent the whole day together and Whitney slept over that night, entertaining each other well into the morning. They used the next afternoon to do each other's hair and must have tried on their entire wardrobe before choosing the right outfit. Her Uncle Robert, Whitney's daddy, had taken that picture just prior to leaving for the graduation ceremony. Bethany's throat became dry. Those days were a lifetime ago.

Placing the picture under contents on the top shelf of her closet, Bethany stood back and paused with her arms crossed. She seemed to stare at the picture's mausoleum for a long time before howling outside directed her attention back to the window. Curious, she returned to the window and her eyes searched the area near the edge of the clearing. There was the sound again. She could see movement along the border between their farm and her grand's, but she couldn't make it out. Then, it vanished into the brush as quickly as it had appeared. Bethany waited, and yet nothing.

CHAPTER 4

Katherine moved hastily toward the barn where Joseph had disappeared an hour earlier. With coffee in hand, she found her way with the help of the dim light under the barn door. Joseph wiped the glue from his hands and looked at his wife's direction as she closed the door behind her.

"Joseph Davies, what is so important it can't wait until daylight and, heaven forbid, warmer weather?"

Joseph smiled and looked down at the near complete baby cradle. "Babies don't wait until the weather clears, Katherine," he said. He looked at the sudden excitement on his wife's face. "I won't have my first grandchild sleeping in a dresser drawer."

Katherine ran her hands over the smooth oak. "Joseph, it's absolutely beautiful!"

He smiled in spite of himself. In all the projects he had completed in his lifetime, and there were many, this was the most rewarding by far. Working with his hands was a passion passed down by his father. As Jeffrey grew older, Joseph found that his eldest took on the same talent for craftsmanship. He was undoubtedly most like his daddy out of all of Joseph's thoroughbreds.

Katherine held the coffee cup out to her husband, and Joseph gasped. Seizing the hot cup into his frozen hands, he shivered with excitement. "Katherine, you are the answer to my humble prayers." Joseph gave her a peck on the cheek. "Can you believe this? I can feel the ice growing at the end of my nose."

Katherine kissed his nose. "There is nothing on the end of that nose but trouble, husband. It worries me that you're out here working alone. You could freeze to death, and no one would be the wiser."

"Now, Katherine, I've worked alone many times before. Besides, I can't have the work piling up around me waiting for the weather to clear." He enjoyed another sip and sent her a gratifying smile. "If you're that concerned, you can bring me another cup." He held the cup out to her.

Katherine took the cup and intercepted his hand. "No, what I can do is bring you in right now before you catch your death." She tugged on his hand. "Besides, it's getting late, and the children are ready for you to say good night. And I don't want you falling asleep during Reverend Michaels's sermon in the morning."

Joseph laughed, touched her cheek, and gave her a quick kiss on the lips. "And we wonder where our children get their stubbornness?"

Katherine sent him a loving smile.

"Okay, darling, let me clean up this mess, and I'll be right in."

Joseph noticed a sudden sadness come over her and questioned it with his eyes, and she sent him a sorrowful stare. "It'll be wonderful, won't it?"

"What's that, wife?"

Katherine moved her fingers into his, trembling, and held his hand tightly. "I long for this war to finally end, to have Jeffrey and Patrick home for good."

"The war will be over soon and then the house will be full again. So full, in fact, perhaps you should enjoy a few less bodies to clean after while you can."

"I think I would do dishes fifty times a day if I knew all my children were home safe and sound. It's hard to sleep at night knowing they're out there somewhere. I'm afraid the war will last so long all our boys will find themselves involved in it. I couldn't stand that, Joseph. I couldn't stand to see Joshua and Jacob in uniform as well!" She panicked.

Joseph placed his hands on her shoulders and squeezed them gently. "Now, Katherine, aren't you getting a little ahead of yourself?" He kissed her on the head. "You are such a worrywart."

"I guess that's what mothers do. We worry about our children, and about failing them. Bethany, for instance, speaks so little. I know she is bothered, but I can't for the life of me know how I can help her through this."

"Bethany will come through in her own time, Katherine."

"In the meantime, I just stand aside and let her hurt? I'm not sure I can do that."

"Not much we can do, except maybe use a little of that faith you're always preaching to your family about." He gave her a soft smile. "We love our kids, wife. Not much else we can do but that. Oh, sure, we want to protect them. But we can't always. Sometimes we have to put our faith in a higher power with the belief that it will all work out in the end, and perhaps hope along the way we raised them to the best of our ability."

"And all this time I thought you were sleeping during Sunday sermons."

He chuckled and squeezed her hands. "I believe this family is going to see a lot of miracles ahead. We just need to have faith."

"You're a smart and wise man, my husband." Katherine moved toward the door.

"Katherine?" Joseph called. Katherine turned to her husband. "I couldn't have picked a better wife or mother for my youngsters if God himself placed you in my arms." Katherine gave him a loving smile. "And my mama thought you'd be no match for me."

Katherine's mouth dropped, and she gasped. "She said that!"

Joseph threw his head in the air and laughed. "No, darling, I was only funning you." He reached out and gave her another peck on the lips with a chuckle over her quick temperament. "I think he did. I think God himself gave you to me to keep me in line." Joseph was nodding in agreement.

Katherine smacked him on the arm. "What a big job it's been too." They stared at each other lovingly for a moment, and Katherine disappeared into the coldness.

When the cleaning was complete, Joseph took the lantern and headed toward the door. "Good night, old girls," he said to Callie and Gracie. He tugged on the latch. Callie began to stir.

Joseph raised his eyebrows toward the door, hearing movement just the other side. He forced the door open with the lantern held high and attempted to scan ahead into the night. Even with the lantern blazing, visibility was limited before being met with darkness. Just there at his feet, he could see several pairs of paw prints. He guessed four sets in all. He scratched his chin and took a deep sigh.

Joseph tugged on the barn door to ensure it was latched. He reached the top of the porch when suddenly a loud wail came from the far side of the valley. He sent his lantern high again, with no avail. Whatever was out there was well hidden by the blanket of clouds that covered the moonlight. Not a star was visible. The lantern nearly slipped from his fingers as he twirled around with the creak of the front door. Bethany had joined him on the porch, looking into the darkness herself.

"Honey, you like to have made me jump out of my skin."

"Sorry, Papa, but I heard a noise," she said, scanning into the shadows. "What do you make of it?" She pulled her robe tighter and shivered.

Joseph waved the lamp in the direction of the wooded area again. "Wolves, I expect, or wild dogs. I'm sure this weather's been hard on their hunting. We'll have to move the cattle closer to the house or we'll see a number of losses."

"I knew I saw something earlier." Bethany gasped and took a few steps toward the top of the stairway. "We should warn the other farms."

Joseph sighed worriedly. "Not much we can do tonight. You best keep Callie and Gracie in the barn until we get a handle on our new neighbors." Joseph blew out the lantern and dropped his arm. "After church in the morning, we'll talk to your uncles and come up with a plan. A pack of wolves have no place this low to the flat lands." He looked back into the blackness. "Let's go in before we both catch a frightening cold." He opened the door and stepped inside.

Bethany heard a last cry deep in the woods, and the sounds seemed to get further away. She hesitated until it was suddenly quiet and then joined her papa inside.

CHAPTER 5

The Farmer's Almanac *had one thing right,* Joseph Davies thought. *It's not going to be an easy winter.* The year-round view of the Smoky Mountains was a sight to see, and on a usual spring day, one could hear the sounds of moving water with the multiple streams, springheads, and creek branches coming in from all directions. But today, it was very silent and everything was frozen solid. He scanned his eyes over miles of farm with nothing but snow for as far as the eye could see.

Joseph would often find time during the summer months to sit upon the wraparound porch, enjoy the scenery, and ponder on a good day's work. The two-story ranch house was erected in the middle of miles of graze land. Twenty-five years had passed since he and his brothers built the large home for his new bride. The hundred-acre homestead was a wonderful wedding gift from his mother and father, but life as a rancher was very demanding, especially in the winter months.

As time went on, Joseph managed to plow sod for a long section of corn, flour, and other garden vegetables. The farm became plush with a large barn, chicken coop, horse corral, and cattle grazing, all of which proved beneficial with the rationing now in effect. The scenery never became weary to the eye with so much change day after day. A good windstorm had a way of making the farm canvas spontaneously transform, and on a beautiful, clear day, the Rattlesnake Mountain would drift into sight.

The days grew darker earlier, but the workload had a tendency to multiply. During spring, summer, and fall, Joseph would gather with his three brothers to work each other's farms, but winter always proved difficult with the snowstorms and distances between homes. He wished for a day of resting, loafing, and sunbathing, although his whole life he hadn't seen one of those days yet.

Dobson's Crossroads was much like any other North Carolina town. The people seemed to live a sheltered life from the rest of the world. Daily chores never changed, and the struggles seemed to shadow every family, some with a darker shadow than others. With the Depression behind them, the struggles continued with the hardships of war. Farming seemed to be the only security that was felt for Joseph in these times.

Money was scarce, but Joseph maintained the ability to feed his family with the farm. He had often made statements of how lucky his family really was. They had a roof over their head, clothes on their back, and food on the table. He also had a tendency to remind himself that neither of the three is any good at paying the yearly taxes on his farm. Nor would the loan be paid following his brother's misfortune with a windstorm. Andrew had been left roofless, and supplies were needed to reconstruct the entire second level of the barn.

Amongst the hardship, the town was cursed with an unforgiving banker who made no qualms about foreclosing if it meant lining his own pockets. Joseph never displayed it, but he was relieved when Bethany had a sudden change of heart over Derek Carson's boy.

Yes, sir, Joseph thought, scratching his firm belly, *life wasn't always easy out here.* He tugged on his beard and knew he could never live anywhere else. Dobson's Crossroads was his home, and they would one day bury him here.

Joseph poured the pail of slop into the pig's trough and sighed. Not a day had gone by Joseph hadn't looked up the street in hopes of seeing Jeffrey come around the bend of the old farm road. Now his son was finally coming home. He felt his recent insomnia came from the knowledge that Jeffrey was coming home for one reason and one alone. It was that reason that worried Joseph the most, for he felt in his gut his eldest would soon find himself knee-deep in the war—perhaps Sicily or somewhere in Europe. Joseph knew there was no protecting his boy from what was about to come.

Returning the bucket to the rusty hook of the barn door, he turned in time to be nudged by Gracie. "Move over, Gracie!" Joseph said sternly, returning a nudge on Gracie's backside. In turn, Gracie stomped her hoof and took a few steps forward. "Don't go giving me attitude. Your turn is up next." Joseph placed some hay in the corner for her and the Jersey took no time in feasting on it.

With a chuckle, he patted Gracie on the stomach. "By the looks of you, losing a day's feeding wouldn't hurt anyhow." He slapped her on the backside as Gracie continued to gnaw on the divine taste of the sweet hay. "You women are all alike!"

"Papa, Mama asked me to bring her the morning milk for breakfast," Katie Anne announced, coming into the barn. Katie Anne, like all of Joseph's children, shared his brown hair and blue eyes. Their slim build and temperament, he was sure, came from Katherine.

Katie Anne wrapped a curl around her finger. "Will the truck make it through this snow, Papa?"

Joseph gave a shrug and put the milking bucket under Gracie. "I reckon we'll find out soon enough." He glanced up at Katie Anne as he continued milking. "You look very nice for church, honey."

Katie Anne smiled happily. "I wanted to look extra special for our talk with Mrs. Henderson, so I put on my best dress," she announced proudly.

Joseph paused and smiled with a nod. "Oh, yes, I almost forgot. Well, if she refuses your employment now there's something wrong. You'll be the best-dressed employee there by far."

Katie Anne gave her papa a huge smile and smoothed out her dress proudly.

Joseph continued to glance up from the pail occasionally, having mastered the talent of milking without looking. "I take it your mama's still set on going to town today?" Joseph asked as if he had hoped she'd changed her mind. "A blizzard wouldn't keep that woman from church, I reckon."

It wasn't that he absolutely hated going to town, it was nice to get off the farm once in a while, but with the weather being so disagreeable and a lot to do yet, it worried him to meddle about when the time was precious. And, in all honesty, his festive mood hadn't come to visit him this morning.

"Yes, sir," Katie Anne said simply. She waited without a response from her daddy. Then in a moment of flair, her papa mumbled something under his breath. "What did you say, Papa?"

Joseph looked up at her. "Nothing, honey, never mind, zip up your jacket before you catch a terrible cold."

"I heard Mr. and Mrs. Henderson talking. They say that rationing is getting so bad we'll all starve, Papa." She pulled the zipper up tightly.

Joseph patted Gracie on the stomach to thank her for the rich milk, grabbed the pail, and stood. "Baby, we're a long way from starvation. There is nothing we need that the farm won't provide. Folks in the city may have a harder time, I suppose. But we don't live in the city, now, do we?" Joseph ran his glove over his daughter's cheek. "Now, how about running this milk into your mama and tell her I'll be along."

Katie Anne gladly took the pail and hurried off toward the house, securely grasping the pale with both hands. Joseph watched his fourteen-year-old with great amusement. Katie Anne tried to balance the milk carefully without spilling a drop, stopping occasionally to adjust her hold.

Joseph chuckled, shook his head, and turned to Gracie. "Okay, old girl. Let's get you watered so I can have my own breakfast." Joseph filled Gracie's water trough and celebrated a job well done with a peaceful sigh.

The path from the barn to the farmhouse wasn't long, but in the bitter cold seemed so to Joseph. The sunlight attempted to peek over the clouds with no success and a worry came over Joseph as it had every winter. Although they all worked hard to store firewood and preserves for the winter, there was always a question in the back of his mind whether or not they had done enough.

Joseph's eyes focused on the small icicles that had formed along the corners of the old farmstead. The quickening breeze carried the smoke from the chimney skyward and away high above the trees that surrounded the house.

He reached the porch and collected as much firewood as his cold hands could carry. With a little juggling, he managed to get the front door open and quickly took a step inside. Slamming the door shut with his foot, Joseph could feel the warmth of the fire immediately. He added the armload of wood to the pile near the fireplace and held his hands over the heat. The sounds of the children at the breakfast table filled the room and everyone seemed to be talking all at once.

"Now that's enough chitchat!" he heard his wife say. "Anymore playing around, and we'll be late for Sunday services."

Joseph chuckled, not knowing how many Sunday mornings he'd heard Katherine say that in the twenty-five years they'd been married.

"Sara Sue, stop playing with your food and eat it!" Katherine growled.

"But, Mama, I'm not hungry," Sara Sue pleaded in a baby tone.

Joseph peeked around the corner to the kitchen, still holding his hands over the fire. "Sara Sue, you're too old for that childish tone. Now do as your mama says."

"Okay, Papa," Sara Sue said, a little snippy. She took a bite of her buttermilk biscuit with a protesting look. Chewing her food, Sara Sue placed her elbow on the table with a disapproving stare down at her plate.

Joseph pulled his gloves off, placed them in his jacket pocket, and returned his hands to the fire. "It's bitter cold out this morning. I want you children to bundle up extra good today." Still shivering slightly, he took off his jacket and hung it by the front door.

The path to the kitchen table was also a usual routine for Joseph. He walked the path so many times that it could be taken blindfolded with every success of reaching his destination. Placing an arm around his wife's slender hips, Joseph noticed her hair was pulled back and clipped, unlike her usual bun or French braid. No matter how she wore her hair, Joseph knew he married the prettiest woman this side of North Carolina. Joseph and Katherine shared a loving kiss, an important affection of love they chose to never hide from their children, and then he took his place at the head of the table.

Joseph's eyes moved around the table and stopped at Jeffrey's empty chair. Katherine placed hot biscuits on his plate and observed the concern on her husband's face. Joseph had a tendency to carry that look most days. She knew his constant concerns—money and the ability to support his family had always been the biggest stress since the day they married. But over the years, troubles increased for him with his mother's declining health, Bethany's somberness since Whitney's death, and the anxiety itself for simply being a part of a world at war. She had always maintained that her ability hadn't been limited to good cooking and fine housekeeping, but the very talent for reading Joseph's mind, a talent which became more difficult with his concerns extended over the years.

Katherine placed a hand on Joseph's shoulder and gave him a reassuring squeeze. "Eat up so we aren't late for services, husband."

Joseph nodded and lifted his fork, taking a bite of the scrambled eggs. Not only was she pretty but the best darn cook this side of North Carolina as well. The biscuit melted in his mouth, and he let out an enjoyable grunt. Only a second later, he realized there was something different about the table. Something, or rather someone, was missing. Joseph quickly looked at Katherine questionably and sat his fork on his plate, partaking of a long sip of hot coffee. "Where has Bethany taken to?"

Katherine found her place at the table next to Joseph and lifted her coffee cup as well. "She's gone to church early. Reverend Michaels asked her to run the Sunday school lesson this morning. Myra Pringle has taken ill. So your brother Andrew picked her up a little while ago." Katherine took a sip of her coffee and then gave him a big smile. "Working with Sunday school children is good practice for a future teacher." He nodded in agreement and continued to partake of the divine meal. "Can you believe she'll be twenty years old very soon?" Katherine giggled. "I was getting married at her age."

Joseph was darn proud of all of his children, but Bethany was the real go-getter. She was stubborn and determined with eyesight for what she wanted and the will to go get it. He and Katherine had had frequent conversations about their daughter. Joseph only wished Bethany hadn't grown up so fast and enjoyed her teen years a little longer. But she had moved into adulthood by the time she was eleven when the twins came. He felt fortunate to have such a good helper in Bethany, but always felt guilty that perhaps they had been too demanding on her so early. Seeing her now, he liked to believe that he had a hand in molding her into such a wonderful teacher-to-be.

Following the scrumptious breakfast, Joseph worked his way outside again to start the old Ford while his children collected their jackets. It was going to be a slow drive to town from the farm. The roads were slick with at least three inches of snow and Joseph was not looking forward to the drive at all.

CHAPTER 6

The Davies family, dressed in their Sunday best, arrived at the church to see others from the congregation gather. The church had a high-rise steeple visible for miles in every direction. From one side to the other, the tombstones spread with the first grave site dating back to 1726. The church was added to the old pioneer cemetery in 1802 as the area grew and was now one of the oldest buildings still standing in Dobson's Crossroads, second only to Korner's Folly. Old Mr. Dobson himself engraved the sign that reads as one enters the gate: *Dobson's Country Church and Cemetery, Established 1726.*

Walking down the long path toward the steps, Joseph could see the graves out of the corner of his eyes. He shook his shoulders, as he did every Sunday, feeling the same familiar chill. The church had a Sunday school annex, which was added in the spring of 1925. The addition also served as the location for many of the town's church functions—bazaars, parties, wedding receptions, and even the upcoming winter dance. With talents from the town's people, including all members of the Davies family, the church was extensively renovated in 1929.

Mary and Jeremiah Davies, Joseph's parents, stood near Reverend Michaels with a look of intense conversation. The reverend grasped Jeremiah's aging hand and shook it as others gathered. The fragile old man gave his best attempt to exchange a manly shake.

"Jeremiah, it's always a pleasure to have you and your family join us for Sunday services." Reverend Michaels was a tall, slender man of forty-five. He had come to Dobson right out of the seminary. It took much work to break him into the "ways of the town," as Katherine put it, but had been "molded fairly nicely." The reverend had a high-pitched voice that sent everyone to attention when the preaching started.

On occasion, the reverend would eyeball a member of the congregation during his sermon to boost the most extensive measure of guilt. On a particular instance, when good old Monty Macpherson was known to have been out drinking and causing disorderly chaos around town, Reverend Michaels gave a long-winded sermon on alcoholism and juices of the devil. Monty had sweat pouring over his brow all through services and arrived the following Sunday a changed man. Although his transformation hadn't lasted more than a week and he was back to the same old Monty.

Michaels gave Mary a warm smile. "Mary, it is always good to see you. How have you been feeling this week?"

Mary was dressed in her usual Christian smile and nodded. However, the tiredness displayed on her face wasn't something easily hidden from the rest of the congregation. It was known that Mary Davies had been feeling poorly for the last few months, and her four boys were greatly concerned about her. At the age of eighty-three, her hair had turned completely silver, and it had become difficult for Mary to stand upright. She would never complain, but many could see the pain she was in by the way she slouched.

Mary held tight to her cane and gave a friendly nod. "I'm holding my own, Reverend," she replied in a weak voice.

Jeremiah placed an arm around his wife. "It's been slightly difficult for her to get around these days. The weather's been hard on us both."

"Well, I believe even at my age, I tend to recognize new creaks in my bones during the winter months. Perhaps an additional prayer would be just the ticket for all of us." Michaels looked toward their sons. "I see all the Davies boys have arrived."

Mary glanced at her boys. "Sometimes I wonder if you'd have a congregation if not for my brood." Mary's boys stood tall over her and thought her very fragile. However, in her time, Mary did her share of chopping, plowing, and baling alongside them all.

Andrew, Danny, and Robert Davies talked, laughed, and talked some more, waiting for the church bell to ring. Children played about the grounds, and the women performed their usual gossip session. Katherine released her husband's hand and moved toward the women's circle. Joseph, pulling on his necktie, looked in his brothers' direction and joined them.

Joseph resembled his three older brothers. Each had a strong, firm build and slight chubbiness of the torso. Andrew was the only one of Mary's boys who fell short of facial hair, and Danny was the tallest of all her babes. The four brothers shared their father's high cheekbones and sunken chin. When it came to hard work, Jeremiah Davies passed that trait down to his boys as well.

The men shared stories of their week—labors, successes, and trials. Joseph filled his brothers in on the recent sightings of the pack roaming the area. They all agreed acting right away was necessary before the town suffered too many animal losses. Andrew agreed he would discuss the issue with Sheriff Grant Masterson, who would be visiting him for dinner following church services that day.

Meanwhile, the women engaged in other giggly chitchat such as new recipes or funny stories of children's adventures. Katherine's eldest daughter, Taylor, eight months pregnant, soon joined them. Noticing that most of the congregation had gone inside, the women instructed the children to move inside as well. Only moments later, the reverend rang the church bell, calling the flock to services.

Bethany stood near the annex door with hands crossed in front of her. Joseph almost failed to recognize his daughter. Her hair was hanging long and pinned back over her shoulders. The floral dress she wore had a belt around her waist that outlined her womanly figure. He had wondered when he missed the day his little girl became a woman.

Services began with a short welcoming prayer, and then the children joined Bethany at the annex door to separate from their parents for Sunday school. Reverend Michaels shared in a long, heartfelt sermon about sin and Christian responsibility. Bethany spent the next hour reading Scripture to the children and telling stories of Jesus and his disciples. Then Bethany returned the children to the main hall and everyone located their offspring.

Bethany took her spot with the choir and contributed two beautiful solos during "How Great Thou Art" and "Shall We Gather at the River." For Katherine and Joseph, it was a very prideful moment. Their daughter had a sweat and angelic tone. She could have sang for hours, and still maintained the congregation's attention. Everyone was in awe as the singing stopped.

Still sitting on the riser with the other choir members, Bethany spotted David Carson as he moved to the front bench, eyes glued on her. She felt on display as he grinned at her. Bethany clenched her hands together uncomfortably and was ever so happy when the reverend dismissed the choir and they were able to return to their families.

Michaels gave a few reminders about the close approaching church dance and gave thanks to those who volunteered to chaperone and prepare the event. Then he reminded everyone to remember the true meaning of Christmas and to keep the soldiers in their prayers. He met the congregation at the door, shaking hands as everyone ventured outside.

"That was a lovely sermon, Reverend." Katherine grasped the reverend's hand and cupped it between her own. "Won't you join us for Sunday dinner?"

Reverend Michaels gave her a thankful nod. "I would love to, Katherine, but I'm afraid I've already accepted at the Wallaby's. Perhaps you wouldn't object to a rain check on your hospitality next Sunday instead?"

"That sounds just fine," Katherine said.

The reverend looked from Katherine to Joseph. "How is that boy of yours?"

Joseph warmed his hands in his jacket and nodded. "We just received word that he's coming home on leave. Our hope is he'll be with us for Christmas this year."

"He is constantly in my thoughts."

Katherine gave him a soft smile. "Thank you, Reverend." Katherine noticed the twins running wild, their energy levels soaring. "A little prayer for those who remain here wouldn't hurt either."

The reverend chuckled. "Always do, Katherine, always do."

Katherine spotted Mr. and Mrs. Henderson approaching, with Katie Anne not far behind.

"Mrs. Davies, may we have a word?" Mrs. Henderson waved an arm and moved briskly toward them.

Katherine had been expecting this conversation all morning and was prepared to make her demands very clear. "Why, of course, Penny. How are you today?" Katherine turned her sights to William Henderson and nodded. "Mr. Henderson."

Willie Henderson returned the nod, yet maintained his silence. He appeared to be a beaten dog when he was around his wife. Many teased that William's graying hair wasn't anything but the signs of stress brought on by the life he lived with his wife. Although William Charles Henderson was a native of the Crossroads, Penny brought her high and mighty self from the Boston area. Everyone knew who *really* wore the pants in the Henderson family.

Penny was in her fifties if she was a day. Her own children were married off and, as many also gossiped, moved as far from their mother and the county as they could get. Being the owner of the only grocery store in the area, Katherine found herself tolerating Penny more than she would have liked. Well known as one of the richest families in the county, Penny made a point of reminding others of that rather frequently.

"Mrs. Davies, Katie Anne has shared interest in becoming employed at our mercantile," Penny said, throwing her red curls to the wind. "Of course, I told her that I would need your permission first." Penny looked around for an audience. Showing a sign of disappointment, she turned back at Katherine.

"We don't need the help of course, but we're always willing to assist a family in need." Penny gave a deep sigh as if, although sacrificing something huge in the way of employing Katie Anne, she was willing to do her Christian duty to be charitable. Her voice echoed, and she glanced around again with the same disappointment.

Mrs. Henderson stroked her fluffy mink collar and watched Joseph and Katherine, awaiting a reply. When no immediate response was heard, she then added, "I do hope that Katie Anne doesn't disappoint us because we can be very demanding of our employees. Any misconduct and she'll have to be dismissed."

Joseph noticed that familiar look of irritability and hoped taking her hand was enough to convince his wife to hold her tongue. "I'm sure that Katie Anne will be on her best behavior." He glanced at Katherine and noticed his wife's fixed stare. He quickly looked back at the Hendersons. "Of course, Katie Anne's employment is under the strict agreement that chores at home… and studies…are kept up."

"Well," Penny snapped back, as if insulted that Joseph felt he had a right to any demands at all, "I'm sure that it'll all work out fine." She glanced back at Katie Anne. "You'll start three-thirty sharp tomorrow. Don't muddle around. I can't stand people under my tutelage to be tardy." It was very clear—Penny was going *way* out on a limb to hire Katie Anne and refused to be disappointed in any way.

Katie Anne smiled happily. "I won't, Mrs. Henderson. I promise." She turned and ran toward her siblings excitedly. Joseph and Katherine could hear Katie Anne going on about her upcoming adventures at the Henderson store to her brothers and sisters.

Bethany delayed the trip toward the church door, waiting for the Carsons to vacate the building. She could still see David moving his eager eyes over her. Bethany pulled her long jacket tighter, quickly concealing herself from the humiliation of his stare. At first, Bethany felt perhaps it was just her uneasiness getting the better of her until she noticed his eyes piercing toward her breasts. He sent her a frightening wink, followed by a cunning smile when he realized he had been caught looking.

David blocked half the aisle at the exit and Bethany had no choice but to walk right by him during her departure. She held her breath to gain courage and fixed her eyes on her parents who stood just outside the exit. Bethany was determined to continue up the aisle without stopping until she was safely past David, giving him no satisfaction in returning his glance.

She reached her parents, and Joseph proudly placed an arm around his daughter. "So, how was Sunday school, Ms. Davies?"

Bethany gave her papa a quick smile. "It went fine, Papa. Are you all heading home?"

Joseph rubbed her back. "I believe we are."

Bethany laid her head on her papa's shoulder and returned his hug. "I'd like to go for a short walk. Can I meet everyone at home?"

Joseph studied his daughter. Bethany was never afraid to speak her mind and always gave great thought to even the simplest of tasks. No challenge was ever denied and most would be completed with great success. She was, for lack of better words, aggressive in the ways she tackled things. He missed his happy little girl who, in the past, carried a frequent smile. It was a time to celebrate when she carried more than a frown.

"Is everything all right?" He pulled himself out of deep thought.

Bethany gave him a phony smile. "Yes, sir, I'd just like a few minutes with my thoughts." Gazing over his shoulder, she could see Whitney's beautiful headstone, carved and crafted by her own papa. Sadness came over her as it did every Sunday. She noticed Uncle Robert and Aunt Page working their way toward Whitney. Their walk, which was a typical Sunday stroll, perhaps saddened Bethany the most. Bethany watched as her aunt knelt down with a bundle of flowers that Uncle Robert had gathered from the car. Removing the withering flowers from the Sunday before, Aunt Page replaced them with fresh flowers. A moment later, Chester and Marty joined them and lingered over their older sister's grave. Holding tight the railing, Bethany felt overwhelmed with emotion.

"Bethany?" Joseph had to call several times.

Her papa's touch made her flinch. Bethany shook her thoughts away and glanced at her daddy, giving him a warm smile. "I'm fine, Papa."

He continued to examine her another moment and kissed his daughter on the head. "Okay, honey, but don't be long. It's getting viciously cold out." She nodded and he held an arm out to his wife. "Shall we?" Katherine took his arm and said farewell to everyone before heading to the truck.

CHAPTER 7

Bethany moved up Main Street, heading away from the church, and turned left at the T-intersection of Old Farm Road. The road would lead her further from home and toward Dobson's Pond. After walking only a short ways, Bethany took another left onto a small trail that brought her into the wooded area behind Korner's Folly. The trail was somewhat visible from Old Farm Road, but overgrowth remained evidence that the area was seldom visited by others.

The pond was an important scenic area of Dobson's Crossroads since the area had been developed. Although situated behind Korner's Folly, Dobson's Pond was a landmark all its own. One had to travel the trail for a long while before reaching the footbridge that crossed the pond and into the clearing on the other side. Bethany looked back at her footprints in the snow and enjoyed the peacefulness of the wild as she continued the long walk. After fifteen minutes of travel deep into the wooded area, she arrived at Dobson's Pond.

The pond was fed by a small waterfall just to the left of a footbridge. On the other side, a large clearing as far as the eye could see was home to many deer, fowl, and other wildlife. The hillside was overflowing with oak and pine that stretched over nearly 150 acres of woodland and pasture owned by Frank Madison. On a beautiful summer day, the clearing would be covered in wildflowers of various rainbow colors, although today all Bethany could see was mile after mile of thick heaps of snow. At the very far edge of the clearing was a large ridge that dropped about ten feet. One could stand at that ridge and look bellow into the Roanoke River. Many times Bethany had sat for hours and looked up at Mount Mitchell.

The area was perhaps the only thing that hadn't changed over time and Bethany dreaded the idea of new owners. This spot was a solace for her. She only hoped the new owners would keep it as therapeutic as it has remained for hundreds of years. Madison respected the land and its natural beauty, and all Bethany could do was hope that the new owners would, as well.

Wrapped up in a world of constant change, Bethany looked fondly on her visits to Dobson's Pond. She had been manipulating a blade of grass throughout her walk, and as she approached the old cedar footbridge that led across the pond to the nearby meadow, she began to pull the grass apart. Bethany stopped in the middle of the bridge, bent over the old cedar log railing, and began to gaze into the waters. Still very cold, the pond had crusted over with ice in certain areas. But the waters continued to move outward and drain into the Roanoke River far ahead. The small waterfall, laced in pretty icicles, continued to drain slowly into Dobson's Pond.

Her reflection showed the womanly features that had taken over her girlish look. Over the last year, Bethany was forced to change shirt sizes twice to accommodate her chest growth, and eventually even outgrew Taylor's hand-me-downs. Although her change appeared to please David at church this morning, it embarrassed her tremendously.

Examining her own reflection, she imagined herself as the teacher she had always hoped to become. Bethany remembered the night Taylor's engagement was announced. What a shame it was to see her sister settle down with the least idea of what life really had to offer. Taylor was smart, still young at twenty-one. She had a lot to discover about herself and Bethany felt marriage would change Taylor's choices forever. Although Bethany had always dreamed as a child of being married at Dobson's Pond, on that very bridge, she knew all that seemed so far away from her now. She was pushed through unfortunate events to find an unwillingness to believe in love and trust. Sure, she wanted a home and a family of her own. Yet, she could never see herself fully accepting the commitment that love would require of her.

Holding her hand up, Bethany studied the withered grass pieces in her palm, how she, in seconds, turned them into bits of nothing. Spreading her fingers apart, she watched as, piece by piece, the grass fell into the pond to be slowly carried away and consumed by the moving water. That is how Bethany felt, consumed by life, and its unpredictability.

It had turned bitter cold in only a matter of minutes and, although her visit was made short, Bethany knew it was time to head home before she found herself way off path and in the dark. It took her a little longer to return to Old Farm Road because the path was covered in more snow than it had been upon her arrival. Finding her way back to the main road, Bethany headed toward home.

When she came upon the T-intersection again, David Carson was coming off of Main Street. Bethany looked around in desperation for an escape route. But, unfortunately, David had already laid eyes on her and was walking her way.

"Who do we have here?" David said with a grin.

Bethany stopped in silence.

"You looked so beautiful in church today." He smiled. "I thought, wow, has she grown up."

Bethany pulled her jacket tighter, feeling the same uneasy feeling she had felt in church earlier, and took a step back. Crossing her arms over her chest, she looked around again nervously.

"You sounded so good up there." He reached out to touch her face, and Bethany pulled away. "I was never so proud. I just can't believe you're mine."

Bethany shook her head irritably. "I'm not yours, David."

David's smile vanished. "Of course, I know we've had our problems. But that's why I'm here. I was hoping maybe we could talk it out."

"We have nothing to talk about."

David was always dressed in the best fashions and continually portrayed a look of confidence with his blond hair slicked back and every hair in place. But he also had a gruff side to him that she'd noticed five years earlier when he and his father moved to the Crossroads. At the time, Bethany thought she understood him. They had talked about how hard it was growing up. David's parents separated when he was very young, with Lorene Carson disappearing from his life all together. He and his father moved around a lot, making it difficult for David to find any sense of security. Derek Carson bought David anything he wanted to make up for his mother's absence, giving his son the false expectation that whatever he wanted was justly deserved.

When he was rude or disagreeable, Bethany took into consideration the hard life he endured. As they moved from friends to a couple, David became suddenly dominating and demanding over her, even violent or threatening when she upset him. Bethany lost all individuality when agreeing to date David and soon became dreadfully afraid of him.

Whitney pointed out the change in David a time or two, sharing her concerns over David's temper, and worried one day he would raise a hand to her. Then one day, he made the ultimate mistake in their relationship. She had walked in on David, finding him in a compromising position with another woman. At the time she hadn't realized it, but that day was a blessing in disguise, allowing Bethany to see the kind of man he had truly become.

David looked fiercely at her. "I think we have a lot to talk about. We had something great between us once." Bethany didn't say anything, but watched him nervously. David folded his arms and stared her down. "If things worked out differently, we'd be getting married some time this year." He took a step toward her, and Bethany quickly moved back. "You're so beautiful, Bethany… amazing to look at." He puckered his lips with a sheepish grin.

"You're making me very uncomfortable." Bethany attempted to hide her fear, knowing David would perceive it as a victory for himself. He was always happier in their relationship when he held complete control over her. Once, last year when they were dating, David struck her out of anger. She never shared that with anyone, but knew it was the road downhill for their relationship. Since then, well, she learned not to put anything passed him. David could be very aggressive, perhaps even dangerous, if pushed to his limit.

"Are you going to ever forgive me?"

Bethany was frozen, afraid to move for fear she would upset him. "There's no forgiveness needed. It just didn't work out for us."

He shook his head in agitation. "Martha and I…we aren't seeing each other anymore. I made a mistake, but I never stopped caring about you. I think we need to work this out. I want us to be together."

Bethany shook her head. "I don't think we should talk about this anymore." David grabbed her arm tightly and pulled her to him. Bethany fought, attempting to loosen his hold, but he simply tightened his grip. "Let me go, David Carson, I mean it!" she said in terror.

"No, not until you listen to me!" His grip got tighter. "Who do you think you're talking to? You should feel very privileged I even take a second look in your direction." Bethany pulled away, but he had a death grip on her. "You're not going anywhere until you hear me out." Bethany tried to force herself loose, and David moved his hand up to strike her.

"Well, it sure is a fine afternoon for a stroll," Sheriff Masterson called from the corner of Main Street in a stern voice. Masterson moved closer and eyeballed David. "Is there a problem, Mr. Carson?"

David quickly stepped away from Bethany, moved his eyes to the ground, and pushed his hands deep into his pockets. "No, sir, Sheriff. We were just having a friendly conversation."

Grant Masterson was a handsome man at the age of forty-two. He came to Dobson ten years earlier with his son, Eric. It wasn't long, and he found himself a prominent part of Dobson's Crossroads. The sheriff looked different dressed in his Sunday best, but even in his sheriff's uniform, he was pleasing to the eye. Talk was that Eric's mother died the day he was born, and Grant loved her so much he refused to ever remarry. Bethany found that very romantic.

Grant tipped his head suspiciously. "Ms. Davies, is everything all right here?"

Bethany quickly moved to Grant's side, still trembling, and gave David a scolding look. "Just fine, Sherriff! He was just leaving," she demanded.

Grant ran his fingers through his dark hair and looked at David. "You know, I was hearing that some commotion had developed in town last night. A few fellows got drunk and broke some windows. You wouldn't know anything about that, would you, David?"

David folded his arms, staring Grant down rudely. "I was at home. My dad can verify that."

"Well then, I guess it couldn't have been you, could it?" he said with a hint of sarcasm. David's cheeks began to vibrate. "Just to be clear, I run a tight ship in my town. Spread the word that if anyone wants trouble, they should take it to Europe where it can do us all some good."

David gave him a cross look. "I said I was at home. Why don't you go hassle someone else!"

"You and I have a problem, David Carson." Grant took a step toward him, and David stepped back with a look of threat. "I think it's time you headed home."

David chuckled and started up Main Street toward the bank. "I'll be seeing you, Sherriff. Bethany, I'll drop by for a visit and we can continue our conversation."

"No, please just stay away from me!" she called his direction. They could hear him laugh up the street.

Grant shook his head in disbelief. "That boy is nothing but trouble. I suggest you stay away from that one."

Bethany watched in fear as David disappeared ahead. "I've been trying, Sheriff Masterson, really."

"I'm on my way to your Uncle Andrew's. Why don't you let me walk you home?" They moved up Old Farm Road toward the ranch. "So, last I heard, the two of you weren't dating anymore."

"That's right, but I guess it hasn't sunk in for him yet." She gazed back, expecting to see David following them. She was quickly relieved to see the empty street.

"You don't have to put up with him, you know. I can speak to his father."

"I don't think that would do any good. In Derek Carson's eyes, his son can do no wrong. I have to admit, I'm glad you showed up when you did."

"Well, still, if he continues to bother you, I want to know about it. I overheard your parents. It's great news about Jeffrey. It'll be good to see him." He stared into the distance as they moved up the road toward the Davies farm.

"Yes, it will. Your son Eric is in the army, isn't he?"

Grant nodded and pushed his hands deeper into his pockets. "Luckily he's spent all his time stationed in Virginia. I'm not prepared to have him sent to Europe."

"Maybe the war will be over before you have to worry about that." Bethany glanced up at him. "It seems like forever since he's visited Dobson's Crossroads."

"He hasn't come for a visit since he was just a boy, actually. It was better for him being raised by my sister. She was always able to give him more of a home than I could. I felt it was important for Eric to have other children to grow up with, and we still spend a lot of time together. I envy your daddy. I always wished I had a large family."

Bethany giggled and watched the ground ahead of her as the two moved briskly past her Grand's farm. "To be honest, sometimes I wonder what it would be like to be an only child."

They stopped at the end of the Davies's driveway and Bethany could see her siblings playing in the snow in front of the house.

"Well, here we are, safe and sound. If you ever need anything, all you have to do is let me know what I can do to help."

"I'll just be happy to see the end of the war and our soldiers sent home. Were you ever in the war?"

Grant paused and then sighed. "The first war was over for a couple years before I joined, but I did some time as a soldier in the army. Mostly I was in France…and London. The Irish War was going on, but I didn't see much action. I guess I was lucky." He looked down pitifully. "It kills me to think we have to do this all over again." His eyes moved back to her. "Well, I best get going. Your uncle owes me a dinner and a chance to win my title back in rummy."

Bethany waved as the sheriff continued up the road toward her uncle's place. "Thanks again for your help, Sheriff Masterson."

Grant stopped and glanced back at her. "You don't have to put up with him, Bethany. Lord knows his daddy doesn't set a very good example for David. Derek raised that boy to think wanting is as good as having. Time he learned a person has to earn his way in this world and that there are consequences." Grant chuckled and waved. "You say howdy to those folks of yours."

Bethany replied with a wave as the two parted and she headed toward the house.

CHAPTER 8

Bethany moved the brush over Callie's back and patted the horse lovingly. Callie threw her head in the air and gave a soft bellow, then stretched her neck to reach the grain that had fallen to the dirt floor earlier that day. With a soft run of her palm over Callie's back, Bethany's thoughts went to three years earlier. She received Callie from Grand and Grams for her sixteenth birthday. What a wonderful surprise she was.

"That's my girl. There's nothing like a good brushing to get the kinks out." Bethany felt the sudden burst of cold wind behind her and looked toward the door.

Taylor pushed the door shut against the draft and moved promptly toward Bethany. "I was wondering where you might be," Taylor said, reaching up to pat the horse. "I come for a visit and you vanish."

Bethany pulled Callie's blanket from the hay bales, throwing the blanket over the horse's back. Without a word, Taylor began to help Bethany wrap Callie. Pulling the corners tight, Taylor stood back as Bethany fastened the belt.

"I figured you'd let out Jeffrey was coming home the second I walked in the door," Taylor said. "Isn't it great news?"

"Yes, it's very good news." Bethany paused for a moment. "I guess I just have a lot on my mind." Bethany patted Callie again and watched Taylor. "How do you do it?"

Taylor and Bethany both inherited their slim figure from their mama—besides Taylor's obvious front bump of one eight months pregnant, that is. They also shared a lot of the same features, including hair and eye color. But Bethany is an inch taller and unspeakably more stubborn. Bethany believed Taylor to be more beautiful, a mixture between glamour girl and country wife. Her sister could find positivity in every situation and seldom lost her temper. Taylor's Christian outlook spread over everything she did and when something bad happened, it was meant to be for a wider purpose. Bethany couldn't live her life so disciplined.

Taylor snatched a handful of hay from the bale and held it to Callie. She gave her little sister a confused look. "Do what?"

Bethany shrugged reluctantly. "I don't know how you can stand having Patrick so far away when you're about to have his baby?"

"I guess it helps knowing what he's out fighting for. When Patrick and I decided to get married, I promised myself I would accept that he wanted to do his part for the war. It isn't easy at all, but I have to respect his wishes. I'm very proud of him." She touched her belly. "I know our baby will be too."

Bethany patted Callie's neck with a sad glance at her sister. "Are you scared?"

"I'm terrified, for me and Patrick..." She placed a hand on her belly again. "And I'm afraid for my baby too. I want our baby to grow up knowing its papa. I know Patrick is being watched over and I have faith that when he can, he'll come home to me."

Bethany gently rubbed Taylor's belly and turned away. "What a Christmas this will be, hmm?"

"I've been hearing talk of David Carson coming around again. Anything there you want to talk about?"

Bethany grinned and began shoveling dirty straw from Callie's stables. "If I hear that name again today, I think I'll just scream!"

Taylor giggled. "I take it there's no interest there?"

Bethany held the pitchfork to her chest and looked at her sister. "Can this stay just between you and me?"

"Of course," Taylor said, nodding suspiciously. "Is something wrong?"

"David's been getting a little weird lately."

Taylor placed her hands together, blowing on them. "What do you mean weird?"

"He's been stalking me and made me feel very uncomfortable in church today." She moved the pitchfork over the hay again. "David has the illusion that we'll get back together."

"Do you ever see that as a possibility?"

Her eyes moved back to her older sister. "David and I dated for a year. In all that time, I had to constantly ask myself if this was the man I'd spend the rest of my life with." Bethany leaned the pitchfork against the stall and turned to her. "In the beginning, I felt he hurt me during a time I needed him most. Then later, I had to question if I ever really loved him at all. When I told him I'd marry him it was a big mistake." It was silent for a moment. "It was a blessing in disguise when I caught him that night."

"If he's making you feel that uncomfortable, maybe you should talk to Papa?"

"I'm not so sure that will do any good. David will only deny it. I just decided to do what I can to avoid him."

"Maybe it's the idea of getting married that has you spooked. Sometimes I wonder if you'll ever settle."

Bethany was silent for a moment and then shrugged. "Taylor, marriage is what you wanted. Being a wife and a mother is what makes you happy. Someday, I'll be ready to make that commitment when the right guy comes along. Until then, I have my eye set on something a little different."

"Oh, and what might that be?"

"Finding satisfaction in myself before, as you say, I settle." Bethany gave her a big smile.

"There is great satisfaction in being a wife and a mother," she reminded Bethany.

"When I decide to get married and start a family, I want it to be with someone I fall desperately in love with." Bethany tugged on Taylor's collar. "I want to be lifted off my feet by a handsome prince and have him fall desperately in love with me." Bethany giggled. "I want to have lots of babies and live in the biggest house."

"I guess there's nothing wrong with dreaming." Taylor laughed and let her arms drop to her side. "You've very high expectations, Bethany."

"I guess I do." She sighed. "I want to fall madly in love and have him be the center of everything I am and for me to be the center for him as well."

"You do realize who you're describing doesn't exist anywhere in Dobson's Crossroads, right?" Bethany glanced up at her and the two laughed. "Are you done out here? I'm freezing to death."

Bethany shut the gate of Callie's stable and cupped her hand in Taylor's arm. "So, how long are you staying?"

Taylor shrugged and they walked toward the barn door. "Mama's set her mind on me staying until the baby comes so I'm not alone."

"That sounds like Mama."

Taylor opened the door. "Bethany, some day your prince charming will come. The question is what will you do then? Prepare yourself, because it's going to hit you like a ton of bricks."

"I guess I'll just have to deal with that when it comes. I hope it's not too soon though. I have enough on my mind already."

They both giggled.

CHAPTER 9

The radio was playing soft Christmas music when Taylor and Bethany entered the house, shaking the snow off their bodies. Instantly, the chill, which had been present in Bethany all evening, subsided. Their mother sent them a soft smile with bodies strung about the room, immensely concentrating on their individual activates. The fire crackled as Jacob added a new log, making the living room quaint and warm.

"I do declare, sometimes I think your Papa walks on his knees for the many times I've mended these patches," Katherine said, holding up her husband's coveralls and pushing her fingers through the tattered knee.

"Where is Papa?" Taylor asked, searching the room as if expecting to see him.

Katherine looked down at the coveralls again. "He had to retrieve Katie Anne from your Grams'. He should return soon." Taking the thread into her teeth, Katherine ripped it from the patch and smoothed the knee with her hand. "There, guess we'll see how long this'll keep."

She sat the coveralls aside and began to tackle the missing button on Sara Sue's khaki shirt. "Dinner is about done. We can eat as soon as your Papa gets back."

Bethany lifted her book from the desk near the fireplace and sat on the floor in front of the warmth. "Did you notice it was snowing again?" Bethany asked with her eyes already moving over the next chapter of Faulkner's book.

"Um-hum," Katherine said simply. "Your papa thinks we'll have a lot this winter." Katherine chuckled. "I remember that Christmas just before your Papa and I were married. He was to pick me up for the Dobson's annual church dance, same dance approaching in a few days."

Katherine looked up, and her children were sitting at attention, extremely immersed in her story. Katherine giggled and sat her sewing deep in her lap, being very attentive to her audience. "The snow was so high that year with nearly no getting through it. Your Papa was beside himself. Lord knows he had tried for months to court me." Their mama giggled again. "Playing hard to get was one of many things I enjoyed about courting your papa, although he found it somewhat trying." Katherine pushed the needle through the buttonhole and smiled. "When I finally said that I'd go to the dance with him…well, he was determined to make it—one way or another."

Bethany smiled trying to picture her Papa trampling through heavy snow. "Mama, what happened then?" she asked, holding her book to her chest with fascination.

Katherine smiled her way. "Well, I'll tell you, Bethany, with snow shoes, fine wool suit, and all, he worked his way to my house with no absence of determination."

Taylor laughed. "I couldn't picture that!"

Katherine smiled and looked at Taylor. "You forget how headstrong your papa is. When he sets his mind, it's but done." She pulled the needle through again and gave a big sigh. "By the time he got to my front door, he was covered from head to toe in snow and had caught the worst cold anyone could ever dread catching!" Katherine looked at the floor and giggled as if reminiscing. "Your Grandpa Joshua was so impressed with your papa, he let him stay to warm, and we held our own dance right there at the house."

Bethany looked at the floor and smiled. That was what she so desperately wanted, a young man to go out of his way for her.

Bethany sighed with the doubts of that ever happening. She looked up and noticed her mama watching her.

"God put us on this earth, two people destined to be united." She seemed to talk to Bethany. "One day, we'll all find our soul mate. We can only find happiness through love. One must have faith that God has his own perfect timing."

"Mama, when did you and Papa fall in *love?*" Sara Sue asked in her baby voice.

"Sara Sue, that's enough baby talk, now."

"I'm sorry, Mama." She bounced excitedly on the hardwood floor. "But when did you, Mama?"

Katherine placed the completed khaki shirt aside and scooped up the next project. "I reckon I knew I was in love with your papa the minute he showed up at my front door covered in snow. From that moment on, I knew that was the man I would one day share a family with." She giggled. "Your papa, well…I guess you'll have to ask him."

Hearing footsteps on the front porch, Joshua quickly stood and ran toward the door. "Look, everyone! Papa's home! It's Papa, he's home!" He opened the door and stood as if paralyzed. Joshua slowly backed away from the opened door, eyes fixed on something just out of Katherine's sight.

Throwing her mending aside, she stood. "Joshua, for the love of heaven, what is it?" She suddenly stopped as if frozen in time. Placing her hand over her mouth, she gasped and then gave a loud screech. "Oh, thank the Lord!" she shrieked. "Praise God, thank you, Jesus!"

Jeffrey Robert Davies scooped up Sara Sue and laughed as he twirled her in the air. She was returned to the floor and Jacob threw himself into Jeffrey's arms. Jeffrey laughed and messed his little brother's hair before returning him to his feet.

Jeffrey, the tallest of Katherine's children, slowly took off his hat as he approached his mama, stopping within arm's reach of her. "Hello, Mama," Jeffrey said in his deep voice. "I'm home," he said softly.

Katherine took a step toward Jeffrey, slowly caressed his face, and then scooped her son into her arms. She began to rock him as if her eldest were still two years old. "Thank the Lord! Oh, thank you, my sweet heavenly Lord!"

Jeffrey released his mama to suddenly be mauled by his siblings. Bethany waited by the fireplace until everyone had their turn, then gave her big brother a hug. He looked around the room. "Mama, everyone, I'd like you to meet a friend of mine." All eyes veered toward the handsome soldier still holding his duffle bag at the door. Scott took a few steps inside and placed his bag on the floor, shutting the door behind him.

"This is Scott Jenkins. You remember? I wrote about him in all my letters. Scott, this is…well…everyone!"

Bethany examined the handsome stranger. His hair was black as night with thick eye brows, his pearly whites were bordered by adorable dimples, and his face outlined by heavy evening shadow. When he smiled to greet them, his smile lit up the room. Bethany was drawn to his dark-brown eyes and million-mile stare. A little ragged around the edges, she thought, but still absolutely handsome.

"Bethany?" Jeffrey said again.

She flinched, suddenly realizing Jeffrey had just introduced her to the guest and Scott's amazing eyes were staring right at her. She smiled in spite of herself. Things were about to get very interesting indeed.

Scott held out a hand. "It's my pleasure, I'm sure," Scott said in his English accent.

Bethany didn't mean to, but dropped Steinbeck with a loud thud against the wood floor. Her face turned red with all eyes focused on her. To make matters worse, she could hear Taylor snickering from behind Scott. At that moment, all she wished for—prayed for—was accurate aim Taylor's direction with a Steinbeck Special right between the eyes.

Scott was just shy of six feet and slightly taller than her. He looked like one of those guys Bethany admired in magazines at the Henderson mercantile, the kind of magazine she would've been embarrassed if caught looking at. She was awestruck by his distinctively muscular build and broad shoulders. *Quite the looker*, she thought.

Avoiding eye contact, she took his hand and gave one quick shake. "It's nice to meet you, Lieutenant," she said simply and quickly moved her hand away before he noticed her palms were sweating.

Scott looked around the room. "I've heard much about you all." He glanced back at Bethany, and for an instant, seemed to look deep into her soul. She quickly moved her eyes to the floor and he looked around at everyone again. "I'm grateful to you for allowing me a place to lay my head for a time."

Katherine smiled. "You are very welcome, Scott."

He caught Bethany staring again and she quickly looked down, smiling in spite herself. She had never seen anything like him.

Joseph and Katie Anne arrived home only moments later. After a short reunion, everyone gathered at the table for dinner. Then, once desert of apple cobbler was finished, the children left the adults to their small talk and retired upstairs to play. Katherine made a trip around the table, filling coffee mugs while conversation echoed the kitchen.

Jeffrey was saddened to hear his old friend Sampson, a red and black hound dog, had met his final days a few months earlier. During an attempt to outrun the hooves of the cattle, he had lingered too long in the pasture. Sampson was unable to move as quickly as he used to and, in the end, the cattle got their revenge for years of hound harassment.

The most popular topic circled around the present happenings of the war. This, of course, wasn't a topic that interested Bethany and soon she moved into the living room to continue her reading by the fire. About an hour later, Jeffrey brought Scott upstairs and showed him where to change out of his uniform.

After getting comfortable in blue jeans and a blue tee-shirt, Scott worked his way toward the stairway, nearly knocking Bethany over as she reached the top of the stairs.

"I'm so sorry," he gasped, grabbing her by the arm before she was completely knocked over. "Are you all right, love?"

Bethany quickly pulled away. "I'm fine, thank you." She concealed her embarrassment by quickly looking down. "Good night," she said simply and walked around him.

Scott's eyes followed her and he found himself admiring her curves. He looked down, embarrassed, when he realized Bethany was watching his stare. "It's still early. I was going to challenge you to a game of chess."

"You should ask Joshua. He's the chess master," she said sleepily.

"Maybe we can go for a walk or something tomorrow?"

Bethany sighed and took a few steps toward him. "We should get one thing straight, Lieutenant. Your handsome charm may work on all those women in London, but I, for one, am not interested." She folded her arms and noticed he had taken her insult with a smile. "What's so funny?"

He shrugged and put his hands in his pockets. "Well, I never had a beautiful woman call me handsome or charming, let alone both in the same sentence."

She had always been her daddy's daughter, or Jeffrey's little sister, but never did she remember being called a woman. His flirting amused her. "I didn't say that."

"Oh, you sure did, love. And for your information, my handsome charm hardly *ever* worked on any women in London." He beamed at her.

Bethany's lips curled, and her arms dropped to her side. "Good night, Lieutenant," she said, attempting to hide her amusement.

Scott took a quick step toward her. "You can call me Scott," he suggested, placing his palm over his chest. "After all, that is my name." He smiled in spite of himself.

They stared at each other in a moment of silence. Then, Bethany moved inside her room, and turned to him with a cunning smile before shutting the door in his face.

Scott put his cheek against her door. "Good night, love," he said softly.

Bethany leaned against the closed door, folded her arms across her chest, and listened. She could still hear him moving about on the other side of the door and she turned, placing her palm on the door panel. "Good night—Lieutenant," she said, still listening carefully.

Scott placed his forehead against the door. "It's Scott." He smiled hearing her laughter on the other side of the door. "Cheers, love."

CHAPTER 10

Bethany pulled a bale of hay apart and placed the pieces in the back of the old truck in sections. Shifting to a comfortable position in the driver's seat, she drove the truck up the fence a half an acre to where the cattle were grazing.

On a mission, she immediately went right to work throwing the hay into the trough where the cattle awaited breakfast. Once finished, she moved to the top of the fence and looked out into the vast prairie. The fields were green in patches, but a thin layer of white snow still remained. A large section of pine trees remained in the far field that connected the property with her grandparents homestead.

Suddenly, in the distance, she could see something weaving in and out of the trees. Bethany stood, balanced herself on the fence, and forced her eyes to focus on what was approaching. She gasped as the vision of two, maybe three, wild dogs came into view. In an instant, she found herself to her feet, located the rifle behind the seat of the truck, and loaded it.

Moving herself through the wood fence, she pushed the cattle to the side and found an unoccupied spot. She stood firm, aimed, and searched the barrel for a visual. *There you are*, she thought, pushing the butt of the rifle deep into her shoulder like her Grand had taught her. Taking aim, she squinted and fired, then fired again. Her body jerked back from the coil of the rifle, feeling a sudden sharp pain move through her shoulder. The pack dispersed and vanished into the trees.

"What on earth?" Jeffrey hollered, coming under the fence with Scott moving quickly behind him. Each took a stand at Bethany's side and looked out to where she was firing. "What are you shooting at?"

"Wow!" Joshua yelled. "Look at all those wolves!"

"They're not wolves," Bethany corrected sternly. "They're wild dogs." She looked at Jeffrey, concern written all over her face, knowing eventually a wolf pack would return to higher ground whereas wild dogs would be a more challenging issue to contend with.

Jacob raced a few feet ahead. "Should we go after them, Bethany? Should we?" He looked back at his older sister. "We can catch up to them, I know we can."

Bethany lowered the rifle. "No need, I'm sure they'll be back." Bethany looked at Scott as he examined her questionably. "What's with you?"

Scott gave her a suspicious smile. "I'm just not use to seeing a woman use a rifle." He raised his eyebrows. "Very attractive, I might say, love, however dangerous it may be."

Bethany handed the rifle to Scott, and he reluctantly took it. "I can handle a rifle as well as any man, Lieutenant."

Scott looked into her eyes, and for a moment, they held the rifle together. "In London, the women have babies, keep house, and take care of their husbands," he said, raising his eyebrows in an almost challenging tone.

"Oh, no, not so sure you should have said that, buddy," Jeffrey warned, as he took a step back from Bethany.

Bethany glared at him, struggling to keep her smile at bay. "I should expect that from some rich English city boy." Bethany let the rifle go and raised her voice in his face. "My mama worked just as hard to put this ranch together as my papa. Out here, you work together to build a home." She took a step away. "We don't buy happiness, but earn it just like any man, Lieutenant Jenkins!"

"Wait a minute. I didn't mean it like that, love," Scott protested.

"Out here, we're just a bunch of ranchers. If you want skirts, go to the city, Lieutenant." Bethany offered him a heated stare as she moved toward the truck. "And stop calling me love!"

"It's Scott," he corrected, watching Bethany slam the truck door. Scott looked at Jeffrey. "What was that all about, mate?"

Jeffrey sighed and shook his head. "You sure know how to talk to a woman, my friend." Jeffrey laughed and watched Bethany stir up dust, heading the truck back toward the house. "There you have it—liberated and direct. Don't say I didn't warn you from the beginning."

Scott sighed and looked at the path the truck was taking at full speed. "Is it just me, or does she hate everyone?" he mumbled.

Jeffrey hit him on the shoulder and placed his hands on his hips. "I told you she doesn't get close to many people. I suggest you stay far away for your own protection." Jeffrey watched the truck disappear over the hill. "My sister's quite the woman. You just have to get through that wall she puts up."

"I sure had no intentions of upsetting her."

"Oh, I don't think Bethany was as upset as she made out. She can come off strong sometimes. If anything, she's setting her boundaries with you, which is good, actually. If she didn't like you, she wouldn't give you time of day."

"Guess I didn't make a very good first impression."

"You don't receive trust from Bethany without earning it anyway." Jeffrey hit his arm. "Don't worry about it. Come on, I'll finish showing you around."

Callie had wandered out of the stall and found comfort in the corner of the barn. "Naughty girl, where do you think you're going?" Bethany said, pulling her sleeves up and patting the horse on the head. The large barn was so peaceful she could hear Callie's breath echo off the high tilted ceiling and hayloft just above the three sets of stalls. The loft and much of the barn was flooded with hay, grain, and corn the family managed to harvest over the summer.

Bethany returned the black mare to her stall, very well aware of Scott's presence by the barn door. She had spotted him out of the corner of her eye a few moments earlier and, after pondering her options, decided to ignore him.

"Easy girl, that's a good girl." Bethany patted Callie on the nose and sent the brush through the mare's coat.

"You're good with her," Scott said and closed the door behind him. "I didn't mean to sneak up on you, love."

Bethany glanced at him and then moved her attention back to Callie. "I asked you not to call me that."

Scott took a step forward. "I'm working on it, I promise."

She grinned at his sarcasm. "You've been standing in the doorway for a while, was there something you needed?"

Scott gave Callie a friendly pat. "Joseph said I might find you out here." Bethany moved the brush over Callie's back. She remained silent, and Scott sighed. "You have a beautiful ranch."

"I'm not one for small talk, Lieutenant. If you have something to say, then please save me the time and just say it."

Scott was taken off guard by her candidness. "Okay, ever since I arrived here, you've been very…unfriendly." He paused. "What is it I may have done for you to dislike me so quickly?"

"Dislike you?" Bethany stared at him for a moment, smiled, and turned back to Callie. "Do you require this much attention from everyone, Lieutenant, or just from me?" His silence made her curious, and she looked back to him. Scott was glaring at her. "I'm sorry about what I said earlier. It was uncalled-for." She turned back to Callie, grinning from ear to ear, and feeling his stare. "It's just that we get a lot of visitors at Dobson's Crossroads with the delusion that a horse and cattle ranch runs itself. I'm not sure what life is like in England, Mr. Jenkins, but out here, the women work just as hard, right alongside their men. It's a mutual partnership. It isn't an easy life, and I'd hate for anyone to belittle it." Her lips curled slightly, and it was all she could do to remove the smile before facing him. "But, I was out of line, and I apologize."

Scott looked deep into her eyes and slowly nodded. "It doesn't look easy at all." He gave her a soft smile and took a step toward her. "And apology's accepted." Bethany didn't move as he reached over her to pat Callie. She took in his sweet cologne. He smelled as good as he looked, in her opinion anyway. "I guess I just like people to get to know me before they pass judgment because of my family and the fact that I'm from London." He glanced down at her, and she was still smiling at him. There was no use hiding her interest anymore.

"Your family—you mean your rich ambassador grandfather," she said sarcastically.

Scott grinned.

Bethany laughed, feeling his extended arm rub against her shoulder. "So what are you, some kind of prince or something?"

"Don't let the title fool you."

She rolled her eyes. "Oh, trust me...it doesn't."

He offered his hand to her. "I'm really sorry if I insulted you earlier. I sure had no intentions of being rude. What say we try again?"

Bethany stared at his hand a moment and then simply turned her attention back to Callie. "Welcome to Dobson's Crossroads, Prince Scotland of London."

Scott looked at his hand and grinned. "Thanks." He took a step toward her and suddenly stopped, perhaps fearing for his own life. "Tell me something, is it just me, or do you offer such a warm welcome to all your houseguests?"

She ran the brush down Callie's strong leg. "Mr. Jenkins, as a friend of my brothers, I'm obligated to be polite and hospitable. But, I'm not lured by charm, especially from a soldier."

"So you dislike me because I'm a soldier?" Scott asked, raising his eyebrows. "I'm afraid there's not much I can do to change that."

"I don't dislike you for any reason. Maybe you just take things too personally." His eyes were magnetic, and for a moment, they gazed at each other. "I'm done here. Was there anything else, Lieutenant?" He was silent. "Good," she said simply, and he watched her leave the barn. Scott stared at the empty doorway in frustration.

CHAPTER 11

Jeffrey sat his coffee cup down and turned the page of the newspaper. "Boy, Kristina sure has a way of reporting the news."

Katherine topped off her son's coffee cup. "She's been very anxious to see you, Jeffrey. It would be nice if you dropped by."

Jeffrey watch Scott move down the stairway. "What about it, Scott, want to go for a ride into town?"

Scott sat next to Sara Sue at the kitchen table and looked a little more civilian in a blue button-up shirt and faded blue jeans. Katherine placed a mug in front of Scott and filled it with coffee.

"Well, sure, why not, mate. What's the mission?"

"I imagine just what I promised when I invited you along, a lesson in social interaction. It may even help your struggles with a certain country girl I know."

Scott grinned. "Maybe I'll just stay here and give Joseph a hand, then."

Katherine squeezed Scott's shoulder. "Scott, would you like some pancakes?"

Bethany hurried downstairs after spending half the morning searching her wardrobe for that perfect outfit. Her black skirt and tight purple blouse left no curve to the imagination. She chose to complete her ensemble by pinning her hair back and adding a dab of her favorite perfume. Scott maintained an undying stare the moment she entered the kitchen, but Bethany moved about pretending not to notice his interest. She smiled in spite of herself, feeling somewhat guilty of the torment she was putting him through, but still pleased with the success of gaining the lieutenant's attention.

"No, thank you, Katherine, coffee is just fine." Scott looked at Bethany when he thought it was safe, only to meet her eyes. She beamed when his face turned red, and he quickly looked away. "Good morning, Bethany."

Bethany pretended to ignore his dumfounded look, but her smile got bigger. She wasn't sure, but felt perhaps it was wrong to enjoy the way he looked at her. She pretended to ignore him for a moment longer and moved about the room, collecting her belongings. Then, she gave him a quick look, not wanting to be totally rude or appear to be playing *too* hard to get. "Did you sleep well, Lieutenant?"

"I slept very well, thank you for asking, Ms. Davies." He winked at her.

Bethany looked away to keep from laughing. "I'm—very glad to hear that," she said with obvious sarcasm.

"Why don't you have some breakfast?" Katherine asked placing some scrambled eggs on a plate for Sara Sue.

Bethany stood over Scott. "I can't, Mama. I have to meet Irene Maples this morning. I don't suppose anyone's going into town?" she asked, leaning over Scott and intercepting his coffee cup. She helped herself to a sip and then replaced the cup on the table in front of him.

"We were thinking about it," Jeffrey answered.

Scott sent Jeffrey a stern look. "Jeffrey—"

Jeffrey squeezed his friend's shoulder to silence him. "Would you like a ride to town?"

"Sure," Scott said, moving his coffee cup to his lips, "we would be chuffed to take you into town."

Bethany giggled. "I'd be *chuffed* to accept," she mocked. Scott grinned at her and she tapped him on the shoulder playfully. "So, are we going or not? I have to meet her in twenty minutes."

She grabbed a piece of toast from the table and headed toward the door.

"What's the occasion?" Jeffrey asked as he stood.

Bethany struggled with her coat, and Scott took it from her, initiating his gentlemanly charm. She accepted his assistance and fixed her eyes on her brother, placing an arm in the jacket. "I'm just giving her a hand in the classroom."

Katherine gasped. "I'm so happy to hear that, Bethany."

"Thank you, Scott," she said simply with her eyes still on her mama. "She asked me to assist in last-minute tasks before closing the school for the holidays."

Scott hurried to the door and held it open for Bethany. She walked past him with a big grin on her face.

Jeffrey shook his head in disbelief. "I think you're taking the social training a little too seriously." He shook his head again and hit Scott on the shoulder, laughing as he joined Bethany outside. Scott could hear Bethany laughing herself from the porch. Scott grinned and joined them.

Bethany sat between Scott and Jeffrey in the truck as they headed out of the driveway and turned right onto Old Farm Road. The road led them past their Grams and Grand's long driveway. The T-intersection was only a few miles ahead and would take them onto Main Street and into the heart of town. The roads, although still slightly frozen, was more slush now than anything. Taking the bend around the corner a little too fast, Jeffrey shifted and hit a pothole. Bethany grabbed Scott's leg for support and turned bright red immediately. She quickly moved her hand in embarrassment, and he gave her a big smile.

"Sorry," she said, looking away quickly.

"Oh, no, absolutely fine, I'm sure," he teased.

She sighed with a smile, shook her head, and gazed out the front window.

Jeffrey pulled the truck next to the curb in front of the school. "Do you want us to pick you up on the way home?"

"I'm not sure how long I'll be so I'll just walk home when I'm finished." She collected her belongings and then gasped when she looked up. "Oh, that's just great!" she grumbled, noticing Martha Walters come out of the Henderson's store looking their direction with extreme interest. "What a way to start a morning!"

"Well, I can see things haven't changed for you and your worst rival. Don't look now, but I think we've been spotted, and she's coming our way." Jeffrey laughed when Bethany slowly slid down the middle of the bench seat.

"Who is she, mate?" Scott asked.

"Her name is Martha Walters. She and Bethany have, how should I say, history."

Bethany frowned and elbowed Jeffrey. "Well, one of you has to let me out!" The hostility in her voice increased as she looked from one to the other.

"What's your hurry?" Jeffrey asked, waving at Martha with a smile. "You don't want to be rude, do you?"

Bethany elbowed Jeffrey again and he held his arm as he laughed.

Martha approached the truck on Jeffrey's side and he rolled down the window with a wave. Scott, noticing Bethany's hostility, quickly exited the truck from his side and assisted Bethany out the door.

"I thought that was you!" Martha gasped and placed a hand on his arm. "I'm so happy you're home from the wars. When did you get here?"

"Last night. How are you, Martha?" Jeffrey politely asked, still very amused by his sister's discomfort.

"Why, I'm just fine, Jeffrey." She looked at Scott and Bethany who were making their way around the truck. "And who might this handsome man be?"

"Martha, I'd like you to meet my best buddy, Lieutenant Scotland Jenkins. He's a paratrooper with the 101st Airborne Division."

Scott offered Martha a hand. "It's a pleasure to meet you, Ms. Walters."

"Oh, my, listen to that accent!" She placed a hand on her chest as if she was about to pass out. Bethany knew the vixen was displaying her naked wedding finger on purpose. "Be still, my beating heart." She looked at Bethany for a brief moment. "Hello, Bethany. Did you do something with your hair?" she said rudely and sent her attention back to Scott.

Bethany squeezed her purse to an inch of its life and glared back at her.

"We don't normally get such handsome visitors in our little town, most especially an English paratrooper." She shook her head vigorously. "That sounds so dangerous!" she said, emphasizing the words strongly.

Scott noticed Bethany's cheeks begin to vibrate as she clenched her teeth. He could only imagine the choice words Bethany was holding back and he just smiled.

"We should get together while you're in town. I would love to do my patriotic duty by entertaining the troops while you're here." Martha played with the pendant around her neck.

"I'm sure you would," Bethany said under her breath. Scott sent a smile her way and Bethany rolled her eyes back at him.

Martha moved closer, "I was just about to get a bite at the café. Would you care to join me?"

Bethany grabbed Scott's arm before he had a chance to answer. "Scott's here to meet Irene Maples, aren't you, Scott?" She tugged on his arm to pull him toward the school. "Come on, she's expecting us and we don't want to be late."

Scott moved his eyes from Bethany to Martha confusingly. Jeffrey suddenly felt very sorry for his friend. "Um, yes. All right, love."

"Oh, don't disappear yet, I just found you! I'm sure I'd be more entertainment for you than a couple old school teachers in a stuffy schoolhouse." Martha smiled, grabbing his hand. "Don't let us keep you, Bethany."

Bethany's mouth dropped and she glared at Jeffrey when he began to laugh. Scott looked at Bethany in confusion. "I think I better go in with Bethany," he insisted. "But we can get together another time."

Scott turned back to Martha questionably when she refused to release his hand. "Now, if I let you get away this time, you have to promise we'll get together before you leave."

"I'll see what I can do."

Bethany rolled her eyes again with no attempt to conceal it this time.

Martha rubbed Scott's hand erotically and Bethany thought she was going to throw up. "Do you promise?"

"Scott, I'm going to be late!" Bethany urged.

Scott glanced at Bethany, grinned from ear to ear, and then moved his eyes back to Martha. "Maybe we could catch some dinner sometime this week?" He could hear Bethany's intense sigh and witnessed her head shake in disapproval out of the corner of his eye.

Martha released his hand hesitantly. "That sounds like a charming idea. You don't look like a man who would make promises he doesn't intend to keep, Scotland."

Only his mother ever called him that. "Yes, ma'am," he said simply.

Bethany tugged on Scott's hand. "Come on, *Scotland*, Irene Maples is waiting."

Jeffrey laughed and put the truck in gear. "I'll meet you at the *Crossroads Chronicle*," he said to Scott before waving goodbye to Martha. "Have a good morning, Martha." Jeffrey looked at his sister with another chuckle before pulling the truck back into the street and toward the library.

Martha took a step back and waved as Jeffrey departed. "Now, let's not be a stranger, Jeffrey," she yelled after him. When she glanced back at Scott, Martha was somewhat irritated that Bethany was pulling him toward the schoolhouse. "Remember, Scotland, you promised." Scott waved back, and she stood, watching in disappointment as Bethany pulled him up the steps. Martha headed down the street alone.

Scott paused at the top of the stairs, tugging on Bethany's hand, and pulling her to a stop. She looked at him questionably. "What was that all about?"

She shrugged innocently and opened the door. "I have no idea what you mean."

Scott grinned and followed her inside. He took a few minutes to speak with Irene Maples and found her to be pleasant enough. During his visit, Bethany spent her time warming at the fire and very quiet. Irene was curious about London and had a few questions for him. All in all, it was a very nice visit.

About a half hour later, he met up with Jeffrey at the *Crossroads Chronicle*, which Bethany was kind enough to direct him to, and Scott made arrangements to return later to give Bethany a ride home. Although she didn't act as appreciative of the offer as he thought she should have, he brushed off her rudeness just as he had many times before.

When he returned, Bethany was sitting at the desk, in deep thought, and hadn't heard him come in. He watched from the coatroom as she chewed on her pencil, occasionally pushing her hair behind her ear. She glanced up from her papers and grinned. "Are you going to make a habit of creeping up on me, Lieutenant?" She seemed annoyed.

He approached her desk. "Sorry, I guess I do consistently do that, don't I? Are you ready to go?"

Bethany walked around the desk, leaning against it with her arms folded. "You're a nice guy, you know that?" she said freely.

"I can be, I guess."

"And, because you're a nice guy I'm going to give you some friendly advice. You'd be better off staying far away from Martha Walters. She has a reputation, if you know what I mean." Scott took a step toward her, and she drew back, quickly returning to the chair behind the teacher's desk.

Scott sat on the edge of her desk. "I'm honored you care enough to warn me."

Bethany was about to say something when she noticed Grant Masterson enter the classroom. Grant was in uniform and held his calico hat in hand as he approached them.

"Good afternoon, Bethany, I was looking for Irene." Grant seemed to stumble on his words and Bethany wondered why he looked pale as a ghost.

"She should be back any minute, Sheriff. Irene went across the street for a moment." Bethany pointed at Scott. "Sheriff Grant Masterson, this is Lieutenant Scott Jenkins. He's here visiting on military leave with Jeffrey."

Bethany noticed Grant's hesitation to extend a hand to Scott. When the sheriff did finally grasp Scott's hand it was with sudden awkwardness. She was puzzled as to why Grant appeared unforthcoming. She had never witnessed this form of shyness from the town sheriff before.

Scott seemed unaware of the discomfort Grant was displaying and simply shook his hand. "It's a pleasure to meet you, Sheriff."

"Jenkins?" he repeated. "You're English?"

Scott nodded and placed his hands in his jeans. "Yes, sir, I was born in London."

Grant squeezed his hat anxiously, and his continued uneasiness made Bethany very curious. "Well, welcome to Dobson's Crossroads, Lieutenant Jenkins." Grant's eyes continued to scan

Scott. "Bethany, I'll just catch Irene across the way." He gave her a quick look and his attention went back to Scott.

"Sheriff, is there anything I can do to help?" Bethany asked inquisitively.

"We've had some reports of wild dogs in the area. Lyle Baker lost some cattle last night. Then early this morning, one of Jack Ackerman's boys found himself cornered in the barn. I'm making visits to warn everyone to be on guard. It's not every day you hear attacks on people, but this weather's made them desperate to find food, I imagine. Desperate enough they don't scare off very easily. Might I suggest you not walk alone until we get this matter under control?"

"We've seen them around the farm the last few nights." Bethany walked around the desk and stood next to Scott. "Any idea how many?"

"Ackerman said he counted at least seven…maybe more… it's hard to say." There was a tense silence, and then Grant shifted toward the door. "Well, Scott, are you going to be in town a while?"

"I have a few weeks and then the 101st will undoubtedly be sent to Europe."

"So, you're a paratrooper?"

"Yes, sir."

"I've been hearing a lot on the radio. You guys sure know your stuff. Any hope it'll be over soon?"

"There's always hope," Scott said reassuringly.

Grant manipulated his hat nervously. "My son Eric's in the army. You remind me of him." There was an awkward silence and Grant suddenly offered his hand to Scott again. "Well, it's good to meet you, Scott. Be on the lookout heading home, now." He placed his hat on his head and walked toward the door. Glancing back, he tipped his hat, studied Scott one last time, and disappeared out the front door.

Grant stood on the porch and behind closed doors for a moment, intense concern on his face. He never expected this day to come, but here it was. He lifted his hat and ran his sleeve over his forehead. Although it was still bitter cold outside, the man was perspiring intensely. Over the years Grant had wondered what kind of likeness his boys may share. Scott was more firm and muscular, perhaps a smidgen taller, but his boys were identical twins just as he believed they would be. Grant hadn't counted on such an awkward visit and hoped they failed to detect his discomfort. He had heard that the Davies family were entertaining a guest, but for the life of him never counted on it being Naomi Jenkins' son—his son! Attempting to collect his thoughts he noticed Irene Maples exiting the Café and placed his hat back on his head. He moved down the steps and toward the teacher as she began to cross the street.

Bethany was still standing next to Scott when Grant departed. When Scott took a step closer, Bethany immediately retreated to her chair to retrieve her jacket. She wasn't sure why, exactly, she felt the need to be distant with Scott. It wasn't like he was ever anything but polite to her. In fact, the indescribable emotions she had when Scott was near confused her, because she was never confused in the presence of a man before. With perhaps the exception of David Carson, of course, but that was different. David made her feel uncomfortable and threatened. Scott simply made her feel—well, emotionally vulnerable. She had to be on guard with her feelings in the presence of Scott, because she could fall for him so very easily, and that was something she refused to do.

"Sheriff Grant seems very nice," Scott said, breaking the silence.

"Are we going to stand around chatting all day or were you driving me home?" she asked, unintentionally sounding rude.

Scott glared at her, sternly shook his head, said nothing, and moved toward the door. Bethany watched him from the desk, knowing she had hurt his feelings. She sighed and closed her eyes for a moment as he disappeared outside. Bethany didn't mean to sound so snippy and, honestly, regretted it the second it came out. A moment later she joined him at the truck. He slammed the door behind her, obviously very upset, and said nothing the entire trip to the house, regardless of how hard she attempted conversation. Needless to say, it was the longest trip Bethany had ever taken home.

CHAPTER 12

When Scott and Bethany arrived at the house a while later, Katherine had colored banners strung over the kitchen table. Scott took Bethany's jacket for her and both approached the kitchen where Katherine was working diligently on her project.

"Mama, what's all this?"

Katherine looked up from the table with a needle dangling from her mouth and her hands full of fabric squares. "It's decorations for the winter dance," she mumbled through the needle and thread. "How was your day?"

"We got a lot done. Didn't we, Lieutenant?" Scott frowned and it hurt Bethany's feelings somewhat, although she knew she had it coming. Bethany sighed sadly, feeling very bad about the tension between her and Scott. "Anything I can do to help, Mama?"

Katherine took the needle from her lips. "You can start by eating your lunch. Scott sat a bowl in the oven to stay warm for you before he left to pick you up."

Bethany briefly moved her eyes to Scott questionably, and he simply shrugged, apparently still offended by the little tiff they had earlier. He was being anything but cordial toward her, and it made her feel even worse about the situation between them. She gave him a sad smile, and he simply walked toward the stove, placing the bowl of homemade chicken soup on the counter for her. Then he walked right by her without saying a word.

Scott was on his way upstairs when Bethany suddenly blurted out, "Thank you, Scott." She waited patiently for a response.

He stopped halfway up the stairs and turned to her. Bethany sighed sadly, noticing the glare he continued to send her. "If you're not in a hurry, I'd like to cash in that rain check on a game of chess," she asked, as if there was no recent stress between them at all. Without waiting for an answer, she intercepted the game board off the top of the refrigerator. Scott reluctantly joined her at the table.

A moment later, a knock came from the front door. The sound of running feet filled the room as Katie Anne and Joshua made a mad dash toward the door at full speed. The girl stuck her tongue out at Joshua in victory and greeted their guest.

"Is Bethany home?" David Carson asked in a chipper tone.

Katie Anne stared at him, suddenly taking a step back. "Bethany!" she screamed with all her might. "It's for you." She snickered and ran toward her sister. "It's for you, Bethany!" She screamed, arriving into the kitchen. With her hands clutching tightly to the back of the chair, she bounced up and down excitedly. "It's David Carson. Quick, it's David Carson!"

Bethany sighed angrily and rolled her eyes. "Tell him I'm not here!" She tightened her jaw. "Never mind, I'll be happy to tell him myself!" she said, placing her palms on the table and throwing her chair back.

Scott's eyes followed Bethany. "Is everything alright?"

"Just peachy!" she said sarcastically. By the time she reached the door, David had taken it upon himself to move just inside.

"Good afternoon, Bethany. How are you?" he said, holding out a bouquet of daisies to her.

She ignored the flowers he offered. "What's it going to take for you to just get the hint?" she snapped.

David looked over Bethany's shoulder, noticing Scott, who had taken a few steps closer to the situation with great curiosity. Then David's eyes moved back to her. "I wanted to ask you something."

Bethany folded her arms. "I told you, we have nothing to talk about!"

"Please, just hear me out. The annual winter dance is coming up. I know it's short notice, but I was hoping I could convince you to go with me."

Bethany's chin dropped. "You've got to be kidding!"

"I assure you I'm not. Let's go outside so we can talk in private," he demanded while taking a step toward her.

Bethany shook her head vigorously and immediately stepped back. "No, I'm not going anywhere with you."

David gave her an angry look. "You seem to be forgetting who you're talking to," he raised his voice, grabbing Bethany's arm. Katie Anne and Joshua, who had been watching with Katherine from the kitchen, moved into their mother's apron in terror.

Bethany attempted a step back, but was unable to move with the hold he had on her. Within a second, Scott was standing between them. David fearfully released Bethany and took a few steps back himself. Katherine, with great concern, quickly approached Bethany who was obviously very upset.

Scott held out his hand. "Scott Jenkins, nice to meet you—David, is it?" David reluctantly shook his hand. Scott gripped it hard, and David tried to pull away, but Scott tightened his grip, turning David's hand blue. "I believe what Bethany was attempting to explain is that she already has a date for the winter dance. I'll be escorting her. But I'm sure she appreciates your invitation." He released David's hand, and the guest quickly stepped back, taken off guard. Bethany looked at Scott questionably, and he immediately took her hand, squeezing it reassuringly. "Was there anything else we could help you with?"

David glared at Scott. "What do you mean she's going with you?" He looked beyond Scott to Bethany sternly. "Let's just go outside and talk for a moment." Scott squeezed Bethany's hand again, and she rolled her eyes at David. "I'm not playing around, Bethany, let's go now."

Scott took a step toward David. "I'm sorry, but you are really being very disrespectful, mate."

"I'm not your mate, and I suggest you stay out of other people's affairs." He gave Scott a stern look.

Scott took another step toward David, and Bethany softly pulled him back. "I think you just wore out your welcome," Scott said sternly. "So, maybe it's time you left." Scott took another step forward, and Bethany pulled him back again. She grasped his right arm into her chest and held him firmly back. Scott looked at Bethany, who at this time looked terrified.

"I don't want you coming by anymore," Bethany said with a soft, scared tone. "I asked you before. Please, just leave me alone."

David took a step toward her, and Scott moved in front of Bethany, holding her hand tightly. Scott tipped his head and stood in a challenging stance, daring David to come closer.

David stopped. "What would it hurt to just talk to me for a minute?"

"I believe Bethany asked you to leave," Scott said with a more stern voice.

"What, are you her bodyguard or something?" David asked rudely. "Why don't we just settle this outside like men?"

Scott took a step forward again, and this time Katherine grabbed Scott's arm, standing between the two. "David, I need you to go."

David glared over Katherine to Scott. "This isn't over, Jenkins." He pointed a finger at Scott. "You have no idea who you're dealing with!"

"Actually, I know exactly what I'm dealing with!" Scott attempted to move forward, and Bethany pulled him back again.

"Scott, please," Bethany pleaded. "David, just *go!*"

David pointed another finger at Scott. "I'll be seeing you," he said sternly.

Scott gave him a daring smile, nodded, and winked at him provokingly. David dropped the flowers, threw the screen door open, and disappeared down the stairs.

Katherine looked back at her daughter. "What on earth was that all about?" she asked in a worried voice.

Bethany, still in shock over the ordeal, shook her head sadly. "Mama, David's been stalking me," she finally shared. Bethany held tight to Scott's hand as she trembled. "He has this idea we're going to get back together. I've asked him to leave me alone, but he keeps following me."

Scott squeezed her hand. "We'll be putting a stop to that," Scott said sternly, feeling her tremble.

"Something needs to be done about that young man. Your papa will be beside himself when he gets wind of David's actions here today!" Katherine said, returning to the kitchen.

Bethany and Scott stood alone by the doorway and she let go of his hand. "I wasn't really planning on going to the dance."

Scott folded his arms and shrugged. "That's up to you. I was just trying to give you a little assistance," he said simply and walked toward the stairway, shooting her a quick look. "I would hate for you to feel obligated," he said in a hurt tone, disappearing at the top of the stairs.

She stormed toward the stairway and grasped the railing. "I didn't mean it that way. I thought we were going to play chess? Scott!" She looked down in confusion.

Katherine wiped her hands and approached her daughter, looking up the empty stairway herself. "Do you realize you're constantly rude toward that young man?"

Bethany looked at her sadly.

"He was just trying to be helpful, Bethany."

"I didn't mean to hurt his feelings. But I seem to be doing it a lot."

"Perhaps now that you realize that, you can change it." Katherine squeezed her daughter's shoulder. "People can't be hurt unless they care."

"I never asked him to care," she said softly, looking up the empty stairway.

"Then why do you look so upset?" Bethany looked at her mama, and Katherine gave her an understanding smile. "Biggest hurt of all is if we feel we've hurt those we care most about." Katherine walked back toward the kitchen and stopped, turning to her again. "If you didn't care, why are you still standing there?" Bethany gazed at her mother, and Katherine smiled, nodding in approval when Bethany ran up the stairway.

Bethany could see movement coming from the boy's room located next to her own. Entering the empty doorway, she folded her arms and leaned against the doorframe. She was in awe. There he was, shirtless and beautiful. She attempted to move her gaze away from his amazing form, his firm and muscular build. It was too late. Scott sent a devilish grin her way when he caught Bethany staring. What could she do but simply smile? Bethany liked what she saw, and now Scott Jenkins knew it. For a brief moment, he stood silent, watching her as if giving her the opportunity to admire him.

"Did you come up here to yell at me some more, love?" he asked, pulling a clean tee out of his duffle bag. He looked back at her, and she was grinning from ear to ear. Scott tipped his head. "What?"

She shrugged and bit her bottom lip out of shame. Scott threw his shirt over his shoulder and walked toward her. Bethany, eyes still fixed on his chest, watched the contracting muscles as he approached her. His skin was soft and perfect, every curve attractive, to say the least. Scott Jenkins was amazing to look at. Now, sharing the doorframe together, her smile matched his grin.

"I'm not the friendliest person sometimes. People have to get to know me." She attempted to apologize with her eyes still fixed on his body.

He moved his face closer to hers and Bethany looked into Scott's eyes. She didn't blink. His sweet breath warmed her lips. They seemed to communicate without words for a moment as he moved even closer.

"Slightly hard to do when you're busy yelling all the time, love," he said, folding his arms.

She stared at his lips and tried to imagine what it would be like to cover them with her own. David Carson was the only one she had ever kissed, and Bethany had no reservations that Scott Jenkins would put him to shame.

"I don't mean to," she said truthfully, still staring at his lips.

Bethany's eyes drifted to his, and they observed each other. No matter how mysterious his eyes seemed to her, there was something trusting in them. She knew those brown eyes locked in a number of secrets—as a soldier, how could they not? But she suddenly realized that she wanted to know all there was to know about Lieutenant Scott Jenkins. He reached up to touch her face, and for the first time, she didn't pull away from him. His hand traced her face and his eyes followed in amazement. Her smile widened when his thumb moved over her lips. Bethany watched him in silence, waiting for him to reveal his next move. Scott placed his hand on her neck and pulled her closer. Her heart began to beat wildly. For a brief moment, she felt the static of his lips.

"Race you to the bed?" they heard Jacob call.

Scott was suddenly pushed aside, leaving Bethany standing alone at the doorframe. Jacob pounced on the bed, jumping as high as the springs would carry him. Bethany's blood began to boil and she was determined her younger brothers would pay dearly. Scott beamed at her, and Bethany blushed, wondering if he had read her mind. He pulled his shirt over his head and nudged her with his hip as he walked past her. With an almost desperate look, her eyes followed Scott down the hallway.

"Where are you going?" She seemed annoyed by their sudden interruption.

Scott stopped halfway up the hallway and turned to her. "I thought we were playing a game of chess?"

She smiled and joined him in the hallway.

He squeezed her hand and chuckled. "By the way, I accept your apology—this time, anyway." He winked at her and she laughed.

CHAPTER 13

"Here we are, my child." Mary placed the tray of cookies and milk on the coffee table in front of the couch. The Davies boys often teased their mother, stating that with just one bite, people would come from all parts of the world for her freshly baked goods. The still warm sugar cookie melted in Bethany's mouth.

Mary joined Bethany on the overstuffed couch and sat her cane aside. "Now, let's have a chat while the men are out fighting that barn door."

Bethany knew that tone. Whenever Grams requested a "chat," it usually meant she had either heard meddling gossip among the townspeople or had something of deep concern on her mind. Bethany simply nodded and filled her mouth with more of her cookie. She studied her grandmother, the frail woman that let only her hardened shell be displayed to many. Mary Davies was good at keeping her feelings locked deep within herself. Perhaps that is where Bethany learned to master it so well.

Bethany remembered being told on many occasions that she and her Grams were very much alike. It wasn't until Whitney's memorial service that Bethany realized how much. The entire town was in tears that day. Her cousin was loved by everyone. Whitney was the sweetest, most compassionate person; her beauty emitted from the inside out. Bethany remembered there were two who shed no tears, two who showed no feeling to the outside world. All the pain and agony of that day was locked up somewhere deep inside Mary and Bethany Davies. Now it was the one-year anniversary of their loss, and the darkness remained, that day unspoken.

Mary smiled and cupped Bethany's hand between her own, holding them in her lap. Squeezing Bethany's hand, Mary gave her a warm motherly smile. "I've been watching you all morning, never seen a child with so much on her mind."

Bethany looked at the floor sadly. "I don't know what you mean, Grams."

Mary sighed and nodded. "We are two of a kind, you and me." Bethany watched her grandmother, the dark bags under her eyes and weariness in her voice. Mary took a deep breath and squeezed her hand again. "Sometimes things happen for a reason. We don't pretend to understand them, but try to have faith and accept them."

Bethany gave her a confused look.

"Bethany, it's time you and I accept what happened to Whitney and move on with our lives." Mary focused on Bethany's quickening movement as she stood and walked to the hearth. Taking a deep breath, Mary felt her granddaughter's torment. "Sweetheart, it's been a year. Have you even mourned her yet?"

Bethany quickly turned to her, sounding somewhat insulted. "I mourn her every second!" she said furiously.

Mary looked down in despair. "I mean to really mourn, Bethany. It was a long time before I could cry myself. When I finally did, I was able to let go. I see it in your eyes, the pain and sorrow. We have living to do, and it's time we got to it."

Bethany stared at the picture of her and her cousin on the mantel and she took it tightly in her hand. Her eyes watered, but she refused to cry. "You, of all people, should understand me, Grams," she said simply.

"There was something I never told you about that day."

Bethany slowly looked at her.

"I used to think that we've had trouble expressing our feelings over Whitney because we're so much alike. But I think it goes deeper than that. We share a similar guilt that we need to let go of."

Bethany replaced the picture on the mantel and took her seat, once again, next to her grandmother. "I don't understand," Bethany said softly.

Mary took her hand again. This time her grandmother's hands began to tremble. "It wasn't your fault what happened…it was mine." Mary's eyes became damp.

Bethany shook her head in desperation. "No, how could it have been your fault?"

Mary looked at their clasped hands and squeezed them. "I asked Whitney to come over that day. Your Grand was off with your uncles, and I was feeling lonely. By the time we finished working in the kitchen, she was running late to meet you, Bethany. I believe she was in a hurry to get to Dobson's Pond because I had detained her…and that's when she fell. If it hadn't been for me, perhaps she would've never slipped."

"Don't you see, Grams? Whether she was running late to meet me or I was late getting there, if I had been there like I should have, I could have helped her." Bethany quickly stood and wiped her cheeks. "I should've been there for her!"

Mary stood as well and held Bethany at arm's length. "You have to let this guilt go, my darling. You can't keep on so."

Bethany was about to say something when the front door opened. She quickly wiped her face and turned away in an attempt to gain her composure. Scott, noticing Bethany's sadness, watched her as he slowly closed the door behind him.

"Well, how is that barn door?" Mary attempted to gain her composure as well.

Scott kept Bethany in his sights, and she noticed his concerned look.

Jeffrey seized a cookie from the platter. "It took some doing," he said with a mouthful. "But it should hold through another winter."

Jeremiah sat in his overstuffed chair. "Thank you, boys, I'd have never managed that door on my own."

Scott and Bethany watched each other and he questioned her with his eyes, but she simply shook her head and looked down.

"You know, Scott and I can come over and help you tackle that rundown fence in the morning, Grand. It didn't look like it'd take much," Jeffrey insisted.

"Oh, you two enjoy your time home," Jeremiah protested. "I'll get your uncles over here in due time." He looked at Bethany. "Bethany, you're awfully quiet, honey."

Bethany gave him a phony smile. "It's just nice to be here, Grand." She glanced at Scott, and he was giving her a concerned look.

Scott looked down at Jeremiah from where he was standing next to Bethany at the fireplace. "Jeffrey's right. If you need, we'd be chuffed to give you a hand, Mr. Davies."

Mary clasped her hands together. "Well, won't you all stay for dinner? I have a wonderful roast in the oven."

"I'm sorry, we can't, Grams," Jeffrey said. "Mama was expecting us home for dinner. Before we leave though, for sure." Jeffrey chuckled. "Besides, Romeo here has a date."

The burning jealousy on Bethany's face told a story all its own. Her jealous stare moved from Scott to the floor, and Bethany remained silent.

"Who's the lucky girl?" Jeremiah asked.

Bethany sighed aloud unintentionally. There was nothing like pouring salt on her wound.

"Do we know her?" Jeremiah sent his eyes up to Scott.

Scott shrugged. "It's not really a date. I'm just going to a movie with Martha Walters."

Bethany's heart dropped.

Jeremiah raised his brows and glanced at Bethany, then back to Scott. "Walters, you say? Isn't she the girl that—"

"So," Mary quickly interrupted, "what's your mama been up to?"

Bethany looked at her grandmother with an almost pathetic stare.

Mary nodded at her granddaughter reassuringly. "I'm sure Katherine has her hands full with the holidays just around the corner. The house is no doubt sparkling with decorations, along with a grand tree on display, if I know her."

Bethany nodded, not really into the conversation, and lifted her jacket off the chair behind her. "You know Mama and the holidays, Grams. It's her favorite time of year. She's got every decoration displayed about the house."

Mary gave Bethany a hug. "And she has already started her fruitcakes, I'll just bet."

"Yes, ma'am, just like every year before," Bethany said in a low tone.

Mary kissed Bethany on the top of the head. "You tell that son of mine that I'd like to see him more than simply church services."

Jeffrey gave his grandmother a smack on the lips. "We'll tell him, Grams."

Jeremiah reached his hand out to Scott. "It was a pleasure to meet you, young man. Don't be a stranger."

Scott shook Jeremiah's hand. "I won't, sir."

Bethany bent down and gave her grandfather a kiss on the cheek.

Jeremiah smiled up at her. "Bethany, are you all right, honey?"

Bethany's eyes held Scott's for a moment and then she looked back to her grandfather. "I'm just fine, Grand, I love you. We'll see you two at church services on Sunday."

Jeffrey walked heel to heel with Scott as they headed up the street from his grand's toward their farm. "You know, William Dobson bought the land in 1771. Why, rumor has it George Washington himself made unannounced visits because he liked the pub so much. 'Course, it's called Greer's Bar and Pub now." He looked at Scott and his friend seemed preoccupied. "Korner's Folly is one of the oldest homes still standing in Dobson. When the family moved away, it was boarded up. Kind of a shame no one lives there, it's such a nice home. I'll bring you there one of these days."

Although listening in part, Scott's attention was focused more on Bethany, who had worked her way ahead of them. She walked at a steady pace and stared sadly at her feet. They approached a large farm on the left and a voice echoed from the porch.

"Jeffrey, is that you, boy?" A man waved.

"Hello, Uncle Danny!" Jeffrey waved and hit Scott on the arm. "Don't wait for me, I'll catch up." Jeffrey moved toward his uncle and, grasping the top of the white picket fence, threw his body over the top, finishing the length to his uncle in a sprint.

Scott picked up his speed in an attempt to catch up with Bethany. In no time, he was walking in stride with her. Bethany glanced up, acknowledging him, and then looked back down at the ground.

"Your grandparents are so great. I really enjoyed our visit," he said, breaking the silence, and she simply nodded. Scott gazed at her for a moment and then ahead. "Are you all right?"

She refused to look at him. "Shouldn't you be hurrying along to prepare for your date?"

Scott studied her animosity and then looked away. "The movie isn't until later tonight. Besides, I'm enjoying my walk with you," he said, noticing her jealous tone. "It's Clark Gable. You're welcome to come along if you'd like."

Bethany laughed rudely and glared up at him in amazement. "Go with you, on a date to a movie—with Martha Walters? I think I'll pass, thanks."

Scott forced her to a stop as he gently took her arm. "It's not a date, Bethany. We're simply going to see a movie."

"I'm sorry. Did it sound like I'm bothered you're going with her?" she growled back.

Scott released her and placed his hands in his pockets. "Aren't you?"

She shook her head in disbelief, leaving him standing alone.

"Will you wait?" he asked sternly.

Bethany stopped and turned to him but said nothing.

"I just know she's not your favorite person, that's all. I didn't want you to think I disrespected your feelings by spending time with her."

She stared at him a moment and then took a deep breath. "I'm a big girl, Scott. You can see anyone you want, it's none of my business." She left him standing alone in the middle of the street.

CHAPTER 14

Bethany hadn't mentioned her discussion with Irene Maples to anyone. She decided it would be best to ensure passing the exam before getting everyone's hopes up. It seemed to her that everything came out jumbled lately. Bits and pieces of thought floated around, but the puzzle never really connected to anything that made sense. She leaned over the railing of the front porch and gazed out at the Great Smoky Mountains and wondered if anything would ever make sense to her again. Running her fingers through her hair, she took a deep sigh to shake the headache that had been forming all day, and then placed a strand of hair behind her ear and out of her eyes.

Bethany, even now, tried to rationalize what was truly bothering her. Was it the conversation she had had with her Grams only hours earlier? How the guilt she felt was long due for closure and needed to be reckoned with.

Perhaps it was even the initial shock of Scott seeing her archenemy, Martha Walters, the one person who had the ultimate goal of ruining her life and had interfered with her relationship in the past. She didn't understand why Martha hated her so much, but was very well aware of the contempt and hostility she had toward her.

Then again, maybe it was Bethany's very own desire to run away. She felt the need to hide from love for fear of it. Bethany wondered what happened to the control over her environment she once felt. Suddenly, she found herself lost in change and no way of controlling the outcomes. It made her very melancholy.

Although many things bothered her at that moment, she had to admit it was the burning jealousy of Scott's date with Martha that confused her the most. She found herself watching the clock for Scott to return. At almost ten in the evening, her blood began to boil. She could only imagine how far that vixen had gotten with Scott by now.

Then, half past ten, Martha pulled the car in front of the house. Bethany watched as she placed the car in park and the two began talking. Scott had reached for the door handle and Bethany witnessed as he was abruptly pulled back by the scoundrel. Martha placed a persistent kiss on Scott's mouth and Bethany looked down when the kiss turned into a passionate moment between the two. She leaned against the railing and stared at the door of the house after hearing the car slam shut. Martha drove off, and Scott ran up the steps.

"How was the movie?" she asked, staring at the front door.

Scott was taken off guard. "Bethany, I didn't see you there." He placed his hands in his pockets and looked shamefully at the disappearing car.

She noticed the sudden embarrassed look on his face.

He took a few steps toward her. "It was okay. Clark Gable flicks are usually entertaining enough." They watched each other in silence for a moment. "Why are you out here in the cold?"

His question stuck in her mind for a moment and she shrugged before veering out into the darkness. She was glad he was enjoying his time while he was at the Crossroads, but wished it was with someone other than Martha "Easy As They Come" Walters. Bethany shrugged for fear he would misinterpret no reaction as an intrusion of her space and go inside.

"I'm glad you had a good time," she said, and Scott nodded. "How was the company?" Bethany was sure he detected a hint of jealousy, because she was sure feeling it. She moved her eyes to him, not really expecting an answer.

Scott looked down and smiled, remembering the warning she had given him about Martha. Bethany rubbed the lipstick off the corner of his lips and held out the thumb smear to show it to him. "Not exactly your shade," she whispered and stormed toward the door. Scott gently intercepted her hand, and she stopped, refusing to look at him.

"Please, Bethany, don't walk away," he pleaded. "Can't we just talk without you storming off like you usually do?"

She stared at him sternly. "If you want to get involved with Martha Walters then that is your business, so what is there to talk about?"

"I asked her to the dance." His eyes moved up to hers, and he noticed the hurt she tried to conceal. "You said you had no plans to go. I didn't want you to feel obligated."

She folded her arms and quickly looked away. "Oh, well, I'm not much for social gatherings," she said, obviously very hurt. Scott said nothing, and she turned to him. "That's why you're here isn't it, to enjoy yourself – to have a last fling before you go off to war?" Bethany stomped toward the door. "I have an early day tomorrow. Good night."

Scott took a step toward her as she pulled the door open. "Bethany, please?"

She stopped, glanced back, and disappeared inside.

CHAPTER 15

The door of the mercantile chimed, announcing Bethany's arrival. It was a cozy store, with an ice cream booth and malt counter to the right as you entered, and the grocery counter to the left. Rationing had a large impact on the shelves up and down the aisles, and although not completely empty, it was surely not as plentiful as it had been since before the war. In the back was a full area drug counter that also accommodated a few tables where Willie Henderson entertained for a friendly game of cards or a round of tall tales with some of the town men.

The entire upstairs was dedicated to the Henderson's living quarters. Bethany had heard, but never witnessed, that Mr. and Mrs. Henderson had their own rooms and slept separately. Bethany found that to be very peculiar and decided if she were to ever have a husband, he would never get away with making her sleep alone. The store had the faint sound of Christmas cheer in the background, and Bethany was sure she smelled the delicious scent of cinnamon apple coming from the upper level.

Penny seemed occupied by last-minute holiday shoppers, and at the same time attempted to assist the Bryant sisters, who appeared to be having trouble choosing a fabric color for their new kitchen curtains. Meanwhile, Willie Henderson was adding a new name to the memorial board near the front door. Bethany stopped, noticing that Owen Stanford's name was being added to the casualty list. She watched sadly as Willie painted the words *Private Owen J. Stanford, Jr., killed in the line of duty.*

Bethany looked down sorrowfully. It had been a long time since she'd seen Owen, at their high school graduation, in fact. Although she found it hard to tolerate him when they were in school together, Bethany still found it hard to believe he was suddenly gone. It made her hate the war that much more.

Penny had moved to the back of the store to assist three men at the drug counter, two of which had the letters POW painted on their pant legs, as well as the insignia from Camp Butner on the back of their jackets. The two German's were accompanied by an American soldier and they seemed to be collecting supplies. Bethany spotted one of the German POW's watching her out of the corner of her eye. It made her sick to think that, while Willie added an American loss to the casualty board, his wife was assisting the enemy who may have very well taken Owen Stanford's life to begin with.

"Ms. Davies, may I help you?"

Bethany hadn't noticed Penny approaching and the store keeper took her by surprise. "Yes, Mrs. Henderson, thank you. I have a list from Mama."

Penny took the list and her eyes scanned it. "Did you want to wait?"

"I'll be at the school for the next few hours. Can I pick them up on the way home?"

"Of course, I'll have it ready when you return."

Katie Anne was stocking shelves in the back room and Bethany waved goodbye, glancing at the memorial board one last time before working her way onto the boardwalk. Bethany hadn't walked long when she heard someone calling her name.

"Well, good morning, Bethany Davies." Martha Walters was working her way down the boardwalk dressed, as usual, in a very revealing outfit. "I must say, you're looking more and more like Ms. Maples every day—very teacher-like, I mean."

"How are you, Martha?" Bethany forced herself to say, doing her best to ignore the rudeness of her rival's last comment.

"Why, just fine, thanks. I wanted to do a little shopping before the holidays get away from me. You know, being so busy with Scott and all, I just haven't had much time to get everything done I had hoped. He is very needy of my time, you know." She gave Bethany a cunning smile. "I do hope you're all right with our dating and all?"

Bethany glared at her. "I'm not so sure I would call one night at a movie dating, but then it's really none of my business, is it?" she asked sternly.

Martha returned the glare. "I was under the impression that you may have some slight feelings for him yourself."

Bethany really disliked her. Choosing not to reply, she took a few steps down the boardwalk, but Martha stepped in front of her. Bethany's shoulder bounced off Martha's, and she came to a dead stop.

"Scotland is nothing like the men around here, and I have full intention of living in the lap of luxury in London as soon as he's out of this war. He's quite the catch. In fact, according to our mutual friend, David Carson, Scotland has more money than either of us could spend in two lifetimes sitting in that bank right over there." She pointed across the street.

"I think he deserves more than a woman who wants him for his money, don't you?" Bethany lashed back. "Most certainly better than any women he could find in this town, and that includes you. I can only assume you feel sharing this information with me is a ploy to hurt me. So for your information, I acknowledge the fact that Scott deserves better…better than both of us!"

Martha stood in a challenging stance. "You have no idea what a man wants. If you did, David Carson wouldn't have come running to me."

Bethany clenched her teeth. "And half the boys in this town from what I hear," Bethany threw back. "Certain things should be shared out of love, but I can see why that is foreign to you."

"You were always the smart one in school—highest grades, valedictorian, voted most likely to succeed...people liked you. Myself, I had to work hard just to get others to notice me. Well, who's in the limelight now, Bethany Davies? Just as soon as I can, I'm leaving this miserable town, and Sir Scotland Anthony Jenkins is my ticket out! We'll see who's who when I become Mrs. Scotland Jenkins." She took a step toward the mercantile door and looked back at her, smirking. "You know, Scotland is a much better kisser than David ever was." Martha laughed and disappeared inside the store. Bethany glared at the empty door before marching off.

Bethany returned her papa's wave from the barn before running up the steps and into the house. Katherine was finishing dinner while Scott played a familiar tune on the piano.

Jeffrey, who was indulging in a game of cards with the twins, smiled up at her. "Hey, how was your day?" Jeffrey asked.

Bethany nodded with her eyes still on Scott at the piano. "It was okay." She seemed distracted. She placed the grocery bag on the kitchen table and joined Scott at the piano. He looked up at her as the song ended.

"That was very nice," she said, still feeling the anxiety of her confrontation with Martha and her tiff with Scott the night before. "You play beautifully."

He placed his hands in his lap and looked down at the keys. "This is what ten years of piano lessons get you."

She sat next to him on the bench. "I was rude and disagreeable last night," she said in a low tone.

Scott stared at her a moment and then looked away. "I'm not your enemy, you know." He glanced back at her. "At least I don't want to be."

"I know you're not, Scott, and I don't want you to be either. You walked in at a bad time in my life. I don't mean to take it out on you. I'm sorry about how I've treated you since you've been here. You haven't done anything to deserve it, and I'm truly sorry."

Scott smiled, but said nothing. Bethany stood, squeezed his shoulder lovingly, and silently moved up the stairs. She stopped when reaching the halfway point and gripped the railing tightly. Bethany stood in a trance as thoughts of the last few weeks came flooding in. Her eyes moved from Scott and drifted to the floor. She squeezed the railing, sighed, and disappeared upstairs.

CHAPTER 16

"Yoo-hoo, Scotland, are you home?" Martha called from the front door and knocked again. Holding tightly to a glass bowl, she quickly straightened her dress as she heard someone approach the door.

Jeffrey opened the door and smiled. "Well, good afternoon, Martha."

"Howdy, Jeffrey, is Scotland home?"

"Come on in, he's upstairs, I'll fetch him."

Martha stepped just inside the door as Jeffrey closed it behind her and disappeared upstairs. Bethany, who was helping her mama at the kitchen sink, shook her head irritably when she noticed Martha at the door.

"Good afternoon, Bethany, Mrs. Davies, I hope you're all having a fine Saturday?" Martha cunningly asked.

"We're doing just wonderful, Martha, how about you?" Katherine said happily.

"I'm very well, thank you. I was sitting around the house going through Scotland withdrawals." She held up the bowl. "So, I used my last ration coupons to make him a bowl of my famous potato salad."

"Scotland withdrawals—good grief," Bethany said under her breath. Katherine nudged her daughter as Scott hurried down the stairs with Jeffrey close behind.

Martha's smile widened. "There he is! I've been thinking of you all day. Look, I brought you a gift."

Scott lifted the glass lid and peered inside. "Well, that looks real brilliant, thank you, love."

Bethany snickered when Martha sent her a triumphant smile. "I was hoping you would like it." She handed the bowl to Scott. "I thought, if you had nothing planned, we could go for a walk. It's a little nippy out, but the sun is shining."

"That sounds splendid," Scott said taking the bowl toward the kitchen.

Bethany's eyes followed Scott as he placed the potato salad in the refrigerator. She made no attempt to hide her disapproval by sighing loudly, but Scott only responded by sending her a quick glance.

"Will you be out long?" Katherine asked. "We'll be starting dinner soon."

Martha took Scott's hand as he returned to her. "Perhaps you can all do without him this evening?" She looked at Scott. "I was hoping we could go to town for dinner?"

"Is that all right?" Scott questioned Katherine.

Katherine heard her daughter sigh in dissatisfaction. "Of course, just don't be out too long. The weather is due to get bad again tonight."

Bethany threw her towel on the counter and stormed toward the back door, forcing it open with a thud as she ran down the steps. Jeffrey watched his sister heave the barn door open angrily and slam it shut in a temper tantrum. Martha maintained her victorious smile.

Scott grabbed his jacket and his eyes veered toward the back door in concern. Then, he looked at Jeffrey. "We'll be back later, mate. Is that alright?"

"Sure, I'm just going to hang out around the house." Jeffrey approached his mama in the kitchen as Scott and Martha left out the front door. "What on earth was that all about?"

Katherine giggled and pulled a saucepan from the stove. "Let's just say that your sister is having some real issues with

Scott's choice in women." She shook her head. "I'm afraid this is all going to come to blows very quickly."

"Why would Bethany care who Scott spends time with?" Katherine raised her eyebrows at her son and his chin dropped. "I see." He looked at the empty door again and shook his head. "I never saw that one coming."

Katherine laughed. "I'm sure Bethany's just as surprised as you are."

Bethany intercepted the bucket off the hook near the stalls and filled Callie's water trough, only to throw it angrily against the barn just above the door. Jeffrey jumped out of the way, placing his arms over his head before being struck by the empty container.

He frowned at the bucket that now lay motionless on the dirt floor and then looked at his sister. "You always did have one heck of a temper."

"I'm sorry, I didn't mean to hit you," she said sorrowfully.

"It's alright I'm use to women throwing foreign objects at me." Jeffrey said sarcastically and then pulled her into his arms when she suddenly burst into tears. "It's alright, no harm done." He held her at arm's length. "I figured you'd be hiding out here."

Bethany sniffed her tears away and wiped the jacket sleeve over her face. "What makes you think I'm hiding?" She picked up the bucket and replaced it on the hook by the stalls.

"Hey, I'm your big brother, remember? You don't think I can tell when a storm is brewing inside you?" He took a step toward her. "If you want to talk about it, maybe I can help."

Bethany collected a handful of hay and placed it in the stall for Callie. After several attempts to latch the stall door, she kicked it impatiently. Jeffrey laughed sympathetically, kissed her on the head, and latched the door for her – only to have her burst into tears again. He pulled her into his arms. She embraced him, speaking and crying into her brother's shoulder.

He caressed her hair. "You'll have to calm down. I can't understand a word you're saying."

Bethany lifted her head and looked up at her big brother. "I just wish you never brought him here!" She released him, took a deep breath, and then moved away, running her palm over her wet cheek. Gaining her composure, Bethany picked up another section of hay and placed it in the trough for Gracie. "Everything was okay until you brought him here." Bethany wiped her cheek again and looked at Jeffrey. "I can't be responsible for him too." She sobbed.

"How many times do you need to hear that what happened to Whitney wasn't your fault? Bad things don't happen because you care. Bethany, it was an accident!" Jeffrey shook his head angrily.

Bethany took a step toward him, shaking her head hysterically. "No, I should have been there!" She pointed to herself. "I wasn't there for her, Jeffrey!"

Jeffrey threw his fist in the air. "There's just no talking to you!"

Bethany turned away. "When Whitney died...I promised myself I would *never* care about anyone again." She laughed in the air with tears still streaming down her face. "I've never been so confused in my life! Do you know what it's like to find yourself trusting in someone...no matter all the promises you made to yourself...only to be so scared that the whole world will come tumbling down on you because of it?"

Jeffrey held her at arm's length. "So you care about Scott. How is that the end of the world?"

Bethany jerked away angrily with her back to her brother. "You're not hearing me!"

"Yes, I am hearing you, Bethany!" Jeffrey yelled.

She wouldn't look at him.

"You're scared that because you care for Scott, something bad will happen to him and you'll have to live with that too." He heard Bethany begin to cry again and knew he was right. "Bad things don't happen to people because you love them, honey. You can't hide from the world and your feelings because you're scared. The kind of guarantees you're looking for doesn't exist."

"I wish I knew how to stop what I'm feeling. If I could, I would in a heartbeat!" She turned to her brother. "He's from England, Jeffrey, and that's a long way from Dobson's Crossroads. He's also a paratrooper and jumps out of airplanes into the backyard of the enemy. How can I believe anything but tragedy could come from loving a man like that?"

Jeffrey took a few steps toward her. "Do you love him?"

Bethany crossed her arms and stared at him silently.

Jeffrey smiled sadly and nodded. "I should have known better than to think you'd answer a question like that." Jeffrey sighed and let his arms drop. "If you care for him, you owe it to both of you to tell him."

Bethany frantically shook her head and turned away.

"Bethany, be reasonable!" Jeffrey pleaded.

Bethany quickly turned to him. "Jeffrey Robert Davies, if you breathe one word of this conversation to anyone…!"

"I wouldn't chance your wrath!" He held up his hands and took a step back. "Just think about what I said." He took a few steps toward the door and looked back. "I think Scott is a very lucky man to have you feel that way about him. I also think that if you found the courage to tell him, he may just be what you need. Maybe he can help you with all you've kept locked up since Whitney died." Jeffrey placed his hand on the door handle and looked at her. "You're a survivor, Bethany, you always have been. Always the strong one, the one everyone can count on to keep her head. Well, maybe it's time you found what makes Bethany Davies happy for a change. You've been hiding inside yourself for the last year. I'd like to see Bethany again. I miss your laughter." He sighed and opened the door. "I guess I just miss you."

She wiped the tears away and yet more followed. "She doesn't exist anymore, Jeffrey."

"You think you have it so bad. You're not the only one who is suffering over this war, you know! You're also not the only one who lost Whitney that day. We all loved her. I think she would be very sad to see all that you have given up because she died. She wouldn't have wanted this, and you know it." Jeffrey paused. "She would have been so happy you found Scott."

Bethany folded her arms and turned away.

"I won't mention our conversation to anyone, but think about what I said."

Bethany watched her brother disappear into the darkness. She looked at the ground and angrily flopped herself on the hay bale. For the first time, she allowed herself to cry. She knew Jeffrey couldn't understand what she was really going through. Bethany was the one that had to live with finding Whitney that day, lying in a pool of blood, at Dobson's Pond. She would never forgive herself for letting her cousin die alone on the rocks, or forgive Whitney for abandoning her, for that matter.

Although she felt guilt for running late and not being there when her best friend needed her, it went much deeper than that. She had grown angry at Whitney for dying. Bethany counted on her, needed her, and Whitney just left her alone to move through life without her. The anger she felt inside consumed her, and Bethany knew, until she was finally able to release it, there would be no room in her life for anyone, even Scott Jenkins.

She had told him he had entered her life at a bad time, and it was true. Bethany knew feelings had become strong for him. She was scared, terrified even, of what would happen when he left. All the denying in the world couldn't hide what had emerged in her heart for him. It ripped her heart out to know he was with Martha. She began to cry harder, lifting the halter from the table next to her; Bethany threw it with all her might, and it bounced off the stable door.

CHAPTER 17

Scott sat in the passenger side of Martha's sports car, beer in hand, and gazed out the window. Persistently rubbing his leg and kissing his neck, Martha took Scott's beer from him and placed it on the dashboard before straddling his lap. Scott was a little tipsy from the alcohol consumption over the course of the evening and returned her kiss with a little less eagerness than she seemed to have. Martha unbuttoned his shirt and ran her palms up and down his strong biceps.

"You are so incredibly handsome," she said, kissing his chest.

He reached for his beer and took another chug as she persistently moved her wet lips up and down his chest. Scott felt her hands move to his belt.

"Martha, I don't think this is such a good idea," Scott said as her hands began to pry on his belt buckle.

Martha, still eating at Scott's neck, smiled. "Why not, honey? Come on, relax, Scotland."

Suddenly, a beam of light lit up the interior of the vehicle. Martha released Scott's belt and looked at the driver's side window in surprise. Sheriff Masterson was peering into the window and tapping on the glass with his flashlight. Martha quickly moved to the driver's seat. She rolled down the window with one hand, and in desperation, attempted to button her blouse with the other.

Grant shook his head. "Well, I guess you're not broke down." He moved the light to Scott. "Scott Jenkins, is that you?"

Scott looked away in agitation over the whole situation. "Yes, sir, how are you, Sheriff?"

Grant grinned sheepishly. "Do Joseph and Katherine know where you are?"

Scott sighed again and looked at him. "I suppose they will very shortly," he said with a slight hint of sarcasm.

Grant moved the beam to the empty beer containers at Scott's feet, and then back to his face, "You been drinking, son?"

Scott said nothing but glared at the dashboard.

Grant moved the light to Martha. "Ms. Walters, have you been drinking too?"

Martha adjusted her blouse. "No, Sheriff," she said, shaking her head. "We were just talking," she said and placed her hands in her lap innocently.

"I can see that," Masterson chuckled. "You do realize it's after midnight?" He flashed the light back on Scott. "A little late to be out with the ladies, I would say, Lieutenant. It's getting awfully icy out on the roads and the weather isn't going to get any better."

"I guess time just snuck by," Scott said as his eyes moved to Grant for the slightest moment and then returned to the windshield.

Grant chuckled as he moved the light to Scott's hands where he was finishing buttoning his shirt. "I guess I can understand that." The sheriff stood. "Martha, you're only a little ways from home. I want you to go straight there. As for the lieutenant, I'll be happy to see him home myself."

Scott didn't hesitate, but departed Martha's car rather quickly. Martha, in turn, looked at Scott nervously before starting the car up the dirt road.

Grant aimed the beam on Scott again. "I don't have to tell you what a bad idea this was. I can understand, a young fellow like you, heading off to the war. Getting in a little fun before you leave is expected. But, Martha Walters might be a little too much for you to handle, if you get my meaning."

Scott said nothing and placed his hands in the pockets of his jeans, realizing he left his jacket in Martha's car. He wished the lectures would end so he could get warm.

Grant smiled and flashed the light on the passenger door of the police car. "Hop in and let's get you home." Grant continued his fatherly lectures as he drove them up the street toward the farm. "Martha Walters has quite a reputation around here," he said, watching the road.

Scott looked at the sheriff. "We were just out for a drive," he said innocently.

Grant looked at him, "It takes quite the talent to drive with a young lady on your lap, I'd say."

Scott stared out the front window. "Believe me, Sheriff, it wasn't the way it looked."

Grant glanced at him again, said nothing, and pulled the car into the driveway of the Davies's farm. He stopped the car at the end of the drive and looked at Scott. "Are you ready?"

Scott shifted positions nervously. "Let's get it over with," he said, knowing full well he would never hear the end of this.

Lights upstairs suddenly came on as the car pulled in front of the house. Within seconds, the living room lights flickered as well, and bodies began to gather on the porch. They were met by Joseph and Katherine as they both exited the vehicle. Bethany had been waiting at her bedroom window for Scott to get home when the police car pulled up. Only a moment later, Jeffrey joined Bethany and their parents on the porch. All were in their pajamas and concerned to have the sheriff at the farm so late in the evening.

"Sherriff Masterson, what has happened?" Katherine panicked.

"Oh, now, Katherine, nothing to concern yourself over," Grant reassured her. "Scott just had a little too much to drink so I thought I'd see him home safely." He hit Scott's shoulder. "You get some sleep now."

Scott said nothing as he began the agonizing walk up the front steps with all eyes on him. He wouldn't look her direction, but could feel the heat on his face from Bethany's burning stare. Katherine and Joseph continued their conversation with Grant and Scott attempted to pass by Bethany, only to have his arm intercepted.

Bethany pulled Scott to a stop and moved the collar of his shirt to the side, exposing the lip prints all over his chest. "It looks like you had an enjoyable evening." Scott could see how distraught she was as he looked into her eyes. He reached for her and Bethany pulled away, "Don't," she said, glaring into his eyes and backing away from him, "Just don't, okay Scott?" Bethany disappeared inside.

"Making out with Martha Walters?" Jeffrey looked at the empty door and then back to Scott. "She's not going to let you off very easily–collaborating with the enemy like that. You do know that you have a problem, right?"

Scott stared at the empty door, "Like she said before, it's none of her business who I see. So, what's the big deal?"

"You really can't see it, can you?" Jeffrey shook his head in disbelief. "Bethany's stuck on you, my friend."

Scott stared at the empty doorway. "Jeffrey, we both know she's better off," Scott said, and looked at him. "I'm the worst person your sister could ever think of falling for." Scott turned his stare to the empty doorway again, and then moved inside.

CHAPTER 18

Bethany paused a moment at the top of the stairs. Taking a deep breath, she began her descend reluctantly. With the spectacle last night, she wasn't in any hurry to see Scott this morning. But, as she reached the bottom step, there he was, sitting at the kitchen table with his head cupped in his hands.

Katherine noticed her daughter as she placed a hot cup of coffee in front of Scott. "Good morning, Bethany," Katherine said in a low tone.

Bethany nodded, eyes still burning in Scott's direction. "Good morning, Mama."

Scott was very still with his head cradled in his hands and staring down at the table in agony. He looked simply pathetic, in Bethany's opinion, and she questioned her mama with her eyes.

"Scott's not feeling so good this morning." Katherine said in a low tone. "I sent your brothers outside so Scott could have a little quiet time."

"What's the matter, did you have a little too much to drink last night?" Bethany asked, raising her voice as she moved toward the table.

Scott frowned up at her and then moved his eyes back to the tabletop. "Just a little, I'm afraid, my love. I think I may be dying."

"That's your fault!" she screamed into his ear without the slightest attempt to hide her dissatisfaction with him the night before.

Scott tightened his eyes and held his head in pain.

Katherine covered her mouth to conceal her giggle. "Bethany Davies, that wasn't nice in the slightest."

Bethany smiled at her mama, a little proud of herself, as Scott moaned. "Maybe next time Reverend Michaels has a sermon on juices of the devil, Scott Jenkins should be sitting in the front row," she said as loud as she could.

Scott sighed and looked up at her. "You really do hate me, don't you?" he said in agony before placing his head on the table in pain.

Bethany laughed and shook her head. "No, I don't hate you. But I do think when you drink irresponsibly you deserve what's coming to you."

Without saying a word, Bethany walked to the kitchen cabinet and located a bottle of pain medicine. Placing two pills in the palm of her hand, she replaced the bottle and returned to Scott.

Bethany held the pills out to Scott and waited with a stern look. "Next time you decide to waste your night making out with Martha Walters and getting ridiculously intoxicated, you're on your own."

Scott looked up at her in agitation and then stared at the pills in her hand. She waited a moment, and when he refused to take them, Bethany nudged him demandingly, moving her hand closer. Scott glared at her defiantly, but intercepted the pills anyway. Bethany crossed her arms and waited, letting him know she wasn't going anywhere until he had swallowed them in its entirety. She knew he recognized defeat when he placed the pills in his mouth and washed them down with a sip of coffee.

Bethany let her arms drop and looked at her mama as Scott grinned up at her. "I'm running late, I'll grab something at the café later." Bethany looked back at Scott. "Good day, Mr. Jenkins."

Scott's eyes followed her to the door. "Thanks for caring."

Bethany stopped at the front door and looked back at him. "Oh, trust me, I have no sympathy for you. I warned you about

Martha Walters from day one. You got what you deserved. I just found myself tired of you crying like a baby." Bethany smiled at him.

Scott returned her smile. "You're heartless, Bethany Davies."

She sent him a bigger smile and they shared a stare for a moment before she disappeared outside.

CHAPTER 19

The house was very still when Bethany arrived home later that afternoon. The children were upstairs playing and her mama sat with Scott and Jeffrey at the table. Bethany's eyes moved from face to face and she could see something was dreadfully wrong. She sat her books on the counter; the three looked up at her, but were silent.

"Mama," Bethany hesitated as she continued to watch the long faces, "what is it—what's wrong?" Her first thought was the possibility of bad news regarding Patrick.

Katherine stood and turned to her daughter sadly. "It's Grams, Bethany."

Bethany's eyes moved from face to face in silence. Crossing her arms quickly, she looked back at her mama in shock. Katherine didn't have to say anymore, she suddenly understood. Bethany's cheeks became wet as her face moved downward to the floor sadly. She shook her head in disbelief.

"Her heart gave out," Jeffrey shared softly. "There was nothing anyone could do."

Bethany turned her back to them. "It can't be. She can't be gone!" Bethany cried.

Scott stared at the table sadly in silence. He remembered how it felt when his mum died and wished he could have spared Bethany this. Bethany made a mad dash out the back door and Jeffrey stood to run after her.

Scott pulled him back. "Please, let me go."

Without waiting for a response, Scott ran full speed out the door to catch up to Bethany. He could see her just ahead, moving up the drive and toward the street as if heading into town. Although it was difficult to catch up to her, he managed to keep Bethany in his sights. Bethany ran past Main Street, and continued up Old Farm Road, to a trail that led them into the woods. Scott had no idea where she was taking him, but knew if he lost visual of Bethany, he may never find his way back.

They must have run up the trail for several minutes. Only trees and overgrowth was to be seen for miles. He could only guess very few people visited the area with all the overgrown weeds and debris that lay over the trail. Bethany was still very far ahead, and Scott suddenly panicked when she turned, disappearing from his sights. Scott reached the location he last saw Bethany and gave a sigh of relief. Bending over and holding his knees, he attempted to catch his breath as Bethany moved over the footbridge, just beyond his reach. Scott took another deep breath and stood, holding his chest a moment as he looked toward Bethany. She was leaning against the railing, weeping as she stared into the water. Taking a few deep breaths to slow his heart rate, Scott moved toward her with hesitation, sure he would meet her with some resistance.

Bethany saw him, said nothing, but gazed back into the pond. Scott approached her cautiously and shared the railing in silence. He could hear her sniffling and wanted to say something to make Bethany feel better. Historically, he knew his conversations with Bethany never really ended well, and so he made the decision to stay silent.

Unexpectedly, Bethany burst into tears and fell to her knees on the footbridge. Scott, dropping to his knees as well, felt his own tears appear.

"I'm so sorry, love." His voice cracked. "So very sorry." Scott reached for her and Bethany allowed him to take her into his arms. Scott rocked her lovingly as she wept uncontrollably. She pulled him tightly into her arms, needing him more than she ever thought she could need anyone. He had come after her and that was all she needed to see.

Scott kissed her head and rocked her again. "I'm so sorry, Beth," he whispered.

Bethany released him with a questionable look. "You called me Beth?"

Scott touched her face. "Yes, my Beth."

Scott wasn't sure if he was seeing anger, remorse, or even fear on Bethany's face. It took him a minute to realize she wasn't looking at him at all, but over his shoulder to something at the far side of the bridge. Scott gazed over his own shoulder in time to hear the snarling of a dog. Twisting his body around, he forced Bethany behind him, his first instinct to protect her.

"Oh, this is just not happening!" Scott gasped as the snarling Rottweiler turned into a pack of three. "Well, this is bloody great!" Scott said as he slowly stood, pulling Bethany up with him. The dogs snarled louder and took a step forward. "Okay, my love, just don't move."

Bethany, her chin still dropped to her chest and mouth opened wide, could only nod slightly in response. Scott took her hand and began to back her up. The dogs snarled louder and Scott came to a stop.

"I thought you said not to move!" Bethany scolded.

"All right, let's just think here for a moment." Scott looked around desperately.

"Here's some good news, there's only three –."

Scott raised his eyebrows at her.

"I'm sorry!" she said sternly. "Usually I'm very good under pressure." Her eyes moved to the ground at her feet and she picked up the stick that had been lying there. The dogs began snarling out of control.

Scott looked at her angrily. "Don't move!"

She placed her hand on her hip. "Do not raise your voice to me, Scott Jenkins."

Scott threw his head in the air in aggravation. "I'm sorry," he said, taking the stick from her hand. "I'll keep them distracted and you make a run for it."

"Absolutely not," she gasped.

Scott looked over his shoulder at her sternly. "Are we really going to have a debate right now? I don't think now is a good time, Beth." He became agitated again and the dogs moved closer.

Bethany looked away angrily.

Scott sighed at her sudden anger toward him. "You know if I didn't like you so much I would be sitting in the house by a nice cozy fire right now."

"Making out with Martha Walters sounds more plausible," she said under her breath and then gave him a stern look.

"I was not making out with Martha—oh, for the love of God," he said angrily and turned to her. "I had a few beers, yes—and she took full advantage of it."

Bethany laughed rudely. "You have got to think I'm an idiot." She folded her arms. "Just out of curiosity, how far did you let her take *advantage* of you?"

"You think I slept with her!" he gasped. "Beth, I'm not so sure this is the right time to have this discussion." He threw his arm out and pointed at the dogs as they snarled again. "Hello, did you forget we have company!

Bethany tipped her head and glared at him. The dogs moved closer and Scott raised the stick higher, moving Bethany back a few steps.

"What is over there?" he asked, looking behind them toward the other side of the bridge.

Bethany held his hand tightly. "Just some trees, wildlife—and a ten-foot drop into the Roanoke River."

Scott sighed in aggravation. "That's just great!"

"Did you?" she asked out of the blue.

"Did I what?" he snapped back.

She was silent and Scott looked over his shoulder at her.

Bethany gazed deep into his eyes questionable. "Did you sleep with her, Scott?" she asked in desperation.

Scott turned as the dogs raced toward them. Lunging with the stick as hard as he could, Scott sent the smaller mutt retreating back from where he came in pain. But the Rottweiler went sailing in the air, landing in Scott's arms snarling and growling. Scott fought the animal, attempting to protect his face, and the dog took a bite out of his arm. Scott called out in pain.

Bethany picked up the stick and began swinging it wildly at the smaller dog, afraid the third mutt would come back to finish them off. Beating the dog as hard as she could, Bethany kept Scott in her sights as he continued to fight the Rottweiler with his bare hands. Scott brought his arm back and laid a heavy fist into the eye of the animal. The Rottweiler yelped and went flying in the air. Pulling himself off the ground, he kicked the dog Bethany was fighting and it moved back over the bridge in retreat.

The sounds of repeated gunfire cracked through the air. Scott and Bethany flinched as the shots fired again. There it was again—a crack in the air and then a sudden yelp of pain in the distance. Joseph, Jeffrey, and Sheriff Masterson came around the corner, guns drawn, as the dogs vanished into the brush. Bethany dropped to her knees in front of Scott and took his bleeding hands, panic stricken, and examined him.

"No," Scott said simply staring at her.

Bethany looked into his eyes confused.

"I've never been with a woman in my life, Beth." He touched her face, "Hard to believe knowing how handsome and charming I am, isn't it?"

Bethany laughed and placed her forehead against his, "I imagine it is."

"Are you two all right?" Joseph gasped.

Bethany helped Scott to his feet, placing her arm around his waist, as her daddy approached, "How did you know where to find us?"

Joseph set the safety on his rifle as Grant and Jeffrey search the brush for the dogs. "I guess you're just too predictable, daughter," He lifted Scott's hand and examined his knuckles. "It must have had some set of teeth, it got you good." He let Scott's hand go. "We have the car at the end of the trail, best be having Doc Malone take a look at you both."

Jeffrey and Grant moved back toward the others and Jeffrey lowered his rifle. "There's blood in the brush so we hit something. But they're gone now," Jeffrey said, disappointed. He hit his friend on the shoulder. "You were lucky there were only a couple."

Bethany pulled Scott closer, "I'm sorry I got you mixed up in all this."

Jeffrey laughed. "Haven't I told you? Saving damsels in distress is what he does best." He looked at Bethany. "Were you hurt?"

Bethany shook her head and gave Scott a thankful smile. He pulled her deep into his arms with a loving squeeze and a quick kiss on the head.

CHAPTER 20

Mary's funeral was a few days later. Following the burial, there was a gathering at Danny's house. Mary had spent her whole life in Dobson and there wasn't one townsperson absent from her services. Early in the socializing, Bethany had left the house, spending most of her time alone by the stables. Joseph found Scott standing on the back porch watching Bethany.

"Best we just let her alone with her thoughts, son." Joseph sighed and squeezed Scott's arm. "It's been hard on us all, but I reckon worse on her."

Scott didn't take his eyes from Bethany, "Yes, sir, I know," Scott said softly.

Joseph looked toward Bethany, "You'll be here, watching out for her?" Joseph asked, somewhat distraught.

"I'll be here, Joseph, as long as you need me to be, and as long as she allows me to be."

"Then I reckon I'll go find my own corner to grieve," he said sadly.

Scott moved his eyes back to Bethany as Joseph returned inside the house. Most of the snow had melted and turned the dirt around the farm into mud. Taking the four steps down the porch, Scott moved toward the stables where Bethany was leaning over the fence. He was glad she had chosen a beautiful floral dress instead of a black and unappealing one for services, although he knew she could make anything look good.

Bethany patted the white mare on the nose.

Scott approached her slowly, stopping a few feet away. He placed his hands in his pockets. "If you'd rather be alone, I can go back to the house."

Bethany glanced back at him and said nothing.

Scott completed the steps to her side and leaned against the fence. "Are you hungry? I can go inside and make you up a plate."

Bethany simply shook her head.

Scott took a deep breath. "I never knew my grandmum," he said softly. "If I had, I would have wanted her to be just like Mary."

A tear escaped Bethany. "Grand always said we were a lot alike," she whispered. "I was always proud of that." She shook her head sadly and looked at Scott. "I miss her terribly."

Scott nodded and leaned his head against hers. "I know you do. I'm not going to lie to you and tell you that time will heal your pain. I do not know that to be true. But I can say that so long as someone is in your heart and thought, they are never truly gone."

Bethany studied his words. "It hurts."

Scott nodded and took her in his arms. "I know it does, Beth."

She held him tightly, weeping softly in his shoulder. He watched as Bethany slowly drew away from him.

"I know you mean well," she cried. "But I can't do this with you." She gave him a sad smile. "You are so sweet and great, but I don't need another person to lose."

Scott looked down sadly.

She touched his face. "I have no strength left, can you understand that?"

Scott was silent.

Bethany ran her palm over his cheek. Turning, Bethany began to cry hysterically as she walked away from him, not looking back.

CHAPTER 21

Scott had gone for a walk the following morning with the weather turning for the better. It still dropped below freezing at night, and patches of old snow still remained amidst the trees, but the walk was less sluggish. Jeffrey had a lunch date with Kristina and said he would catch up with him later. Bethany seemed to be avoiding Scott by leaving well before he woke, which he didn't understand at all, because he felt they were finally beginning to be friends. Walking toward town, Scott spotted Jeremiah Davies struggling to repair a hole in his fence. Jeremiah was bending down to retrieve the hammer from the ground when Scott hurried to his aid.

"Here, Mr. Davies, let me assist you."

Jeremiah gave him a sad smile. "It's a shame a man was born with only two hands."

Scott smiled back and hammered the nail in to hold the fence together.

"That's it, put one more right there, my boy." The man pointed and gave him a warm smile. "Thank you, Scott. I would've been here all day."

Scott studied him. "You're very welcome, sir."

Jeremiah chuckled and turned out into the field. "You know, I've been standing here I don't know how many times. Strange, somehow the view is different when you're older, and alone."

Scott wasn't sure how to respond, so he didn't.

Jeremiah smiled at Scott. "Mary has been after me for weeks to fix this fence, but I always put it off believing I had plenty of time. Time has a way of catching up to you. Never take a minute of it for granted, son."

Scott nodded sadly. "I won't, Jeremiah."

The old man sighed and looked around his farm. "When Mary and I were courting, there wasn't a day she was ready on time. I learned soon enough not to show up early, because even on time I'd be waiting on that woman." Jeremiah chuckled. "I guess it should be some conciliation to know that she's sitting up there, this time having to wait on me for a change." He chuckled again. "I'll bet you a wooden nickel she's planted herself right by the pearly gates, sassing and ordering the angels around, that was my Mary. She was always worth waiting for, though. She was two of a kind. My little Bethany is just like her. I'm sure you'll find her worth waiting for too."

Scott sighed. "I'm not so sure Bethany wants me to wait for her. She's very bullheaded."

"You certainly have a job on your hands, that's for sure. You might as well be trying to tame a wild stallion, but I have faith in you."

Scott shook his head. "As much as I'd like to think Bethany and I could ever be close, I don't see that happening. She's very withdrawn, when it comes to me anyway, and I'm not sure why, mate." Scott shrugged. "I think Bethany and I could be great friends, if she didn't spend all her time pushing me away." He sighed. "Maybe it's better for her in the long run. A lot of men won't be returning from the war," Scott said sadly. "But I'd like to think I'll be one of the lucky ones."

Jeremiah hit him on the arm. "Just keep reminding yourself of that." He sighed, "Women have a way of making it tough on us men, that's for sure. I think it's an unwritten law." Scott laughed. Jeremiah squeezed his arm. "I have some hot water on. How does a hot cup of cocoa sound?"

Scott smiled. "That sounds real good." Scott followed Jeremiah up the steps and into the house.

Jeremiah sat the cup of hot cocoa in front of Scott, lifted a picture off the mantel, and handed it to him. He recognized Bethany right away and remembered thinking how beautiful she was from the moment he first laid eyes on her. But when she was smiling, Bethany took Scott's breath away. The girl next to her seemed just as happy and very pretty, but Scott couldn't stop staring at Bethany.

"That picture was taken a year ago, just before the accident." Scott looked in Jeremiah's direction. "The young girl next to Bethany is my other granddaughter, Whitney. They were always very close." Jeremiah smiled and sat in the chair across from Scott. "I can see the way she looks at you. There is no hiding a feeling like that. Mary could see it too. But, there are some things you need to know about Bethany."

"How do you mean, sir?"

Jeremiah sighed. "She cares for you, very much I think."

Scott shook his head. "I don't believe that. All we ever seem to do is argue. I annoy her and she's always angry and rude toward me, I'm not sure why." Scott looked at his cup. "She always seems so unhappy."

"She's not angry at you, son, she's angry at the thought of you." Scott sent him a puzzled look and Jeremiah nodded. "I think you're probably the only one she's let get this close, but she's cautious. Bethany has had to deal with much loss this last year." Scott looked at the old man questioningly. "I gathered no one's told you about Whitney?"

Scott slowly shook his head, slightly confused. "No, sir, no one has."

"Whitney was my son Robert's oldest. She and Bethany were best friends since grade school, connected at the hip, you might say. Both wanted to be teachers, in love with children, and so very good." Jeremiah smiled. "Bethany and Whitney sang in the church choir together. Oh, my, talk about the voice of angels.

My Bethany…she has the heart of gold. But she hardly lets it show anymore."

Scott looked down sadly. "Jeremiah, what happened to Whitney? Will you tell me, because no one else seems to want to talk about it?"

Jeremiah sat his cup down on the coffee table in front of him. "Well, it was just a few weeks after Jeffrey went off to boot camp. Bethany was supposed to meet Whitney at Dobson's Pond that afternoon. But Bethany was running late helping at the school." Jeremiah took a sad sigh. "By the time help got Whitney to the doctor, our little Whitney was gone." Scott looked down sadly. "Doc Malone said she must have slipped. Whitney suffered major trauma to the back of her head." Jeremiah sighed and shook his head sadly. "My Bethany was the one that found her."

Scott gasped in disbelief. "That must have been so difficult for her."

"Bethany's never been the same. She always finds herself drawn back to Dobson's Pond. It's almost like the place she feels closest to Whitney." Jeremiah stood and walked to the fireplace. "Bethany feels it's her fault bad things happen to those she cares about." Jeremiah looked back at Scott. "She tries to protect those she cares about by pushing them away."

Scott moved to Jeremiah, placing the picture back on the mantel. He studied the old man. "What do I do?"

Jeremiah paused and thought very hard. "What are you willing to do, Scott?"

"I care about her, Jeremiah, very much."

Jeremiah squeezed Scott's arm. "Don't let her push you away, Scott. As long as she thinks there's a chance you'll leave her, Bethany will never open up to you. Find a way to make her hear you, son."

"Yes, sir, I will." Scott walked toward the door.

"There's one more thing. When you keep company with that young lady, Martha Walters, no good can come between you and Bethany."

"I don't understand, sir."

"It's not my place to say. But perhaps you should ask Bethany."

Scott sent him a confused look, thanked him for the hot cocoa, and moved out the door with a huge determination on his face.

Jeremiah smiled and nodded.

CHAPTER 22

LONDON, ENGLAND, 1943

Tyson was nearly knocked to his feet when he opened the door of the Jenkins's manor.

"Is he here?" Jameson Flannery asked in desperation. "He has to be here!" He looked over Tyson's shoulder in panic, searching the room. He proceeded to walk the foyer nervously.

Bradley, holding the daily paper, pulled off his glasses upon entering the room. "What is all the commotion out here?"

Jameson hurried to him, flinging the file in Bradley's face. "We really did it now!" Flannery began to pace nervously. "It's all over!"

Bradley placed his paper under his arm. "What are you getting on about?"

Flannery took a long breath. "I just came from the bank. I gave them the signed papers like you demanded. I think the bank clerk was suspicious. She said the money couldn't be immediately distributed without further verification. We might as well sit here and wait for the constables to arrive." He looked down pitifully and ran his fingers nervously through his hair. "It's all over!"

Bradley shook his head. "You probably said something stupid as usual!" He looked at Tyson. "If we have guests, we are unavailable."

Flannery followed Bradley into the study, and Bradley slammed the door shut. "It would appear we have no choice."

Bradley turned to him. "You find out where Scotland is... immediately."

"Do you have any idea how difficult that'll be? He could be anywhere fighting this war!"

"Why do you think that is my problem?" Bradley glared at him. "You have your orders. I'll be in a meeting in Oxford for the next few days. When I get back, I'll expect this handled, do you understand me?"

Flannery clenched his teeth. "Yes...sir!" He moved toward the door.

"Mr. Flannery?" Bradley said calmly.

Jameson Flannery stopped in his tracks and turned to his employer.

Bradley took a few large breaths. "Find out what happened to the other one. We can't have any loose ends." Jameson studied him, confused. Bradley sat behind his desk. "Scott is to never find out he has a brother. Do you understand?"

"We're getting in a little over our heads, don't you think—and for what?" Flannery protested.

"Only a few years ago, Churchill wrote a short essay about Hitler and his choices. He says that perhaps Hitler may be a way to help the Germans restore peace and honor. Well, look at Hitler now! It's the misjudgment of many that brought on this war, and I for one made a lot of mistakes, but I sure don't intend to have them come back to haunt me the rest of my life." Bradley sat back in his chair. "Eventually, the British government will be looking for powerful men to rebuild this country. Churchill isn't going to be in office much longer. His health is failing, and I've heard rumors...Hitler has a book known as *The Black Book* and he's looking for those who have fallen from favor with the Third Reich. I heard Churchill's name is listed. It's only rumor, but I fear fact."

Bradley stared at the ceiling. "If Hitler follows through with his plans and wins in the end, he'll be looking for powerful men to run Britain for him. Little men won't be noticed, and I sure don't intend to be seen as little." Bradley took a puff of his cigar. "I have to maintain my position in the political parliament at least long enough to be seen as an acceptable leader for what is about to transpire. Do you think I'll stay long in the parliament if anyone finds out what I did back then…what *we* did?" Bradley didn't wait for Flannery to respond. "I want it all to go away, Jameson…now!" He sat forward and placed his palms on his desk, cigar to the side of his mouth, giving Flannery a stern look. "Do I make myself clear?"

The man's jaws tightened. "I refuse to kill simply to clean up your mess!"

Bradley sat back in his chair again. "I don't care who pulls the trigger. I only care about the job being done." He picked up his paper again, turning the page. His eyes were drawn back into the headlines. "Remember, you're in it as deep, if not deeper, than me."

Flannery gave Bradley a look of hatred, for he knew he was right. Bradley gave the orders, but it was he who constantly got his hands dirty. If anything was to surface, it would come directly back to him first. He had no choice but to cover any tracks, or in Bradley's words, clean up the mess. Flannery left with an utmost look of contempt on his face.

Bradley heard the front door slam and sat deep in his chair again, blowing his smoke into the air. Grant Masterson made the mistake of coming to London twenty-three years ago. He had warned him then that his love for Naomi would be his undoing. But like an American, he refused to listen. Bradley was simply protecting his own interests. It was, after all, a Brit's prerogative to protect his own. Masterson was asked, warned, to stay away. Even after Naomi announced her pregnancy, Bradley continued to be understanding. Then when twins transpired, things got a little more complicated. But Masterson got what he wanted—he got the other one. But he was too persistent, what was Bradley to do?

Scotland had a choice as well. When he decided to join Churchill's band, he was warned it was a bad time to leave his mum. It did, however, work in Bradley's favor when Scotland blamed himself for Naomi's death during the bombings and ran off to join the American paratroopers. Bradley almost felt sorry for the other one though, but war has its casualties. Bradley shook his head and inhaled the cigar again.

CHAPTER 23

DOBSON'S CROSSROADS, NORTH CAROLINA, 1943

It had been a long time since Joseph set foot inside the school. Katherine was always the one who kept in contact with Irene Maples and the children's progress in their studies. The door creaked open. When he came around the corner and entered the classroom, Bethany was cleaning the chalkboard.

Joseph smiled. His daughter looked so natural standing in front of a classroom. "You missed breakfast."

Bethany, caught off guard, quickly turned in the direction of her papa's voice. She sat the eraser down. "Papa, this is a surprise." She took a few steps toward him.

"Can't a father come by and visit?" He smiled and took a few steps toward her. "You've been missed the last few days."

"I guess I just have a lot going on."

"Do you want to talk about it?"

Bethany stared at him but said nothing.

"It's been some year for the Davies family, that's for sure. Truth be known, you've had a huge burden to carry. I only wish you'd talk to someone about it, get it off your shoulders a little."

Bethany sat on the edge of the teacher's desk and folded her arms. "You want me to tell you what's wrong—I don't know," she strained and stared at the floor to fight the tears. "Actually, I guess maybe I do. I've no control over what's happening in my life anymore, Papa. I only know I never want to feel what it's like to lose someone again."

"The last few days I've been feeling rather sorry for myself as well. There's been so many times I got too busy to visit my mother. We have to accept that death is a part of life and go on. Shutting everyone out, acting like you don't care, doesn't work, honey. You can't protect them by pretending you don't care."

Bethany ran a hand over her brow, but said nothing.

"Sometimes, when things get out of control, we can get scared—especially for you, Bethany. You're a planner…you prepare for everything…you like to be in control." Joseph took a deep breath.

"I sure never planned on Scott. I can't be hurt again." She wiped her cheek. "I'd rather have Scott hate me than to go through that again."

"He's not David, honey, and Scott would never hate you."

"Sometimes I think he should. I've treated him so awful since he's arrived."

Joseph sighed, paused, and then looked at her sternly. "A telegram arrived for Scott today and he's being sent to Langley Field. He'll miss Christmas with the family."

Bethany quickly looked up at him and the tears she'd been fighting couldn't be stopped this time.

"Scott has no idea where he's going from there, but I can only imagine he's a little concerned about it. He's slightly upset he won't be here to celebrate the holidays with us. I'm sure he could use a friend right about now."

Bethany looked at the floor in despair.

"Now, you can spend the next few days avoiding him and feeling sorry for yourself," Joseph paused, "or you can be the friend I know you really want to be and help him get through this."

Bethany stared up at him, shaking her head in disbelief.

"For your own sake, don't put off what's most important. You're scared of being hurt again, I can see that."

Bethany cried like a baby and Joseph took her in his arms.

"Maybe in the long run, you'll be hurt—or maybe not. Maybe Scott won't make it back from the war, or maybe he'll decide to go back to England when it's over. The question is do you think he's worth taking the chance?"

Bethany wiped her cheek with the back of her hand.

"I can stand here and tell you that caring about someone is a blessing, but it can be a curse in these times too." He gave her a sad smile, his eyes becoming wet. "I know it would be nice if you could make it home for dinner tonight. We've all been missing you gracing the family table."

Bethany wiped her cheek and nodded.

Joseph moved toward the door and then turned to her. "You're my special little girl and I've been trying to figure out for weeks when you grew up on me. I'm very proud of you, honey. I know your Grams was too."

Bethany wept as Joseph left the building.

CHAPTER 24

"Do you want to be alone?" Bethany asked, poking her head out the front door.

Scott reached for her and Bethany took his hand as he pulled her to his side. Taking off his jacket, he wrapped it around her shoulders.

She stood close to him. "What are you thinking about?" she whispered.

Scott shrugged. "Just everything that's happened since I arrived, I suppose." He looked at her. "I guess you've been pretty upset at me."

"I wasn't upset with you, Scott. I was feeling sorry for myself." She tried to control her emotions.

"I've never been close to anyone before," he confessed. "Apart from maybe Jeffrey and he has to tolerate me most days."

She gave him an understanding smile. "It's not just you. I think we share in the misery we put each other in. I know I've been horrible to you since you got here."

Bethany looked into the darkness and stood silent. Scott noticed, for the first time, how vulnerable Bethany really was. He moved a loose strand of chestnut hair from her face and hid it behind her ear. "You're so beautiful, Bethany." He thought it, but to his surprise, it came out of his mouth. It wasn't that she hadn't heard it before, but hearing it from Scott gained her attention. He reached to her face and gently played with her soft hair.

Bethany smiled, still looking out into the darkness. "I bet you say that to all the girls. You probably have twenty women waiting for you to return to London right now."

"The only one I want waiting for me is a beautiful country girl who spends most of her time pushing me away."

His words took her off guard and she touched his face lovingly in response. "She doesn't mean to. Is it true, you got a telegram today?" She wanted to cry.

Scott took a deep breath and looked into the sky again. "Yes, love, I sure did."

Bethany looked into the sky with him. "It's hard to believe it's the same sky shining down all over the world."

Scott watched as she spoke, the panic in her voice, the pain in her tone.

"Over the last few years, it's been hard imagining the war going on. But most days, I could just pretend it away. If I didn't listen to the radio, and made believe Jeffrey was just away at college, it helped me get through it." She looked at him, tears suddenly streaming down her cheeks. "How do I pretend with you, Scott, knowing you're out there somewhere? Knowing so many people are trying to take you away from me and there isn't even a way I can help fight them. I'd just be left here helpless and waiting. I'm not so sure I could emotionally do that." She wiped her cheeks to only have them soaked again. "I know I couldn't!"

Scott touched her face lovingly. "You've been avoiding me," he said.

She sighed and squeezed his hand. "I've been avoiding—this." She continued to weep. "But I can't avoid how I feel anymore, no matter how confusing and scary it may be. I hurt people, Scott, and I don't want to hurt you, or have anything bad happen to you because of me."

"You can try if you want, but you can't push me away. I've let people I love push me away my whole life, Beth. I won't let you. You're just too important to me."

She looked deep into his eyes and smiled through her tears.

Scott squeezed her hand and moved closer. "Can I ask you something?"

She looked at the tight grip she had on his hand. "Can I stop you?"

He laughed. "I suppose not."

A large smile peeked through her tears.

"Tell me what happened between you and Martha Walters."

Her smile turned to a surprised look.

He squeezed her hand again and his throat became knotted. "Beth, you've become the most important person in the world to me no matter how challenging you've been." She smiled and looked down. "I haven't much time left before I'll be leaving, and I don't wish that time spent being cross with each other. I told Martha I wasn't going to see her anymore because I know it bothers you. But, I do think I deserve to know why it does." Bethany touched his face lovingly. "Does David Carson have anything to do with why you always seem to push me away?"

"That's two questions." She sent him a sad smile and he laughed. With a deep breath, she attempted to veer the tears away. "Scott, don't make that decision because of me. If you like her, I have no right to prevent you from seeing her. You deserve to be happy."

He placed his palms on her hips and pulled Bethany closer, "I don't wish to see Martha Walters, Beth Davies, I want to be with you," he said as she ran her palms over his chest lovingly. "Please, help me to understand."

Bethany nodded; she rubbed his arms and paused. "David and I saw things differently," she began, wiping an escaped tear on her cheek. "He wanted more than I could give him. Then one day, he found it with someone else."

Scott looked at her in confusion.

Bethany examined his reaction. "We were going to get married, Scott." She noticed his surprised look, but Bethany also detected slight jealousy in his stare. "I was naive and stupid. I had a lot going on last year, and I guess he felt I was neglecting him. One night we'd planned to go out, but I had a long day and just wanted to turn in early. Later, I felt bad for standing him up so I went to his house. He was, how should I say, very intensely occupied by another woman in the library." Bethany watched Scott's shocking look and she took a deep breath. "Scott, I believe intimacy is a gift that two people share when they're in love...and married. I'm just glad I found out what kind of man he was before I married him."

Scott moved his hand up and wiped her tear away, giving her a confused look. "What does all this have to do with Martha?" Bethany held his hand to her cheek and stared at Scott until suddenly his chin dropped. He gasped angrily and fell forward against the porch railing. "I am so stupid! Martha was the one you caught him with. Oh, Beth, I am so sorry!"

Bethany gave him a sad smile and looked down. "To be honest, it stopped bothering me quite a while ago." Her eyes moved back to him again. "That is, until you started seeing her." She took his hand. "Scott Jenkins, you have to understand. Something is happening between you and me and I can feel you tugging on my heart. It's the first time I felt this way about anyone my whole life. Ever! But, Scott, I don't think I'm ready for it, I really don't. I'm terrified that I would be taking a chance on losing you too." She placed a hand over her heart and her eyes pleaded with him. "But I don't know how to stop what is happening between us or how I'm feeling. My heart wants this so much. But it's scaring me to death, Scott."

"I'm not sure what I can say to make you feel better. I can't make you promises I know isn't in my power to keep." He placed his arms around her waist and pulled her deep into his arms. "I know you're scared, I am too, because you are the last person on this earth I ever want to disappoint. This war is going to be what it is, I can't control it. I am at a huge disadvantage to try and convince you that everything is going to work out the way we want it to." He pulled her closer with one arm around her waist and sent his other hand up to her face lovingly.

She closed her eyes and soaked in his touch.

"I can only tell you that I'll work as hard as I can to never let you down."

She looked deep and lovingly into his eyes.

"I'm not like Carson, Beth." His voice broke. "You are the most important person in the world to me and I would never do anything intentionally to hurt you."

She welcomed the security of his touch. "I know, but it's not that simple, Scott. David Carson is just one of the barriers I have to work through."

"You're talking about Whitney?"

Bethany pulled away from him.

"Your grandfather told me." She walked toward the door and Scott grabbed her hand. "Beth, please, we should talk about this."

"What is it you want from me, Scott? Is it to confuse me, is that why you came to Dobson? Am I being punished for something? Tell me what you want from me!" She covered her mouth to control her tears.

He held her eyes for a minute. "I want you to be happy. I care about you so much, Beth. More than I ever cared about anyone my entire life. I think more than I will ever care about anyone again."

She turned away. "I can be a lot of work."

Scott forced her to look at him again and nodded in agreement. "You sure can!"

She gave him a sad smile.

"I don't know from one day to the next what's going to happen in this world, Beth. I only know wherever this road seems to be taking me in my life, I want you in it. I want you to be a part of my life. That's what I want from you!"

She took him in her arms, and Scott held her tight. It was the first time in a long while she felt absolutely safe.

"You're not the only one who lost someone," he whispered, rubbing her back. "I've never spoken of this with anyone before, but I think you need to hear it."

Bethany stared at him questionably.

"My mum's name was Naomi Jenkins. She'd been very sick, but was slowly coming back from a bad case of pneumonia. But she died because of me," he struggled to say.

"What do you mean?"

Scott was trembling, and she took his hands in her own, squeezing them reassuringly. He looked down at their clasped hands. "When I was seventeen, I was approached by a man. He worked for Winston Churchill. I was invited to join what was called the Churchill Auxiliary Unit. It was a resistance group Churchill put together before Britain was bombed. Eventually, there were over three thousand of us all over England. I was a rebel as a kid, Beth. I never got along with my grandfather and it caused a barrier between me and my mum." Scott pulled Bethany deeper into his arms. "I spent a lot of time away because it just wasn't home anymore. When the bombings started, I went home to check on my mum. I soon found out she had been killed during the bombing the day before."

Bethany gasped.

"You see, Beth, you're not the only one who has to live with being just a little too late. I should have been there for her. Instead, I abandoned her when she needed me the most. I was eighteen years old the last time I saw my mum. It was a terrible time in my life, Beth. I learned to hate myself and everyone around me. I took chances with my life out of spite because I didn't care anymore. When I heard about the 101st, I just left England. There wasn't anything for me there anymore."

Bethany wiped a tear from Scott's cheek.

Scott intercepted her hand, holding it tightly to his face. "You and me, we have to move on and realize that the past can't be changed."

Bethany looked deep into his eyes, wondering how, in so little time he could know her so well. How did he learn to look right into the very soul of her?

"We have an obligation to those we lost, a sense of duty to live life to the fullest. You taught me that, Beth. I was alone in the world until you came along." He kissed her hand. "Maybe Bethany Davies doesn't need me, but I need her."

"I do need you, Scott." Bethany buried her face in his chest, and he rocked her in his arms. "Your father, where is he?"

"I have no idea. My mum would never speak of him. I only know they met after the first war and that he's American." He rubbed her shoulders. "I want you to know that you're not alone. I understand that I am a high risk for you and I might not be worth the risk. I was just wondering if…maybe you could care about me anyway."

She began to cry. "Caring for you is easy, Scott Jenkins. You make it so very easy!" She wiped her cheek and gave him a big smile as she straightened his collar. "So what you're telling me is you have no date for the winter dance?" She sniffed.

"I guess maybe I don't," he said, suddenly realizing it himself.

She put her arms around his neck. "We could always go together."

"I thought you said social gatherings weren't for you?"

She moved her lips close to his. "I guess you changed my mind on a lot of things." Her heart began to beat faster at their closeness. "Will you be my date?" she whispered.

Scott played with her hair and gave her a big smile. "I would really like that."

She laid her head against his chest and pulled him close. He kissed the side of her head and smiled as they looked into the darkness together.

CHAPTER 25

Bethany had a nasty habit of biting the end of her pencil when in deep thought and by midday the poor thing was nearly unrecognizable. She looked up, pencil dangling from her lips, and sent Scott a big smile as he stood at the door. Scott leaned against the doorframe, his arms hiding behind his back. She admired him from the teacher's desk and slowly removed the pencil from her lips.

"Well, where did you come from, handsome?"

Scott smiled and admired her in return for a minute. "I had some business at the bank and thought perhaps you were free for lunch."

She placed her pencil on her notebook and looked at the clock on the far wall. "I didn't realize how late it's gotten." Her eyes drew back to him. "I'm starving!"

He approached her desk and laughed, lifting her pencil to observe the mangled end. "I should say you are, my love."

She sat back in her chair. "What did you have in mind, soldier?"

"I thought we could eat at the café. That way, the whole town could see us together, and we could give them something new to talk about for the next few days." Her laugh made him smile. "But, then I thought that would mean having to share your attention. So, I decided to bring lunch to you." He pulled a brown paper bag out from behind him.

He smiled shamefully and placed the large brown bag in front of Bethany as he sat on the corner of her desk. She watched as he began digging into the bag. He pulled out a sandwich and handed it to her. "I got you Molly's special—turkey on wheat, light mayo, cheddar cheese, and three sprinkles of black pepper." She took the sandwich in amazement and watched him continue to dig into the bag. He pulled a bottle opener out of his pocket and popped the top on a Bubble Up, placing it in front of her.

Bethany sat back in her chair and gazed up at him. "Three sprinkles of black pepper and light mayo…someone's been talking."

He smiled, digging into the bag again. "It's interesting what one can discover if one only asks. So, did I gain any brownie points or have I crashed and burned?" He pulled his own sandwich out of the bag.

She beamed at him and folded the sandwich wrapper back. "I think you did splendid." She wiped her mouth on her napkin, noticing the bruising on his right hand as he lifted his own sandwich to his lips. "You must have hit that dog pretty good. It almost looks worse than it did a few days ago," she said in concern.

Scott looked at his fist. "Oh, it's nothing," He looked around, obviously changing the subject. "Are you working alone today?"

She placed her sandwich down. "I'm not really working," she confessed and closed her book as she held it up to him, *How to Take the Educator's Exam*. She waited for his response.

Scott nodded and looked down at his sandwich. "That's quite a challenge you've set for yourself."

She paused for a moment, trying to establish the tone she was hearing. It wasn't sarcasm, but he almost sounded disappointed. "I told you I wanted to be a teacher." Scott placed his soda on her desk. "Yes, yes, you did. I guess I'm just not used to women working."

"Are we really going to have this conversation again?" she asked with an irritable voice.

Scott sighed and said nothing.

Bethany nodded, walked around the desk, and sat on the corner with him. "Scott, women can do both, you know?" She gave him an understanding smile. "Look at where we are now. The men are off fighting the war, and the women are here on the home front, taking care of the children and keeping things going."

Scott nodded vigorously. "That's because it's necessary, Beth," he defended.

"Are you saying that if we were to get married, you'd want me to stop teaching?"

Scott tried to process her question. "I think there would be a lot of things to consider, my love."

"Like what?" she asked impatiently.

He shrugged again. "Well, for starters, I want a large family. I always have. I'm in a good position to provide for a large family, and you would have no need to work. I feel ten, perhaps twelve, little tykes that look just like you would be an acceptable amount—to start anyway." He smiled sheepishly.

She threw her head in the air and laughed. "I'd have to think long and hard before agreeing to give you twelve children, Scott Jenkins."

Scott looked deep into her eyes. "Is it the amount of little ones you'd need to consider, or the topic in its entirety?" He moved his mouth close to hers, and her heart began to pound fast. "I can most certainly compromise when the situation requires it."

"For some reason, I thought we were talking about an exam." She smiled and stared at his lips. "Would you have so little faith in me that I couldn't take care of our family and teach at the same time?"

He folded his arms and thought for a moment with a smile. "I have faith that you could accomplish anything you set your mind to."

She smiled.

"Beth, I would want you to do what would make you happy, so long as at the end of the day you came home to me."

Bethany blushed and looked at the table top, "I would always come home to you."

Scott took her hand and Bethany squeezed it lovingly. "And, Beth, I would always support you in anything you want to do. But, I don't wish to see you hurt when the war finally ends and all those soldiers come back looking for teaching jobs."

Bethany ran her palm over his cheek and leaned into him as if telling him a secret. "I guess I just have to be better than all those men." She gave him a big smile and held the book up to him. "Maybe one day I'll want to be a stay-at-home mother and wife like my mama, or perhaps I'll still want it all. Until then, teachers are needed. I read an article just yesterday. Over seven thousand male teachers throughout the country joined the war and need to be replaced immediately." She held the book to her chest and she looked deep into his eyes. "Besides, Ms. Maples is getting married, and she asked me to take over for her right here." She moved closer to him. "Scott, I'm not saying that how you feel wouldn't matter to me, because it would matter greatly, or anyone I marry as far as that goes. I believe that a relationship demands compromise on both sides too." She giggled. "You want twelve children, and I want to teach. Perhaps there's a compromise there somewhere."

"Do you want children?"

"You mean with you?" she teased. Scott grinned, and she laughed and suddenly became serious. "Of course, not only is it a need I would feel as a woman, but also an obligation and a pleasure I would feel as a wife. But I sure wouldn't want my entire existence to be limited to the two."

"Of course you wouldn't," he said sarcastically.

She grinned. "It sounds like we would have some big barn burners to overcome if we ever started talking about getting married."

Scott shook his head, "No, not at all." He took her hand. "Marriage is a voluntary commitment we would make to each other, it's not a prison sentence. I would want you to be who you are and would never want you to change for me."

"Is there a *however* in there somewhere?" She waited.

Scott shook his head. "No, Beth, I accept that you have goals in your life that you set for yourself. I'd never try to come between that. I would only hope that you accept that, as your husband, I would have goals I'd want us to meet together as well."

She beamed at him, "Then can you help me with something?"

He nodded. "Yes, love, if I can."

She held the book out with a smile. "Drill this stuff into my head."

He took the book and flipped through it, nodding. "I can do that." He glanced at her, and she smiled at him. "How long do we have?"

She took a sip of her Bubble Up. "We have until Friday at eleven a.m. At which time I will be in utter panic," she said nervously.

Scott sat the book down and rubbed her hand. "No worries. Lieutenant Jenkins is on the job."

"I was hoping you were going to say that." She sighed. "Why did it take so long to say something about this?"

She shrugged. "Ms. Maples has been teaching here for years, as long as I can remember. I just hope I can measure up to her, if I'm lucky enough to pass the teaching exam, that is."

He took her hand gently and held it in his lap. "I think you could just about measure up to anything you set your mind to." He played with her hand, and she watched him lovingly. "You know, Beth, being a civilian in these times is hard. I'm almost glad I'm a soldier."

Bethany wondered if he had found immunity to his feelings when it came to the war, a way of distancing himself from the pains of his experiences. "I'll be in line for the biggest party at the Crossroads when this war finally ends, that's for sure."

"And I'll be there to escort you."

She looked down. "I've noticed, Scotty, there isn't much weariness that comes from you when we talk of the war. You make accepting the war seem easy." Her eyes moved up to him.

Scott was silent for a moment. "Nothing is easy, gorgeous. Just some things are necessary." He looked up at her and found that she was studying him. Scott gave her a sad smile. "I wish I could be around to see you with your own children someday. I bet you're going to be just an amazing mum."

She looked deep into his eyes. Suddenly, the thought of not having him there for all the important aspects of her life seemed so very sad and somewhat unnatural. "It's a big world out there. I guess sometimes I forget you're just on a stop in our little town," she said, a little agitated, and stood, moving to the window.

Scott watched her from the desk. "I did not mean to upset you."

She folded her arms to keep from trembling. "You didn't. This war is what upsets me." She wouldn't look at him.

Scott watched her, how she stood tall and assertive. "I plan on coming back to visit as much as I can, you know."

She turned and gave him a phony smile. "Of course you will." She walked back to the desk and sat with him. There was an awkward silence for a moment. "You'll be going back to England when the war ends?" she whispered.

Scott gazed at her and she looked at him when he didn't respond. He took a deep breath and touched her face. "Honestly, I never really thought about it." He looked away. "I never really thought I had a reason to make any plans."

She wanted to cry. "Why, because you think you won't make it through this war, is that what you're saying?"

Scott quickly looked at her, noticing the tears in her eyes.

"You can't do that to me." She raised her voice. "You can't just walk in here and make me care and then say things like that and think I'll let you get away with it!"

Scott remained silent for a moment. "Perhaps we should change the topic."

"No, I want to talk about this!" She demanded.

Scott quickly stood.

"Scott!"

"You want to talk about this?" he said angrily and turned to her. "I always believed this war would get the best of me in the end."

Her eyes became wet.

"You said I show no weariness when it comes to speaking of the war." He stared at her for a long moment. "I've been at war my whole life, Beth. My grandfather and I have never gotten along. I'm not so sure I understand why he hates me so much, I just know he does."

Bethany wiped her tears away but they kept coming.

"Somehow, I think I disappointed him, but I don't know why. Thing is, I would give it all to him, every dime, if he would just love me. Maybe I'm just tired of fighting to be happy."

Bethany walked to him. "What would make you happy?"

Scott touched her face and took a step closer. If he had any idea what his touch did to her, he could understand how sad his words had made her.

"I would be happy if I could be someone else," he said simply.

She slowly shook her head, not accepting his answer.

Scott turned away. "My family's money has been a curse. Bradley married into wealth. After my grandmother died, it went to my mum. Bradley hadn't been exactly responsible in his endeavors and my grandmother didn't trust him. Then when mum died, it was all handed down to me." He looked at her again. "I think he resents me for that. I don't mean to disappoint people, Beth."

Bethany's eyes pleaded with him. "If you had no money, would you be happy?"

Scott rubbed her shoulders and then wrapped his arms around her waist tightly. "I promised myself one day I'd make sure that money did some good in this world. That would make me happy." She stared deep into his sad eyes and Scott reached a hand up, running it over her neck. "Fact is none of us could know what will happen when we get to Europe." He laughed sadly and looked into her eyes. "I just know I'm tired, Beth. I just need something else…to *be* someone else…than what I've been my whole life." He gave her a sad smile noticing the worried look on her face. He shook her in his arms. "I would hope you would stay in touch when I leave."

There was so much she wanted to tell him at that very moment. How much he had changed her life in just the short time he had been there. Scott was a godsend to her, and she hated that something deep inside was holding her back from screaming to the world how she really felt. But she also knew that the last thing Scott needed was a distraction. He needed to clear his head of everything but coming back alive.

She nodded in reply. "Of course I'll write." She looked at his lips. "Just come back, okay?" She buried her face in his shoulder and held Scott for a long time.

CHAPTER 26

When Scott and Bethany arrived back at the house a while later, Sheriff Masterson's car was parked in the drive.

Bethany gave Scott a questionable look. "I wonder what's going on." Scott shrugged but didn't seem very surprised to see the car.

Grant Masterson took another sip of his coffee and looked toward the door from the kitchen table. He stood as Bethany and Scott walked into the kitchen.

"Mama, is everything all right?" Bethany asked, concerned, as she pulled her jacket off.

Grant put his hands on his hips and looked from her to Scott. "Scott, how have you been?"

"Real good, thanks." Scott failed to control the smirk on his face, and Grant saw right through him.

Grant looked at Bethany and grinned. "Has he been with you all day?"

Scott folded his arms and smiled, looking at the floor. Bethany looked at Scott confused and then back at Masterson. "The last two hours. What is this all about?"

Grant grinned and looked from her to Scott. "I received a visit from Derek Carson just a while ago. It appears his son showed up at the bank with a real nice shiner." Scott moved his eyes up to Grant, and the sheriff grinned at him. "You wouldn't know anything about that, would you, son?"

Bethany raised her eyebrows and then looked at the floor herself as a large smile developed on her face. Things suddenly made sense.

Scott shrugged with a smile. "Wow, really. A shiner, you say? I sure hope he's okay."

Grant sighed. "Yes, a shiner. He'd been beaten up pretty good. I'm wondering where you were before you met up with Bethany."

Scott smiled and glanced over at Bethany. She didn't look up. "You know..." He looked back at Grant. "I think maybe I did run into Carson just after leaving the bank. We were talking... and stuff."

Grant folded his arms, trying to lose the grin. "What kind of *stuff*?" He waited, but Scott said nothing. "You see...David isn't saying a word. I can only speculate that maybe he's too...how should I say ...scared." He tipped his head and studied Scott. "Do you have any idea why that is?"

Scott looked from Grant to Bethany, and she shook her head in disbelief, quickly turning her smile to the floor again.

Grant grabbed Scott's right hand and turned the knuckles upward. "Not healing very well, is it"

Scott smiled and pulled his arm away. "Sure is tough about Carson. Do you think he'll be okay?"

Grant sighed and shook his head in disbelief. Bethany nudged Scott, and he couldn't hold back his chuckle. "Oh, he's okay. What were you two talking about?" Scott froze, and Grant had to laugh. "You do realize you're lucky David Carson is keeping quiet? I might suggest you limit your 'conversations' with David Carson. It doesn't seem to be good for his health."

Scott pointed at Grant. "See, that is what we were talking about...his health," Scott said cunningly, and Bethany couldn't control her laughter.

Grant sighed. "Well, I think he got the message." He looked at Bethany. "I can only gather it had something to do with you?"

Bethany held her hands up. "I'm innocent. This is just as much a surprise to me as all of you."

Grant turned his gaze back to Scott. "I'm not really very surprised," he said sarcastically.

"Scott?" Joseph asked from the table. "Do you know anything about this?"

Scott looked at Joseph. "Yes, sir, I know that David Carson came over here the other day being very disagreeable. I just thought I would give him a lesson in English manners."

Katherine looked at her daughter, and Bethany was smiling shyly. Lord knows Katherine didn't condone violence, but she witnessed firsthand the vindictiveness coming from David that day.

Grant shook his head disagreeably. "Next time, let me handle it."

Scott let his arms fall to his sides. "There better not be a next time! I don't like him bothering Beth," Scott said sternly.

"Seeing it myself, I understand. But I can't have you beating him up every time he looks Bethany's way."

"Scott was just standing up for me," Bethany said softly and glared at Scott sternly. "But I'll make sure it doesn't happen again, Grant."

"Oh, no worries about that," Scott said looking down at her. "Because I told him if I hear him blinking your direction, I would find him."

Bethany shook her head and looked at the floor with a smile.

Grant took a quick step toward Scott. "Why would you admit that in front of me?"

Scott smiled and shrugged. "I'm not admitting anything."

Everyone watched curiously as he sat on the couch and began reading the morning paper. Grant looked at Bethany, and she smiled, shrugging innocently.

Grant laughed and placed his hat on his head. "Scott Jenkins, do what you can to stay out of trouble, will you please?"

Scott gave him a wave, turning the page of the newspaper.

The sheriff turned to Bethany. "I might need a little help from you. He doesn't seem to listen to anyone else." He looked at Scott and raised his voice. "I can't have people going around taking the law into their own hands."

Scott sent a grin his direction.

Grant tipped his hat. "Have a good day, all."

Bethany closed the door behind Grant and walked over to Scott. With her arms folded, she looked down at him and shook her head. Scott smiled without looking up at her, and she nudged him with her leg.

"I never knew you were such a troublemaker," she teased.

Scott chuckled and turned the page of the paper.

CHAPTER 27

Friday came quickly, and with a few late nights of study, Scott was sure Bethany was very prepared for her exam. Scott had been wondering around the college for the last three hours, patiently waiting for Bethany to come out. He hoped that the positive energy he was sending, along with the good luck hug before she went in, was enough to bring her success.

Scott leaned against the truck, arms and legs folded, focusing on the mud puddle directly in front of him when he heard her screech. Bethany had the biggest smile on her face and was running to him the moment she hit the door. Scott stepped away from the truck, and she jumped into his arms.

"That was the most amazing three hours of my life!" He twirled her around, and she squealed again happily. "It felt so… amazing!" He sat her down, and she gave him a huge smile. "I feel so good!"

He put his head against hers. "You think you did well?"

She closed her eyes, enjoying his closeness. "I knew all the answers. Thank you for this. Thank you for being here. It means so much to me."

He took her hand. "I'm very proud of you, Bethany." She smiled. "How would you like to get lunch to celebrate?"

"Oh, yes, I'm so hungry!" He laughed at her bouncy excitement, and Bethany smiled up at him. "Thank you." She held his eyes for a moment.

Scott simply smiled back. They chose the small café across the street from the college. The sign said "Farmer's Café" and it offered a sit down area. Scott was pleased to see that there were only a few vehicles in the parking lot. Sitting at a corner table by the window, the waitress offered them a menu, but Scott simply ordered two burgers with fries with chocolate shakes. He watched Bethany, how she looked around the café in amusement, and could tell she didn't get out of Dobson very often.

Bethany caught him staring and sent him a loving smile. "I hope you weren't too bored waiting around for me," she said, breaking the silence.

He looked down, a little embarrassed. "No, it was fine. I looked around the college a little." Scott liked the idea of getting her alone for a while. Although he loved the Davies family, there were so many of them. He would never admit it but found himself jealous of the time everyone else got with Bethany.

She stared at the table. "Scott, you made it a good day for me. Thank you."

He sent her a huge grin. "You're making it a good day for me too. Besides, I made good use of the time. I checked into their veterinarian program while I was waiting." He reached over and squeezed her hand.

She raised her eyebrows. "Veterinarian, wow, I never knew that interested you!"

Scott glanced down in embarrassment. "I want to have my own ranch. I thought it would be good to know a little something about treating my own animals." He lifted his head, and she was smiling proudly at him. "What?"

Her smile got bigger. "I'm just happy to see you're making future plans."

He smiled back. "I guess I am. Can you keep a secret?" She nodded. "When the war ends, I want to come back to the Crossroads."

Her heart pounded with excitement. "That's so wonderful!" She hardly got the words out.

He took a deep breath. "Do you think that sounds crazy?" He chuckled. "Of all the places in the world, who would have thought this was where I wanted to be. I just feel at home here, more than I ever have anywhere else."

She shook her head. "No, it doesn't sound crazy at all." Her eyes got wet, and she quickly looked down to conceal it. "That sounds so great, Scott," she said as their food was delivered.

He played with his straw. "'Course, it might not please David Carson."

Bethany wiped her mouth with her napkin and gave him a confused look. "Why do you say that?"

Scott was silent for a moment. "I'm very protective of you, Beth."

Bethany giggled. "I noticed." It got awkwardly silent. "Why is that?" she decided to ask. She watched as he sat back in his chair and stared at her, as if he were choosing his words very carefully.

Scott looked deep into her eyes. "Because, Bethany Davies, you're all I think about."

Bethany was taken off guard and almost dropped her milkshake. She didn't know what to say, so she said nothing, knowing she would be too excited to get the words out with embarrassing herself anyway. She sent him a huge smile.

He sighed. "I know things are complicated right now." He looked into her very soul. "I think we've gotten very close in a very short time, and I know we have a lot of personal issues to deal with. But I never thought I could ever feel this way. You asked me what would make me happy. You do, Bethany. I am happiest when we're together."

She looked up at him, not able to hide the tears any longer. Scott questioned her tears a moment. Reaching over the table, he ran his palm over her cheek. She touched his hand and held it there.

He smiled and sat back in his chair, folding his hands over the table nervously. "I know having a relationship is the last thing you need right now. But I was wondering if you thought after the war–do you think I could be someone you would be interested in having a future with?" Bethany wiped her cheek and stared into his eyes. He waited, and she didn't answer. Scott looked down and nodded.

Bethany took his hand, holding it tightly. "Having a relationship with anyone has been the last thing on my mind."

Scott became very sad as he moved his eyes up to her, and Bethany was beaming from ear to ear. "I just wanted you to know how I feel. How I've been feeling." He leaned into the table impatiently. "When I'm apart from you, I want to be close. I go crazy trying to sleep at night, wondering what you're doing—if you're thinking of me. I can't wait to get up in the morning so I can see you."

Bethany never lost eye contact with him. Her smile lit up the room.

"I've never had a relationship before, never been in love, and never desired to know love until you. I don't know if I'm in love with you, Beth, because I don't know what that should feel like. I only know things are better when we're together."

She stared at him but said nothing.

"Will you please say something?" he suddenly asked impatiently.

She laughed. "Well." She smiled. "You're definitely right about one thing. We both certainly have a lot happening in our lives right now."

Bethany watched Scott's heart fall to the table. The look of disappointment coming from him filled the room. Scott nodded in agreement. He sat back in his chair and pushed his fries around. Bethany giggled softly and looked at her plate. She knew what he was waiting to hear, but her mind kept drifting back to the story her mama had told her, how she played hard to get before she finally agreed to a life with her papa. Bethany was going to make Scott Jenkins work for it, and honestly, she was enjoying the torment she so often put him through. She wondered what he was thinking. Scott had suddenly become very quiet, and when she glanced up at him, he was actually pouting.

"I'm not the person I was before you came to Dobson, Scott." she said out of the blue, and he looked up at her. Bethany paused. "I was willing to be alone the rest of my life if it meant I could just protect myself from the pain I went through in the past. You are so kind and sweet and trusting. You've become my best friend, Scott Jenkins." Scott nodded sadly, and she knew that wasn't what he was waiting to hear.

Bethany stood and sat in the chair next to him. "If it's possible to fall in love with my best friend I think we are in a lot of danger of that happening." She placed a palm on his cheek. "I'll be ready to move forward with you when you get back…because, you see, Scott…I do my own dreaming about you too." He smiled happily and she drew him into her arms. "You helped me trust in love again." She felt the tears. "I need you in my life. Don't let me down, okay?"

Scott held her tight. "Never, Beth, I promise."

Bethany kissed his cheek and looked at him, holding him at arm's length. "I'm scared to death to think what will happen when you finally leave. Do you know what losing you would do to me?" She wiped the tear from her cheek.

Scott put his head against hers. "If I could just stay here with you, I would. With you is where I want to be."

She caressed his cheek.

"You make me want to live so badly. When I go over there, I'm going to do everything I can to end this war so I can get back. You just have to hold on a little longer, okay?"

With her forehead still against his, she nodded. "Let's just promise each other something." Holding him there, she looked deep into his eyes. "Whatever happens, we'll be together again." She closed her eyes.

"I promise, Bethany Davies." He took her into his arms and held her so tightly. Scott moved her food from across the table and placed it in front of her. She sat close to him and held his hand in her lap as she took a bite of her burger.

Scott noticed three African American soldiers come into the café and sit at the bar. The waitress, standing behind the counter, pulled out her pad and pen with a smile at the three soldiers. "Gentlemen, may I take your orders?"

A large man, wearing an apron and wiping his hands on a towel, appeared from the back and stood next to the waitress. "Chris, I'll take over up here. Why don't you finish up in the back?"

The waitress handed him the pad and pen, then disappeared in the back. Scott watched curiously as the man, who Scott assumed was the owner, simply sat the pad on the counter and began clearing dishes as if the men weren't even there.

"I'm sorry, but we're closed," he said without making eye contact with the three soldiers.

The men looked at each other, confused, and then the older of the three gave him a cross look. "Closed?" He looked around at the other customers. "Then why are you serving them?"

Bethany watched as Scott pushed his chair back and stood. The owner simply finished clearing off the counter. "I said we're closed," he repeated rudely.

"I'll be right back," Scott said, squeezing Bethany's shoulder. He approached the counter observing the men's uniforms.

"Are you refusing to serve us?" the soldier asked.

The owner wouldn't respond.

"We're only asking for a hot meal! We can pay our way."

The owner glared at him.

Scott placed a soft hand on the soldier's shoulder. "Would you gentlemen care to join us?" Scott pointed at the table where Bethany sat and held out his hand. "I'm Lieutenant Scott Jenkins with the 101st Airborne."

The soldier shook his hand. "It's nice to meet you, Lieutenant. I'm Staff Sergeant Ed Farley, 761st Tank Battalion." He looked at his friends. "This is Private Max Blackwell and Private Carlyle Watson."

Scott pointed at Bethany. "My friend Bethany Davies and I would really like it if you would eat with us." The men nodded at her, and she returned a smile. "Please, come join us at our table."

The owner became agitated. He watched as Scott pulled up an extra chair at their table and began talking to the soldiers. Scott looked up at the waitress, who was coming from the back. "Can I get some burgers and shakes for my friends, please?"

"I said I'm not serving their kind here!"

Scott glared at him. "Well, you're not serving them. You're serving me!" Scott said angrily. "And I just ordered three burgers and three chocolate shakes."

The waitress looked to the owner, and he angrily shook his head. She looked at the table. "I'm really sorry," she said sympathetically and went in the back.

"These men have fought for your country. The least you can do is feed them a meal," Bethany shouted.

The owner came around the counter, standing over Scott. "You can just leave with them."

Farley stood, "Lieutenant, we should just go."

Scott stood and took a step toward the café owner. "No, you have a right to be here as much as anyone. Please bring three burgers—on me," Scott repeated.

The owner pushed Scott into his chair. Taking a step forward, Scott pulled his arm back and came in with a hard blow across the man's eye, sending the man to the floor.

Farley pulled Scott back. "We should all go before the MPs arrive."

Scott glared down at the owner and flung a handful of money at him. "Thanks for your hospitality!"

"I'm going to call the sheriff!" the man yelled from the floor, holding his eye in agony.

Scott and Bethany gathered near the truck still parked at the college, and after speaking for a while, it was determined that Farley and his friends were due to ship out in a week heading for Europe. Scott had never realized how wrongly African Americans had been treated during the war until talking to the men. Scott had determined that if he was to ever come across a life or death situation where he really needed to count on a man, he would want one of those men to be on his side. Farley, Blackwell, and Watson…they had more heart than any soldier Scott had ever met.

Farley shook Scott's hand. "Thank you for your help, Lieutenant. Perhaps we'll see each other in Europe."

Scott grasped his hand. "Next time we meet, I hope it's under better circumstance, that's for sure."

"Ms. Davies, I apologize for interrupting your lunch." Farley shook her hand. "I hope your exam brings results you need."

"Be safe, Mr. Farley." The others said goodbye as well, and the soldiers headed toward their car.

Scott opened the door for Bethany, and she started to get in. Stopping, she turned to Scott. "I'm so very proud of you." She placed a soft kiss on his cheek.

CHAPTER 28

Grant took off his hat, waiting for someone to answer the door at the Davies's home. A moment later, Taylor greeted him at the door with a smile. She pushed the screen door open and invited him in.

"Good afternoon, Sheriff Masterson."

"Miss Taylor, how have you been?" Grant asked, stepping in and closing the door.

Taylor touched her belly and sighed. "Feeling like a beached whale actually. Mama and Papa are in the kitchen."

Grant looked toward the kitchen, noticing everyone seated around the kitchen table. "I was actually looking for Scott."

Taylor's eyes drifted toward the stairway as Scott was just coming down. Grant met him in the kitchen.

"Grant, can I get you a cup of coffee or something to eat?" Katherine asked.

Grant shook his head and sent her an appreciative smile. "No, thank you, Katherine. This isn't a social call, I'm afraid. But I have to admit something sure does smell good." He looked at Scott who had just sat next to Bethany. "I received a call from the sheriff's office over in Durham County. It seems you had a falling out with a man named Carter Basils earlier today?"

Scott looked at Grant as Katherine placed a cup of coffee in front of him. He thanked Katherine and took a sip. "I have no idea what his name was, Sheriff. But if he was the owner of the Farmer's Café, then that would be correct."

Bethany turned in her chair. "Sheriff, Scott was just defending himself!" she argued with tense irritation in her voice.

Grant looked from her back to Scott. "He's claiming you attacked him."

Joseph studied Bethany. "Girl, what were the two of you doing in Durham County?"

Bethany froze a moment. Scott started to defend her, and Bethany took his hand. "No, Scott, it's okay. Papa, Scott took me to take the teaching exam." Her whole life, the one person she hated to disappoint was her papa. "Ms. Maples wants me to replace her as teacher once she's married. I didn't want to say anything and disappoint you if I didn't pass the teaching exam."

She looked from her papa to her mama. Katherine, seeming very pleased, looked down at the table and smiled. Bethany looked back at Grant. "Scott has been helping me study all week. After taking the exam, we went to the café to celebrate. That man was very rude to those soldiers just because of their skin color!" She looked around the table. "They could die defending this country, and they weren't even allowed to eat in his restaurant!" Bethany shook her head and squeezed Scott's hand. "Scott was just trying to defend them. He pushed Scott. Scott was defending himself," she said sternly.

Grant looked from her to Scott. "Well, it certainly sounds like self defense. You're saying it was necessary to hit him?"

Scott sighed, stood, and looked at Grant. Bethany's mouth dropped, wondering if anyone else noticed the extreme resemblance between the two men, even more so why she hadn't noticed it herself in the past. Scott and Grant shared the same cheekbones, eye and hair color, facial expressions, even their posture when irritated was the same.

"He should consider himself lucky I only had one shot," Scott said and folded his arms. "A man like that has no right serving the public." Scott let his arms fall. "In fact, I would like to submit my own personal complaint. After all, he did push me first," Scott said sarcastically.

Grant sighed. "Scott, please, let me just see what I can do to calm things down," Grant said slowly and put his hands on his gun belt with a shake his head. "I need you to stay out of trouble, you hear me, son?"

Scott glared at him. "Trust me, I heard that enough from my own grandfather growing up, I don't need to hear it from you as well," Scott said angrily and took his seat, and Bethany rubbed his back reassuringly.

Grant looked around. "Katherine, Joseph, I'll be seeing you." He looked back at Scott. "You'll be around if I have more questions?"

"I'll be around for a few more days."

Bethany's eyes followed the sheriff to the front door, and then she glanced back at Scott. Standing, she hurried out the door after Grant, who was getting into his car.

"Sheriff Masterson," she called from the top of the porch.

Grant stopped.

"Do you have a minute?" Bethany quickly worked her way down the steps. Grant waited at the car as she approached him.

"The other day at the school, you acted like you knew Scott. I didn't notice it then." She folded her arms. "But there is an extreme resemblance between you two."

Grant manipulated his hat nervously and then looked to the ground. "I don't know what you mean, Bethany." He gave her a phony smile.

Bethany nodded, realizing Grant wasn't going to give in easily, although she didn't understand why. "You know, Scott never knew his father, only that he was an American." She took a step toward him. "You stand the same, have the same facial features. You even carry the same innocent mannerisms when you're put on the spot." She let her arms fall to her sides, and

Grant looked up at her, his expression that of a child caught in the cookie jar.

"All extremely coincidental, I'm sure." He stumbled on his words. Grant turned, threw his hat in the front seat of the car, and proceeded to get in.

Bethany took another quick step toward him. "She's dead, Grant," she said quickly. "The woman you claimed to love, the reason you never married, she's gone!"

Grant quickly looked at her. "What did you say?"

"You're all Scott has left. I can't understand why you would deny who you are." It was silent for a moment. "You're Scott's biological father. I can see it plain as day."

Bethany could hear the sorrow in his voice. "Naomi's dead?" Grant continued to stare at her in disbelief.

Bethany folded her arms and took another step toward him. "How did you know her name was Naomi?" Bethany asked in a whisper, not so much curious as hurt. Grant had all but admitted that he wasn't the man she thought she knew at all. Grant just stared at her. Bethany took a deep breath. Her heart suddenly ached for Scott. "Grant, I have known you half my life. You've been an important part of this community, and we have all grown to trust and respect you." She pointed at the house, her voice hoarse. "That man…a man I have grown to care for very much, has been living with the unknown his whole life. Please, help me give him some of those answers and lay some of his pain to rest."

Tears formed in Grant's eyes, and he sighed. "It isn't as easy as that, Bethany. Naomi kept things from Scott for his own safety."

Bethany had a look of confusion.

"If you don't want Scott hurt, if you care anything for him, forget about this conversation."

"That's just it, Grant, I do care…I care very much. You're his father, and he deserves to know. Grant, he has a right to know!" Grant just stared at her. Bethany became very angry. "What about Eric? You don't think he has the right to know he has a brother?"

Grant shook his head. "I mean it, Bethany, don't open up this can of worms. You need to let it go." He shook his head angrily and slammed the car door.

She watched as he drove off.

"Bethany, is everything all right?" Jeffrey asked from the porch.

Bethany glanced back at him and then turned again to the departing car. "I'm fine, Jeffrey," she said, still confused. She ran her fingers through her hair.

Jeffrey moved toward her and they watched the car disappear at the end of the drive. "Jeffrey, what do you know about Scott's mother? Has he ever said anything to you about why his parents weren't together?"

Jeffrey put his hands in his pockets and shrugged. "I don't think that Scott even knows. He said he asked his mother many times about his father and she would never speak to him about it."

Bethany folded her arms and stared at the ground.

"Bethany, what's going on?"

"I'm not sure," she said as she shook her head. Bethany looked back at the empty driveway confused.

CHAPTER 29

LONDON, ENGLAND, 1943

Bradley Jenkins slammed his palms on his desk. "What do you mean the accounts are closed?" He whipped around his desk and dived toward Flannery.

Flannery, feeling threatened, took a fearful step backward. "He beat us to it." Jameson Flannery held up a piece of paper. "The accounts were transferred and closed a few days ago."

Bradley shook his head and slammed his palms on the desk again. "Transferred to where?"

Flannery shook his head vigorously. "How am I to know? It was all there, Bradley. My last trip to the bank, it was there!"

Jenkins slammed his chair into the desk. "This can't be happening to me!" He looked at Flannery. Holding out a finger, he shook it at Flannery. "You find my grandson. I want to speak with him…now!"

"Bradley, there's no telling where Scotland could be. We're in the middle of a war, remember?" Flannery said.

"I want you to go back to that bank. You find out where my money was transferred to…*today!*"

Jameson sighed. "Maybe we should just let it go? The more we probe, the worse things seem to get."

Bradley stared sternly at him. "Never…" He paced the floor. "William…what was his name—William Hill. You find that friend of Scotland's. See if he knows where my grandson is!"

Bradley continued to shake his head with the steps he took toward the large window that overlooked the streets. "I'll find you, grandson of mine." Bradley pushed his head into the glass panes. "No matter what, this isn't over!"

CHAPTER 30

DOBSON'S CROSSROADS, NORTH CAROLINA, 1943

Everyone woke Friday morning with a huge agenda. Christmas was approaching, and the church dance was that evening. Last-minute decorations were being collected and food prepared. Joseph and Katherine left for the church dance an hour early to add the last of the decorations, help the reverend unpack the food, and greet any first arrivers.

Uncle Andrew picked up Jeffrey early to deliver any additional supplies that Joseph couldn't carry in the truck. Jeffrey was going to meet Kristina at her place after and walk her to the dance with intentions on meeting Scott and Bethany there. Feeling very pregnant and less than social, Taylor offered to stay home and sit her younger siblings. She was upstairs helping Bethany get dressed.

Scott, dressed in his uniform, paced back and forth in front of the fire, waiting for Bethany to come downstairs. He straightened his uniform and looked up. There was Bethany, standing at the top of the stairs. She was smiling down at him, with Taylor close behind grinning from ear to ear.

Scott tried to catch his breath, for Bethany took his breath away. She was holding a white sweater in one hand and clinging to the railing with the other. Bethany looked flawless. Her elegant red dress stopped just below her knees and was flowing over every curve of her body. The black heels made her slim, soft legs look an inch taller. She had her hair lay over her shoulders and pinned back in a pretty bow. The pearls around her neck matched her earrings and bracelet. Scott slowly moved to the bottom of the stairs, admiring Bethany as she carefully walked down to him with Taylor following close behind. He smiled and held out his arm to her. Bethany gladly took it. She giggled at his awestruck stare.

Scott stumbled on his words. "Bethany, you look in—incredible," he gasped.

Taylor giggled, and Bethany nudged her. "You look very handsome yourself, Lieutenant Jenkins." She looked around the room. "Where is everyone?"

"They already left," Taylor said, grinning.

"Oh, well, if we're walking, maybe I should take my other shoes?"

Taylor giggled.

Bethany looked from Taylor to Scott suspiciously. He just smiled and took her hand. Scott watched her face as they reached the porch. Taylor giggled again. Bethany's mouth dropped. In the driveway sat a brand-new, bright red, two-door Chevy coupe.

Scott turned to Bethany. "Merry Christmas."

Bethany's mouth fell open. "What did you say?"

Scott took a step closer. "Every teacher should have a car." He touched her face. "I thought you might like the sports model best."

She gasped, covering her mouth, and looked back at the coupe. "Scott, it can't be for me!" She looked back at him. "It's too much. I can't accept it!"

"You have no choice." He smiled. "But, I reserve the right to drive it during all my future visits."

She couldn't breathe. "You shouldn't have done this." She quickly looked at him. "Really—it's truly mine?"

He smiled, waving the keys in front of her, and nodded. "It's truly yours, Ms. Davies. If you don't like the color, I can exchange it."

She laughed and grabbed the keys from him. "Not on your life!" Bethany drew him into her arms. "I love it, thank you so much!" She kissed his cheek and gave him another big hug. Then, she looked back at the car and screeched as she raced down the steps to her new wheels. She started the car and began playing with all the buttons and gadgets.

"I love my sister, Scott. You started something I hope you intend to finish," Taylor said worriedly.

Scott nodded and placed his hands in his pockets as he looked out at Bethany. "I'm in love with her, Taylor. I haven't admitted it to her. I only recently began to admit it to myself—but I love her." He looked at Taylor. "I'm not sure how this whole thing will work out. All I can promise you is that I'll do the best I can."

Taylor rubbed his arm, "Maybe you should start by telling her how you feel."

Scott took a deep breath and looked back at Bethany. "I started to the other day. I guess I'm just waiting to be sure it's something Beth really wants to hear."

Taylor gave him a sympathetic hug.

When they arrived at the church, Scott pulled the car up to the front of the annex. Bethany played with the car radio like a new toy all the way there. Scott pulled the passenger door open for Bethany and held out his arm to her. She proudly took it.

The inside of the annex had been decorated with several streamers, balloons, and confetti. The walls were lined with table after table of various foods and refreshments. Many were dancing, but many more were enjoying the town fellowship.

Joseph squeezed his wife who was dancing in his arms. "Our daughter's here."

Katherine gasped. "Oh, Joseph, look at how pretty she is!"

Scott helped Bethany off with her sweater and hung it at the door. They were met by Jeffrey and Kristina.

Kristina gasped. "Bethany, you are breathtaking!"

Bethany smiled and tugged on Kristina's pink silk collar. "So are you, I love this dress!"

Jeffrey, also in his uniform, nudged Scott. "Let's get the girls some punch."

Scott rubbed Bethany's arm. "We'll be right back."

She smiled and nodded, watching Scott and Jeffrey walk across the room.

Kristina put her arm around Bethany and watched the guys. "I'd say we both have keepers. You and Scott sure make a cute couple."

"We do, don't we?" Bethany blushed with a smile.

"Do tell," Kristina said anxiously.

Bethany giggled. "We talked about moving forward with our relationship when the war ends."

Kristina bounced in excitement.

"Scott and I agree we have a lot to work out first."

"Well, I think it's great. After all, everyone knows you're in love with him," Kristina said happily.

"I don't know what you mean," she said innocently.

"Oh, please." Kristina laughed. "It's written all over your face."

Bethany said nothing but smiled.

Kristina squeezed her arm and jumped up and down. "Oh, my goodness, Jeffrey told me what Scott got you for Christmas. Did you just die?"

Bethany laughed happily. "It hasn't sunk in yet. I was playing with the radio and all the little gadgets all the way here!"

"Well, I hope you know I expect you to give me a ride home."

The two giggled as the guys came back with the punch.

Joseph and Katherine danced by. "You both look beautiful!" Joseph complimented. "Make sure you each save me a dance." He gave Katherine a dip and moved back onto the dance floor.

Jeffrey took Kristina's glass and sat it on the table. "Come on, woman, let's boogie!" Kristina giggled as Jeffrey danced her out onto the floor.

Scott smiled at Bethany and held out his hand. "Ms. Davies, may I have this dance?"

Bethany smiled and sat her glass on the table as she took his hand. Scott gently put his arms around her waist, and she lovingly ran her hands across his back. They moved with the slow of the music and he pulled her closer. Scott put his head against hers, and she smiled. Bethany closed her eyes, cherishing every second in his arms. Scott noticed David and Martha come in the door together and shook his head in disbelief.

"Beth?" Scott whispered.

She opened her eyes looking up at him.

"You have an audience."

Martha was in an angry stance, tapping her foot, and sending a stern look their direction.

Bethany shook her head in disbelief. "Do you think she'll be glaring at us all night?"

Scott pulled her closer. "Let her."

She giggled and played with his hair.

"Have I told you how beautiful you are?"

Bethany continued playing with his hair as she looked deep and lovingly into his eyes. "A few times, actually."

He kissed her on the head, and Bethany witnessed Martha stomp her foot in aggravation. Bethany shook her head and giggled, closing her eyes.

Scott moved his lips to her ear. "I'm glad I'm here with you," he whispered. "I think this is the best moment of my enduring life."

She looked at him, tears formed in her eyes as she ran her palm over his cheek. "One day, I want to dance with you in the rain."

He held her tight. "It's a date."

She laughed happily, placing her head on his shoulder.

Grant Masterson approached them and gently tapped Scott on the shoulder. "Scott, do you mind if I cut in?"

Scott shrugged and looked at Bethany, "Well, I'm going to leave that up to Beth," he said with a smile. Bethany nodded, and Scott gave her hand to Grant. "Just don't get too comfortable because I'll be back."

Bethany giggled and began to slow dance with Grant.

"You look very pretty," he said with a smile.

"Once again I get to see you out of sheriff's uniform," she teased.

He chuckled, and it was silent for a moment. "I don't want to say something to put a damper on the evening," he finally said. "I just wanted to thank you for keeping our conversation between us."

Bethany took a deep breath. "Grant, I don't pretend to understand what is going on, but I do know you're a good man. With that said, eventually I'm going to be seeking out answers, if not for my own sake, for Scott's."

"I find that fair enough." He gave her a sad smile. "I want you to know it hasn't been easy. I loved Naomi very much. I see her in both my sons."

"That's something else I just don't understand. If I had children, I could never leave them. How could she just let Eric go like that?"

He sighed as the song ended. "I guess I just need you to trust me."

Bethany let him go. "You were right about something, Grant. I do care for Scott, very deeply in fact. I'd do anything for him." She gave him a stern look. "Do you have any idea what kind of life Scott had to live because of his grandfather or, for that matter, continues to suffer for?"

"Yes, I suppose I do."

Bethany took a step back. "Then I guess you can see how upsetting this whole thing makes me." Bethany turned and walk back to Scott.

"Well, how are we doing over here?" Reverend Michaels asked. "Bethany, you're as beautiful as ever." He held a hand out to Scott. "Mr. Jenkins, I think you're the luckiest man in the room."

Scott smiled at Bethany and nodded. "I know I am, sir."

Bethany gave him a loving smile.

Scott shook the reverend's hand. "Reverend, everything looks great."

"All thanks to Bethany's mama." The reverend paused for a moment and seemed to have something on his mind. "You know, Lieutenant Jenkins, every year we always have a special baptism. All are welcome in our congregation." He held his palms up. "No pressure, I promise. I just wanted to extend the invitation."

Bethany looked at Scott with a hint of hopefulness on her face.

He glanced at Bethany, noticing how happy the idea made her, and looked back at the reverend. "Well, sir, for generations, my family has been raised Catholic."

Michaels nodded. "So you're baptized a Catholic?"

Scott shook his head. "Honestly, I don't know if I was ever baptized."

Michaels raised his eyebrows. "Then you don't practice the faith?"

Scott shook his head again. "I think being at the Crossroads is probably the most I've ever set foot inside a church."

"I'll tell you what, you think about it." He grasped Scott's hand. "These are terrible times for our soldiers. I sure would like to send you off baptized in the grace of God." Michaels shook his hand again. "If you have any questions about baptism or you just need to talk, come by and see me."

Scott smiled and nodded. "Yes, sir, thank you, I will."

"Now, if you'll excuse me, Bethany, I'm going to see if I can tear your mother away for a dance. You two enjoy yourselves." Michaels gave Bethany a loving handshake and moved on.

Scott noticed Bethany's big smile. "What do you think?"

She put her arm around his waist. "I think it's ultimately your decision, but I would really feel better if you left here baptized."

He put his arm over her shoulders. "I'll think about it."

"Maybe take his advice, go in and talk to him more about it." She smiled up at him, pulling him closer; she placed her head on his chest. "I think you came to the Crossroads for a reason. At first, I thought it was for me. Maybe I was wrong. Maybe you needed to be here. Maybe we needed each other. Mama says the Lord works in mysterious ways."

"That he does, my love." He kissed her head, "How about another dance?"

She smiled and took his hand, leading him to the dance floor.

David watched from the refreshment table how happy Scott and Bethany looked. Taking the flask from the inside of his jacket, he took a big swig. Martha approached him from behind, a little uneasy about the display on the dance floor herself.

"One of us really needs to break up the party," she said, grabbing the flask and taking a huge belt herself. "What does he see in her anyway?"

David didn't take his eyes off Bethany. "She's beautiful," David said and looked at Martha. "Not to mention the smartest woman in Dobson."

"Obviously, she broke up with you." Martha looked over the dance floor at Bethany. "I don't think she's that pretty."

David snickered and took another belt, handing it to Martha. "I'm going to ask her to dance!" he said bravely, walking a little off balance toward the dance floor. Martha watched with great interest as David approached Scott and tapped him on the shoulder.

"May I cut in?" he slurred, smiling at Bethany.

"Go away, Carson." Scott pulled Bethany closer and kept dancing.

"You're not playing the game right, Jenkins. When a man asks to cut in on a dance, you oblige him, or do they do it differently in London?"

Scott ignored him, and David grabbed Scott's shoulder, pulling him away from Bethany. Scott sighed. "Now, why did you have to go and do that? I really don't want to ruin the dance by fighting with you."

"David, I don't want to dance with you!" Bethany insisted. "Go away."

David grabbed her arm, and Scott placed his hand on David's neck, pushing him into the wall with ease.

"I've about had it with you, Carson. You *ever* place a hand on Beth again, and I will end you!"

"Scott, please, let him go. He isn't worth it," Bethany said, pleaded with him.

Katherine looked at her husband from the far corner of the room where they were dancing. "Joseph, do something!" She took a step toward Scott. Joseph grabbed her hand. "What are you doing?" She gasped back at her husband.

Joseph shook his head. "David Carson has had it coming for a long time. You let that boy alone, wife."

Scott tightened his grip on David's throat. "Show me some acknowledgment, Carson," he said as people began to gather. "You want to breathe, you show me you understand what I'm telling you!"

David nodded, struggling to breathe, and Scott released him. David fell to his knees, holding his neck as he attempted to catch his breath.

"What is going on here?" Grant asked, hurrying from the other side of the room.

Scott grabbed David by the collar and pulled him to his feet. "I was just having a man-to-man discussion with Mr. Carson here, mate. No harm," Scott said, straightening David's tie and slamming his palm into David's chest. David fell backward against the wall, still attempting to catch his breath. "Isn't that right, Carson?"

David nodded, still coughing and holding his neck. "No harm, Sheriff."

Scott winked at Grant and took Bethany's hand. "Shall we dance?" Scott said simply and led Bethany back to the dance floor.

CHAPTER 31

Bethany pulled the coupe in front of Henderson's Mercantile the next morning. Scott hurried from the passenger side to get the door for her. "So, I'll meet you back here when you finish your visit with Reverend Michaels." She gave him a hug. "Are you sure you don't want me to go with you?"

He shook his head. "I'll be fine. I'll meet you back here in an hour?"

She smiled and nodded. "Okay, one hour. Say hello to the reverend for me." Scott waved in response and Bethany sent him a smile. She proudly watched as he moved up the boardwalk toward the church. Her eyes veered to the sheriff's office and Bethany moved across the street. When she opened the door, Grant looked up from his files and quickly stood.

"Bethany," he greeted.

"Hello, Grant. I was hoping we could talk." Then tears filled her eyes as she noticed the picture on Grant's desk. She angrily picked up the picture; Grant looked down sadly as she stared at it. Bethany looked at him. "I don't understand." She waved the picture at Grant. "He isn't just Scott's brother. He's Scott's *twin*!" Bethany sat in the chair near his desk and stared at the picture for a moment in shock, in disbelief, in anger. She held the picture tightly and looked up at him demandingly. "You tell me what is happening, or I'll get Scott and you can explain it to him!"

Grant sighed and nodded, sitting on the edge of his desk. "Okay." He folded his hands in his lap. "Scott and Eric are twins, you're right. Eric is a little more immature than Scott, but they are very much alike. And every time I looked into Eric's eyes, I wondered how my other son was. You have to know I did everything I could to get Scott. I wanted them both."

Bethany covered her mouth to calm herself. "You tell me right now why I shouldn't show this picture to him." She started to stand, and Grant stopped her.

"If you do that, Scott will be in grave danger, so will Eric."

Bethany stared at him and slowly sat the picture back on his desk. "Tell me!" she demanded.

Grant ran his fingers through his hair. "I met Naomi when I was stationed in London following the first war. We fell in love, but Bradley Jenkins refused to allow us to see each other, so Naomi and I met in secret. We'd been secretly seeing each other for about three months when we found out she was pregnant," Grant said, he stood and moved behind his desk. He raised the coffeepot, offering Bethany a glass. She shook her head in responds. He filled his own cup and sat at the edge of the desk. "I asked Naomi to run away with me, but she was afraid of what Bradley would do. She refused to put all of us at risk."

Bethany stared at the desk. "Surely he can't be that dangerous?" she asked, confused.

"Bradley Jenkins was a very powerful man back then. He still is, from what I hear. He forbade us to see each other, but Naomi and I kept meeting in secret, and each time I tried to convince her to run away with me. Later, there was no hiding her pregnancy anymore because she was getting so big." He got teary-eyed and looked down. "I wanted them, Bethany, so very much." He looked at her, and Bethany also had tears in her eyes.

Sitting his cup down, he took a deep breath. "When we finally told Bradley, he was furious. The last thing he wanted was an heir to stand in his way of the family money, much less two. Bethany, I tried to have my family. I even finally convinced Naomi to meet me at the shipyards. I was going to bring her back to the States, and we were going to get married." Grant stood and took something out of his desk and handed it to her. "Bradley must have found out because she never showed."

Bethany stared down at a travel ticket. She handed it back to Grant. "Did you find out why?"

"Bradley had a man named Jameson Flannery meet me instead. He had a letter from Naomi saying she had changed her mind and for me to go back to the States and leave her alone. To this day, I don't believe she wrote that letter." He stood and stared out the window. "I got beat to an inch of my life that night by some men that came along with Flannery. But I refused to leave!" He looked back at her. "Every time I tried to see her and my boys, she was heavily guarded. Then a few months later, I got a message from Bradley. I was to meet him at the shipyards."

He clenched his hands together and held it to his mouth as if to control his tears. "When Jenkins arrived, he had Eric with him. He said that he was giving Eric to me in exchange for me leaving London. I kept thinking how awful it must have been for Naomi, knowing Bradley had just torn her son out of her arms like that."

Bethany looked at the floor, horror stricken by the thought herself.

He shook his head and angrily ran his hands through his hair. "I had to decide what to do. I almost refused because I couldn't take him away from Naomi. But I thought if Eric was safe at my sister's, then it would be much easier to get Naomi and Scott out of London later. So I brought Eric to the States and left him with my sister. The very next day, I was back on that ship, determined I would never give up until I could bring Scott and Naomi back with me."

Bethany began to cry harder and looked down. "I am so sorry, Grant!"

Grant tried to control his composure. "Bradley had men watching the shipyards, I guess, because when I arrived in London, I was beaten severely. Later, I woke on a ship halfway back to the States. There was a note in my pocket saying if I set foot in London again, Scott would be killed." Grant looked down at her. "I loved Scott, Bethany, that's why I had to let him go."

"But what about now?" she pleaded. "Scott is here. Surely he isn't in danger now." She wiped her eyes. "Grant, he should know!"

"Bradley only has one love, and that's money. As long as Scott comes between him and his goals, he'll always be in danger. Bethany, I'm not as worried about Scott as I am Eric. The minute Scott finds out, he's going to want to see his brother. Bradley will never tolerate two heirs. Bethany, I also believe Scott and Eric need to know. I'm only asking you to give me a chance to figure out a way to tell them that doesn't put them in jeopardy."

Bethany looked down.

"Please, until I know my boys are safe, this has to be between us."

Bethany wiped the last of her tears away. "You have no idea how hurt he's been by his family. I won't allow him to be hurt anymore!"

"Then give me some time to make sure he isn't." He held her at arm's length. "I promise, when the time is right, I'll tell Scott he's my son. I want him to know more than anything in this world! When I saw him in the school, I just couldn't believe it, after all these years." His voice cracked. "Scott is my son, Bethany, but for now, only you can know that."

"I understand, but he's going to Europe, Grant. Don't you think he deserves to know before then—to know he has a family?"

Grant released her. "Just a little more time, that's all I ask." He smiled. "When are you going to be honest with him?"

Bethany was silent for a moment. "I don't know what you mean," she said innocently.

"You're in love with my son."

Bethany was silent a moment longer. "I've yet to really understand love, Grant. But, if it's this fear and emptiness I feel just thinking of a life without him, then I guess I am in love with him."

David Carson, holding a large smirk, quickly moved from the sheriff's window as Bethany and Grant finished their conversation. He whistled happily as he moved toward the bank. His father, Derek Carson, finished writing in the ledger and looked at his son. "Where have you been? I've been waiting half the afternoon for you to get here so I can make my errands!"

David stepped back in fear as Derek move from behind the counter. "Do you think it's easy being mother and father?" Derek grabbed his arm and shook him. "I count on you to be here on time."

"Sorry, Father." He took a step back when his father finally let him go.

Derek grabbed his jacket. "Your mother deserted you, not me!" He looked at his son and pointed a finger. "You can at least express some appreciation!" Derek walked toward the door. "I expect you to do some cleaning around here while I'm gone. I'm tired of your laziness!"

David nodded. "Yes, sir," he said, taking a step back as his father moved toward the door.

Derek threw the door open. "You look after things or else, young man."

"Yes, sir," David glared at his father as he left the bank. "You foolish old man," David said aloud. "One day I'll make you sorry you pushed me around!"

David sat at his father's desk and seemed to stare at the phone for a long time. He tapped his fingers on the desk and placed a hand under his chin, thinking about what he just over heard, and wondering how it may come of great use to him. David stared at the receiver for a long time before finally lifting it.

He took a deep breath. "I'll be better than you one day!" His cheeks vibrated. "I'm tired of being pushed around, its time you all seen who you're dealing with!"

He waited as it rang twice, "Yes, get me Bradley Jenkins in London, England, please." David smiled in spite of himself. "Yes, operator, I'll hold."

CHAPTER 32

Bethany was startled by the patter of feet running over the floor of the schoolhouse. "Howdy, Bethany," Jacob hollered from the door.

Bethany smiled at Scott as he followed close behind her brothers. "What are you boys up to?"

Joshua placed his hands on her desk and jumped up and down. "Scott's taking us for ice cream!" he said excitedly.

She looked at Scott with a smile. "Ice cream, what's the special occasion!"

Scott planted himself on Bethany's desk and smiled as Irene moved toward them from the book shelf in the far corner.

"Your mum needed," he paused, looked at the boys and laughed, "some peace and quiet. I offered to get them out of the house for a while." He squeezed her hand. "I thought maybe we could persuade you to join us."

She gave Scott a long smile, and then looked at her rambunctious brothers before questioning Irene with her eyes.

"Oh, go on ahead. I can finish up here," Irene insisted.

Bethany stood happily. "Are you sure?"

"Absolutely, go on now." Irene smiled. "Have a good time."

Scott helped Bethany with her jacket. "Would you like us to bring you back a dish of ice cream or something?"

Irene shook her head, "Thank you, Scott, no. Bethany, I will just see you in the morning."

Bethany took Scott's hand. "Have a good evening, Irene."

When they arrived at the Henderson store, there were a few people shopping, but not as many as Bethany would have thought with Christmas coming in only a week. They each took a stool as Willie Henderson came in behind the ice cream counter.

"What can I get you folks?" Willie asked, wiping his hands and placing the towel on the far side of the counter.

Scott looked at the boys. "How about a round of chocolate malts for the lot?" Scott looked at Bethany, and she nodded in agreement.

Willie began preparing their malts and Scott looked at Bethany. "So, how's your morning?"

She smiled looking at the counter. "It's been very quiet. We're going to finish up a few things tomorrow and then I have the rest of the time to spend with you." She looked at him and he was smiling. She returned his fleeting look as Willie placed the malts on the counter and Scott handed him some money.

"What would you like to do?" she asked.

"It doesn't matter. I just want to spend time with you."

Bethany reached over the counter and took his hand.

He lifted her hand to his lips and kissed it. "I'm going to miss you, Beth."

Bethany looked at her malt. "New rule, we don't waste a second of time we have together discussing you leaving."

She leaned into his touch.

Scott picked up a napkin and wiped Joshua's ice cream-covered face.

"You'd make a great father, do you know that?" she whispered.

Scott smiled. "Someday, I hope. I'd really like that, actually. I wasn't kidding when I said I wanted twelve children. Trick is to find someone who wants them as well, aye then?"

Bethany squeezed his hand. "I'm sure there is someone out there crazy enough to give you anything you ever wanted."

They held each other's eyes a moment and then Scott looked at the boys. "How are the malts, mates?"

Joshua sucked up what was left of his drink right to the bottom, and the sound echoed throughout the building. Scott's eyes drifted back to Bethany and she was watching him.

"What are you thinking?" He asked.

Bethany paused a moment. "I'm going to miss you too." Her voice cracked.

He put his head against hers and sighed.

CHAPTER 33

Katherine hurried downstairs as Scott and Bethany came in. Taylor was calling out in pain. Bethany looked the direction of her sister's voice.

"Mama, what is it?" Bethany asked in a panic.

Katherine took her hand and looked at Scott, then to her young boys, "Scott, how would you like to take the children to see their cousins at Uncle Robert's while Bethany stays here to help me with a few things? Jeffrey took Sara Sue and Katie Anne over there a few moments ago."

Scott heard Taylor calling out from upstairs again. "Sure, I'd be glad to." He looked at the boys. "Why don't you two head out to the truck." He waited until the boys were outside. "Katherine, anything I can do?"

"I reckon Taylor is the one with the job to do."

"Where's Papa?" Bethany asked.

"He's with your Uncle Danny, they had a sighting of those wild dogs at the Pritchard farm. I guess Pritchard took down a few of them."

"Scott, Bethany and I will be here, if you could just keep track of the children?"

Scott swallowed nervously. "I'll take good care of them." He looked at Bethany. "Call over there if you need anything."

Bethany nodded, heading up the stairs behind her mama.

"Bethany?"

She stopped, looking back at him.

He paused. "I'm here if you need me."

She smiled lovingly. "We'll be fine. Someone will let you know when the baby comes."

They stared at each other for a long moment before he nodded and headed toward the door. Bethany watched lovingly as he slowly disappeared outside.

The next few hours went by slowly, until Taylor found herself in active labor. Then, Whitney Mary Katherine Langley was born. Joseph sent word to Robert and an hour later Scott and Jeffrey brought the kids home. They were able to see the baby for a few minutes and then Katherine sent the children to bed. Scott, standing back from Taylor, who was already up and resting in the living-room, watched from afar as the rest of the family made a fuss over the baby.

Taylor looked over Jeffrey's shoulder at Scott. "Scott, would you like to hold her?"

Scott gave her the look of terror and quickly shook his head. "I've never been around a baby before in my life," he said quickly.

Bethany giggled. "There's always a first time." She took Whitney from Taylor and walked her over to Scott. He stared at the baby in bewilderment.

"Hold out your arms," she directed him, and then laughed. "It's a baby, not a bag of flour." He smiled and adjusted his arms out further. "Now, just make sure you support her head." Bethany gently laid the baby in Scott's arms and sat next to him. She watched his face, how gentle he was. Bethany kissed Whitney softly on the head. The baby had Taylor's small nose and blue eyes, but Bethany felt her chubby cheeks came from Patrick.

"She's so small," Scott gasped.

Bethany smiled. "Trust me; it's much better that way." Scott looked up at her and they laughed. Bethany took Whitney's fingers in hers. "Isn't that right, Whitney Mary Katherine Langley?"

The baby made a cooing noise and Scott looked at Bethany quickly. "Beth, what is she doing, love?"

Bethany laughed. "I think she just initiated you, Scott Jenkins." She stood. "I think you might want me to take over from here." She gently took Whitney in her arms. "Let's go find you a clean diaper, little girl."

Scott looked up from the paper as Bethany came down the stairs and she sat on the couch next to him.

"Got mama and baby all tucked in," she said exhaustedly.

Scott placed the paper on the coffee table, "You look wiped out." She glanced at him and he smiled. "Beautiful, but tired."

She laughed. "I'm very tired." She stood. "I think I'm going to turn in. Maybe you should too, you have a big day tomorrow. Good night, Scott." He said nothing, but stared at her. "Are you all right?"

"I was just thinking how awful it would be to become a father and be so far away. It isn't fair to Whitney or Patrick."

"Hopefully Patrick will be home soon." Bethany could see in his eyes he had something else on his mind. "What is it, Scott? Please tell me."

Scott looked at the floor. "I guess I've just been thinking about my own father; if he ever thought about me or even knew about me."

Bethany gently took his hand. "I can almost promise you he does."

Scott looked at her. "How can you be sure?"

She gave him an understanding smile. "You're a great and wonderful man, Scott Jenkins, and I can only imagine your father is just like you."

"I wouldn't have just left my son, no matter what. One day, when I'm a father, I'm going to be the best ever. I'll be there for my son."

"Or sons," Bethany giggled. "Twelve children, remember?"

Scott's laughter made her smile. "What woman in her right mind would give me all the children I wish for?"

Bethany touched his face. "A woman who is desperately in love with you, Scott," she said, and gazed into his eyes. She moved her lips to his, holding them there a moment, she ran her palm over his lips. "You should get some sleep, tomorrow is a big day for you."

Scott grabbed her hand and quickly stood as well. "Beth?"

She turned to him.

Scott took a step toward her, holding her hand lovingly. "I've learned a lot about myself being here, and it's opened my eyes to a lot I missed out on—a home and a family."

Bethany touched his face.

"I know what kind of a husband and a father I would want to be." He got very sad. "But I also know that this war has a way of changing a man."

Bethany shook her head. "No, Scott, not you. We've helped each other through a lot the last few weeks. And I'll be here to help you when you get back."

"Do you promise?"

His words broke her heart. "I promise, Scott Jenkins." She stared into his sad eyes. "You're a part of this family now—a part of my family. You don't ever get to be just Scott Jenkins again." She watched as his eyes began to tear and he turned away. Bethany ran her palm over her cheek feeling her own tears. "It's not going to be easy for me when the day comes I have to watch you leave." She walked toward him and stopped. "I've never been very good at saying goodbye."

He turned to her, noticing the tears in her voice.

"There were times I regretted that you ever came here, because I didn't want to feel this way." Scott started to say something but she placed her fingers on his lips. "I would have missed a lot if you hadn't come here, and the last few days I've thanked God for you over and over again." She ran her palm over his face, "You've taught me a lot about myself too."

He moved closer. "Like what?"

She stared at his lips, running her palm over them. "What it means to love." She stared deep into his eyes. "To trust, and to need someone." She let her arm fall to her side and gave him a sad smile. "You're an important part of who I've become, just don't go disappearing on me, okay?" She kissed him tenderly on the side of the mouth, holding her lips there for a moment.

He watched as she quietly moved up the stairs.

"I won't, Beth," he whispered.

CHAPTER 34

Scott was baptized the next morning in the presence of the entire congregation. He, along with three other members, stood by the back door as one by one the congregation shook their hands in congratulations. On several occasions, Scott had been asked if he felt any different. Although he would state that he had not, he knew deep in his heart that something had changed within him.

As Bethany approached, beautiful as ever and beaming with pride, Scott thought perhaps the change in him went a little deeper than merely a baptism. Bethany had opened something up for him that no one ever could. And, as Bethany hugged him and told him how proud she was, Scott's only thought was she was home to him. His whole life, no one ever made him feel like he belonged. How he wished the day would stay new forever.

Bethany released him, still holding him at arm's length. "Mama is making a special celebration dinner in your honor," she said, happily kissing him on the cheek.

For an instant, they were alone, captivated by the mere presence of each other. Her heart pounded, and all she wished at that moment was that they were alone so she could speak freely everything she had been feeling the last week. She smiled when he touched her face in response to her silence and turned her attention for a moment to those still waiting in line to extend their joy to him.

Bethany, wearing a large smile, nodded her head and looked back at Scott. "I'll be outside when you're ready." She squeezed his hand. "You can walk me home, Scott Jenkins." She laughed, turning to look back at him before exiting the door.

Scott shook a member of the congregation's hand, his eyes still fixed on Bethany. Scott gave her a huge smile.

Although slightly chilly, the sun was shining as Scott moved outside with the others. He spotted Bethany with her father and was moving her direction when Martha took his hand.

"Scotland, I just wanted to tell you how happy I was for you today." Before he could say anything, Martha grabbed him by the lips. Scott didn't kiss her back, but gently pushed her away.

"Martha, please," Scott said agitatedly.

"What is it with you? I have never had someone reject me as much as you." She almost seemed hurt.

Scott took her hand. "Martha, you're very beautiful and deserve so much, any other place and any other time it may be right."

"But you're in love with Bethany," she said for him.

Scott slowly released her hand. "Yes, and I'm working very hard to gain her trust." Scott took a deep breath. "You and Carson hurt her very badly." Scott shook his head. "I don't understand, Martha. It's Christmas; it should be a season of love and kindness."

She said nothing.

Scott looked down. "I'll be leaving the day after tomorrow and it's going to be very difficult. I consider you a friend, and you're right, I do love Beth very much. More than I have ever loved anyone my entire life. I have no idea what's going to happen in the future with this war. I just know when I leave I don't want to think she's being bullied and tormented by you and Carson."

Martha looked down shamefully.

"I'm asking you to put the past aside. I think you and Beth could be good friends if you would only try."

Martha was very still for a long moment and then slowly nodded her head, "You're a good man, Scott Jenkins. Bethany's very lucky."

"Can you look out for her, please?" Scott was almost desperate.

Martha smiled. "Of course." She took his hands. "I think you're right, it's time we put our childish troubles behind us. I only hope that one day I can find a man to love me as much as you seem to love her." She squeezed his hands. "You go fight this war and leave Dobson's Crossroads to me."

Scott gave her a hug and Bethany was standing behind Martha. He had no idea how long she was there, but by the look on her face, she overheard plenty.

She smiled lovingly. "Scotty, are you ready to go?"

Scott nodded and looked back at Martha. "You'll come by and see me off at the bus, won't you?"

Martha nodded and looked at Bethany. "Would you mind?" she asked sincerely.

Bethany shook her head. "Of course not."

"You take care of yourself, Scott Jenkins." She kissed him on the cheek and headed toward her car.

Scott held his hand out to Bethany, and with a huge smile, she took it.

"Martha's right," Bethany said as they began up the street. "I am very lucky."

"Yes, I do believe you are." Scott smiled at her.

She laughed and Scott kissed her on the head.

CHAPTER 35

Scott stood on the porch, observing Bethany as she strolled up the drive toward the street. He raced to the steps and skipped them, jumping in midair and landing on his feet in the dirt drive. Within seconds, he caught up to her. Bethany smiled and looked at him. "I thought everyone was still sleeping."

Scott looked up ahead at the long distance that remained before reaching the road. "You've been very quiet since your trip to the library with Taylor, love. Did something happen?"

She shrugged. "I guess reality's just set in."

Scott gently took her hand and stopped her. "Before you know it, the war will be over and you'll be sick of having me around."

"I'll never be sick of you, never." They began up the drive. "I didn't sleep much because it finally hit me last night that you're really leaving in the morning." She felt the tears develop, but refused to let them show.

He forced her to look at him. "I made a promise to you and I intend to keep it."

She covered his hand with hers. "It's not only that, Scott." She grasped his hand and held it as they once again continued up the drive. "It seems everywhere I go there's a bad memory I wish I could just forget. Dobson's Crossroads is my home. I would never want to be anywhere else." She glanced up at him, and he was listening very attentively. "But how do you forget?"

He noticed her momentary glare at the shambles of the tree house to her left. Scott stopped her by the large oak tree, and she looked up at him questionably. "You don't forget, love. You replace bad memories with good ones." He looked over her shoulder to the tree house. "One of those memories is right here, isn't it?"

She looked from him back to the tree house. "It's just a stupid tree house withering away. Jeffrey and I built it when I was a little girl."

Scott gave her a sad smile as she looked back at him. "So it holds good memories?" His eyes traced hers and waited.

She grinned. "A little of both, I guess."

"Carson kissed you in the tree house, didn't he?" he said sheepishly. She just looked at him silently. Scott tugged on her arm. "Come on, shall we go up, then." Scott released her hand and started toward the oak tree.

"Are you crazy?" She laughed. "That thing can barely hold itself up much less the weight of the two of us."

He looked down at her as he began climbing the ladder. "Come on, Bethany Davies, live dangerously and come make a memory with me."

Her eyes moved up the ladder with him. She placed her hands on her hips and then laughed. *Heaven, help me*, she said to herself, giggling. She began climbing the ladder herself. When she got to the top and into the tree house, Scott was holding onto a thick branch above his head, trying to keep the whole thing steady. Then, her weight added stress to the base, which sent it swaying back and forth. Scott gripped the large branch tighter with an attempt to steady the structure. They laughed, and she held onto him for support.

Sitting on their knees, they looked around. The walls were slumped over, and branches had started growing through the base of rubble. "Well, that was a little scary," he said making a face.

She threw her head in the air and laughed hysterically. "Scott Jenkins, you're crazy." He smiled lovingly at her. She took a deep breath and gazed into his eyes. "So, tell me again why we risked our lives coming up here?"

Still holding onto the thick branch above his head, he reached out and touched her face. "Like I said, so we can replace that bad memory with a better one," he whispered.

She looked deep into his eyes. "What did you have in mind?"

Scott swallowed nervously. "I thought we could replace his kiss with mine." Bethany's lips curled, and he took a deep breath. "Then maybe when you walk by, you can think of me and not him."

She tipped her head, and her eyes got wet. "Scott," she gasped.

His voice cracked. "I don't want to be forgotten, Beth. So, perhaps this could be a favor to me."

His words broke her heart. "I could never forget you, Scott, not ever! Besides, you told me you'd come back. You didn't lie to me, did you?"

"I would never lie to you."

Scott took Bethany off guard and grabbed her lips deep into his, tender and passionate. Bethany's lips responded in hunger as she closed her eyes, enjoying him immensely. Scott gently moved his tongue over the inside of her mouth and Bethany pulled him closer, never knowing such pleasure. She moaned softly, placing a palm on the side of his head. Then, when their kiss slowed, she took his lips deeper.

When the base began to wobble uncontrollably, he grabbed her and pulled her into him, hanging on for dear life to the branch as half the base hit the ground below. Bethany watched in utter terror as the remnants shattered into pieces at the bottom of the tree trunk. She looked surprisingly at Scott and both suddenly laughed uncontrollably.

Scott gave her a big smile. "Maybe we should go down before we kill ourselves."

She touched his face lovingly. "Thank you, Scott Jenkins," she said, giving him another quick kiss.

"Did I crash and burn?"

Bethany laughed and leaned her forehead against his, "It was a very good memory."

He smiled proudly. "Well, all right then." He held the branch tighter, "Why don't you start down before this whole thing goes?" Scott held Bethany's hand, trying to keep her steady while grasping onto the branch over his head. When she reached the ladder and began climbing down, Scott released the branch and moved toward the ladder himself.

The force was just too much, and in an instant the whole base gave way, sending Scott passing Bethany, who was already halfway down the ladder. He landed with a hard thump at the ground below.

"Scott!" she called and moved briskly down the remaining steps, releasing her grip at the bottom. He was lying on his back, slowly sitting up as she fell to her knees next to him. She gasped, "Are you all right?"

"Ouch." He laughed, half out of breath. He had a gash on his forehead where the railing hit him coming down. "I think I've been rendered paralyzed." He attempted a moment of humor.

She scanned him. "Is anything broken? Can you move?" She panicked. "That was a stupid idea...I knew it wasn't safe!"

He smiled and touched her face. "Well, we wanted a memory." He laughed and pulled her to him, kissing her deeply.

"You're lucky you didn't break your neck!" Katherine scolded as she cleaned Scott's forehead. "Whatever provoked you two to go up in that thing? It's been falling apart for years. Bethany, you should have known better!" Bethany stood next to her mama, watching as Katherine finished up with Scott's bandaging. She looked at her daughter. "Well?"

Bethany smiled and looked down.

"We were making a memory," Scott said, smiling at Bethany.

"I sure hope it was worth it!" she scolded. "Bethany, hand me the scissors, please."

Bethany took the scissors off the table and handed it to her. "It was, Mama." Bethany smiled at Scott. "I think the best memory ever."

Scott and Bethany shared a loving stare. She had always wondered why, when her parents were apart, they would find it difficult to function. She had learned a lot from Scott in the time since he arrived. For the first time, Bethany knew what love really was…it was Scott Jenkins.

CHAPTER 36

The bus pulled up in front of the bed-and-breakfast as the long faces gathered. Scott said his goodbyes to Taylor and the children before they headed to town. Now, Katherine, Joseph, Jeffrey, Kristina, and Bethany waited with Scott as the bus prepared to load. Scott noticed Martha pull up and he met her at the car.

Martha gave him a sad smile. "I do so love a man in uniform."

Scott gave her a hug. "I'm glad you made it."

She nodded her head and held him at arm's length. "You taught me a lot, Scotland Jenkins. I'll never forget you."

Scott gave her another hug. "I hope not." He kissed her on the side of the head. "Why don't you join us?"

She looked at all the eyes watching her. "Are you sure they won't mind?"

Scott shook his head. "Not at all." He took her hand and led her to the group.

"Hello, Martha." Everyone seemed surprised at Bethany's cordial greeting. Martha sent her a friendly smile.

"All aboard," The bus driver called.

Scott looked from the bus driver to all the faces. "I'll write as much as I can. I wanted to thank you all for allowing me to be a part of your family." He looked at Joseph and Katherine. "It's meant a lot to me to be here these past weeks." He gave Katherine a hug.

Katherine held him tightly. "You come home as often as you can, do you hear me?" she said sternly.

"I will, Katherine."

Jeffrey gave him a hug. "I can't believe they're separating the team." He hit Scott on the back and held him at arm's length. "Who's going to keep you out of trouble?"

"Well, at least I won't get caught with my pants down again, mate."

Jeffrey laughed and looked around at the questionable faces, "I'll share that story with you all later."

Scott nodded at Jeffrey. "You stay out of this war as long as you can. I won't be there to cover your back."

Jeffrey squeezed his friend tightly.

Scott hugged Kristina and gave her a quick kiss on the cheek. Then he grasped Joseph's hand. "I'll see you soon, sir. Maybe you can write me how Jeremiah's doing?"

Joseph nodded. "Pa said you dropped by this morning to see him. He'll be missing you—we all will."

Scott looked by the front of the bus as Grant move toward him. "Grant, whatever it is, I didn't do it. I promise."

Grant chuckled. "This is a social call, Scott." Grant held out his hand. "I'll be sending some letters your way, I hope you don't mind?"

Scott shook his hand. "Not at all, I would like that. I can't guarantee I'll receive them though. It can be hard for mail to catch up to me."

"When you get back this way, I'd like you to come by, maybe meet my son, Eric. I think the two of you would have a lot to talk about." Grant glanced at Bethany who was waiting alone closer to the bus, and then back to Scott. "In fact, I think you and I will have a lot to discuss, as well." Grant gave Scott a hug, taking the soldier off guard, "You take care of yourself, son."

"I will, Grant. Take care of Bethany for me?"

Grant squeezed his shoulders. "Best care ever."

Scott looked from Grant to Bethany, who was fighting her tears with all the strength she could muster. Scott placed his bag over his shoulder and walked to her. As he reached her, Bethany placed her palm on his cheek.

"You be safe. Don't go taking a lot of chances, you promise?"

Scott nodded and put his palm over hers. "I promise."

She held up a brown paper bag. "I used some of my ration coupons to get you a few things," she said over her tears, trying to be brave. "It'll be hard to get coffee and I know how grumpy you can get without it."

Scott gave her a sad smile as she began to cry.

"I also got you a sweater, I was going to give it to you for Christmas—" She wept like a baby and Scott took her in his arms. "I'm sorry. I promised myself I wouldn't do this."

Scott held her tightly. "Time is going to fly by very fast, you won't even have time to miss me."

She shook her head in his shoulder. "Not true, I miss you already!"

Scott forced her to look at him. "You make sure you let me know the second you find out about that teaching exam. When I get back, we'll go out and celebrate. Only I think we'll stay away from the Farmer's Café." Scott didn't get the laugh from Bethany he had hoped.

She only nodded, still weeping uncontrollably.

"And I want updated pictures of Whitney so I can see how fast she's growing," He fought back his own tears.

"I will," she cried. "I promise."

Scott drew her into his arms again. "I want a picture of you too," he gasped, "So all my mates will see I have the best looking girl in North Carolina."

Bethany pushed him away, placing a palm on his cheek, she reached into her pocket. He laughed happily as she handed him a picture of herself. Scott held up the picture of Bethany, as beautiful as ever, in the red dress she wore at the dance.

"Taylor took it for me. I'll be here waiting when you get back, because I'm in love with you, Scott, desperately. I think I have been since the second you almost knocked me down the stairs."

"Then I guess I shouldn't feel too guilty about doing it on purpose to gain your attention." Scott threw his head in the air and laughed, managing to get a smile from her.

She slapped him on the shoulder and his laugh amplified.

"Just one of many stories we can tell to our children, Beth." He touched her face, "That is, if you've had, as you put it, a chance to think long and hard about giving me children?"

Bethany responded by placing her arms around his neck and pulling his lips deeply into hers. He took her far away to a place all their own, a safe haven of love and security that she could only find with him. There was no loneliness where he took her, but an everlasting love that she was finally willing to accept from him with open arms. She searched for his tongue, and when he offered it, Bethany moaned under their breath. When the kiss slowly melted away, her eyes remained closed in a last attempt to preserve every second they had left. Scott was smiling at her when she finally opened her eyes. Her heart began to pound. Panic-stricken, she knew in only seconds he would be leaving her, and they would both be meeting a world of uncertainty and loneliness until he returned to her.

He placed his arms tightly around her waist. "I'm going over there and earn my right to come home to you, because I am completely in love with you too, Bethany Davies."

She placed her hands on his cheeks, "Say it again." She pleaded, desperately searching his eyes for truth.

"I'm crazy in love with you, and one day I'm going to come back and I'm never leaving you again."

"Promise me!" She pleaded. "Promise you'll come back to me."

Scott pulled her tighter and looked at her sternly. "I promise you!"

She closed her eyes tightly, locking his words deep into the heart of her. She knew, without those words on reserve for the hard times to come, she would never make it through a day without him.

"Lieutenant, we really must get going," the bus driver announced.

Scott threw his bag over his shoulder, and Bethany's eyes called to him in desperation.

"I love you, Beth," he said suddenly and kissed her deeply. He touched her face one last time, and jumped into the bus. Bethany could see him through the back window. He had slammed himself into the rear seat of the bus and then proceeded to punch the back of the seat in front of him in anger.

Bethany wrapped her arms around herself, watching as the bus door closed and the engine started. She became hysterical as the bus slowly moved forward and away from her. Her mama attempted to console her as a feeling of helplessness came over her, a helplessness she had never felt before.

Scott placed a palm on the back window as the bus moved forward slowly. "I love you," she saw Scott mouth the words to her, and she waved back in reply.

Bethany waited until the bus was out of sight. Then, she released her mama's hand and began to move up the street.

"Bethany, do you want some company?" Kristina yelled toward her.

Bethany waved to Kristina in reply, didn't look back, but left the others behind as she moved toward the solace of Dobson's Pond. There, she spent hours alone in her own thoughts, making it home just prior to dark.

When she entered the house, the family was loafing about the living room. It went silent when she shut the front door behind her. Bethany was lost. Her eyes focused on the stairway, and without a word, the family watched as she retired to her room alone.

CHAPTER 37

The New Year came and went, yet Bethany heard nothing from Scott. She had found herself glued to every radio broadcast in hopes of hearing some news she was starving for. But soon listening seemed too hard to endure.

The day before Valentines, Patrick came up the road returning from the war. He had taken scrap metal in the right leg and, although his wound would heal in time, his limp was permanent. Bethany watched Patrick weep holding his baby for the first time and Taylor was so extremely happy to finally have her family together. Of course, Bethany was happy for her older sister, but it made her heart long for Scott that much more.

Then news came that Friday that she had, in fact, passed her teaching exam. As she held the confirmation letter in her hand and realized that she was finally a teacher, Bethany found it didn't seem as important anymore, not without Scott there to share it with her. When she arrived home, she merely handed her mama the confirmation letter and went upstairs alone.

On June 6, 1944, a special broadcast was repeated over the radio all morning. The American and Allied forces were finally invading the beaches of Normandy, France. Bethany knew Scott was there somewhere, she felt it in her heart. All her uncles gathered around the radio, and her mama kept the coffee coming. Taylor, knowing what Bethany was feeling, stayed at her sister's side. Even Martha had arrived to support Bethany, for since Scott's departure the two had developed a special friendship and bond.

"In an extreme turn of events, the German army has fled Rome and been pushed back. The 101st Airborne Division, along with hundreds of battalions, is en route as we speak to cut off the German empire. A spokesman for Eisenhower has stated that this could very well become the bloodiest standoff since the beginning of the war."

The radio announcer was describing the destruction and loss of the invasion as bodies, American as well as German, spread over the beaches and were washed away into the ocean. Bethany quickly stood, not able to hear any more. It was all so overwhelming for her. Going into the kitchen, she threw her palms on the counter and bowed her head. Jeffrey placed his head against her back as they prayed together. With her eyes still closed, head still bowed, she reached behind her and squeezed Jeffrey's hand tightly.

The announcer said that nearly fifty thousand soldiers stormed the beaches at Utah and Omaha with an attempt to stop the enemy in its tracks. Bethany began to cry. Of those fifty thousand, Bethany's heart intensely ached and longed for one.

Bethany still hadn't heard anything from Scott as D-Day came and went. Then June 17 was right around the corner, and Bethany wished she could just cancel her birthday. The kitchen was filled with the aroma of freshly baked spice and applesauce cake, which was Bethany's favorite. She had hidden in her room for most of the Saturday morning but could hear the gathering of people downstairs as Sara Sue beat on her door. Sara Sue waited, but Bethany never responded.

Slamming her fist on the door again, the child screamed with all her might. "Mama says you need to come down for your birthday!"

Bethany frowned and placed her book on the nightstand. She threw her feet over the corner of the bedside and moved to the window. There were a lot of cars parked out front, and she could see Grant's vehicle coming around the corner and up the drive.

She sighed and opened the door with all the chatter drifting up the stairway. It sounded like the entire town was over, but the last thing she felt like doing was celebrating.

When she made it downstairs, everyone began to cheer and wish her a happy birthday all at once. Her uncles and aunts were all there, along with cousins and friends, as well as her Grand.

Bethany attempted to smile with all the pats and hugs, but noticed when her mama opened the door for Grant he wasn't alone. He was wearing his uniform—an obvious sign that it wasn't a social call. Reverend Michaels was with him as they both came in the door. Grant leaned into Katherine and whispered something into her ear. Then he looked at Bethany sorrowfully. Grant's eyes were sad, almost lost.

Bethany couldn't hold the tears back as she slowly shook her head in denial.

When Grant began to approach, Bethany's heart stopped. She grabbed the railing and slowly sat herself down on the bottom step of the stairway, her legs giving way. With eyes blurred and pointed downward, Bethany shook her head in utter shock of what she knew was about to happen. For the last week, Bethany felt something was dreadfully wrong, but in her desire for Scott to be okay, she forced the fears aside at an attempt to grasp some form of hope.

"Bethany?" Grant said as he approached her.

Bethany shook her head hysterically, knowing what he had to say wasn't something she wanted to hear. Grant sat beside her and took off his hat, holding it tightly between his fingers. Bethany could hear him, how he took several breaths to keep from breaking down himself. She fought the tears but when the reverend began to speak, her heart broke.

"We received a telegram," Reverend Michaels said gently as the entire room went silent. "There's no easy way to say this. Scott Jenkins was reported missing in action just following the Normandy invasion."

Jeffrey quickly knelt beside Bethany, but she wouldn't accept his comfort as she pushed him away and stood.

Jeffrey made another attempt only to be pushed away again.

"No!" she screamed, "Don't!" She raced upstairs and the house vibrated with the slam of her bedroom door.

Jeffrey moved into his mama's arms for comfort; weeping for his best friend.

"Go away and leave me alone!" Bethany screamed, but the knock on the door persisted. "I said go away!" She screeched with all her might and buried her face in her pillow.

Martha opened the door and peeked around the corner. "Surely, you don't mean me?" Martha had been crying herself. She shut the door behind her and sat next to Bethany on the bed. "I don't care what they say, Scott is coming home," she said demandingly.

Bethany covered her mouth, but couldn't stop the tears that consumed her. Martha held her tightly as they cried together.

Taylor rocked little Whitney coming down the stairs, "I don't know what to think about her today. She's being awful fussy this morning."

Katherine held out her arms. "Let grandma try it on for size," she offered as Taylor placed the baby in her arms and began rocking her granddaughter.

Katherine sent her attention to Bethany who was sitting quietly at the fireplace. "Bethany, would you like to join us?"

Bethany stared into the fire. "I'm fine, Mama," she whispered.

Taylor's eyes were drawn to the front door. "I wonder who that could be so early." Katherine continued to rock Whitney while Taylor moved to the front door. A stranger in coveralls and a baseball cap was holding tightly to a clip board.

The man scratched his chin. "Good morning. Are you Bethany Davies?" The man appeared to be in his early fifties.

Taylor sent him a curious look. "Just a minute please." She turned to her sister. "Bethany, it's for you."

Taylor opened the door wider for Bethany and their mama joined them, still rocking the baby.

"I'm Bethany Davies, can I help you?"

"Good morning, Ms. Davies, I had some questions for you and was wondering if you had a minute to come out to the property and have a look?"

Bethany was confused.

"I'm sorry," the man said, clunking his own head with his clipboard and then held out his hand. "My name is Gary Powell, with Powell Construction. I've been hired by Scott Jenkins to do the construction at Jenkins Lane. I was told if there were any issues I should direct them to you personally."

Bethany shook her head. "Jenkins Lane? I'm sorry, I am very confused."

"Yes, um…" He looked at his clipboard, "Let's see, yep—that's what it says all right. Previous owner, Frank Madison, had it listed as Dobson's Pond and Breezeway." Powell held his clip board out to Bethany. "Scott Jenkins purchased the land and left strict instructions to see you for all details pertaining to construction."

Bethany's mouth dropped as she looked at Scott's signature on the work order.

Katherine laughed happily. "Well, I'll be!"

Powell looked a little confused himself. "You are Bethany–Bethany Davies?"

Bethany smiled as Taylor gave her a hug. "Yes, I am. Mr. Powell, what exactly are you building at Dobson's Pond?"

"A two-level log home, ma'am, rather large one, I might add." Powell sighed. "Jenkins has put us in quite a predicament. He said we are to do everything we can to keep the natural beauty of the area. We need to bring the equipment in and need your guidance on the best way to do that." He pointed at the clipboard. "See here, he said '*absolutely no unnecessary harm to surrounding wildlife.*'"

Bethany turned away to keep from crying. She handed the clipboard to Taylor and walked toward the fireplace alone.

Powell watched questionable when Bethany left him standing there. "Miss Davies, we really need to get this taken care of today."

Taylor handed the clipboard to Mr. Powell. "We'll meet you up there shortly, Mr. Powell."

Powell smiled and nodded, heading back down the steps toward his truck.

Bethany continued to shake her head and Taylor placed a hand on her sister's shoulder. Bethany turned to her sister, tears on her cheeks, and the sisters screeched loudly and began to jump up and down in place excitedly.

"I can't believe this!" Bethany screamed and began to fan her face with her hand. "I can't breathe. What did Scott go and do?" She shook her head in disbelief.

Taylor laughed. "I told you one day it would hit you like a ton of bricks."

Bethany's mouth dropped. "What are we doing—let's get going!" she screamed and grabbed Taylor's hand as she pulled her sister toward the door.

Bethany met with Mr. Powell and after an hour of conversation, it was decided they would begin construction immediately. Because much of the building materials were under rationing laws, the timber would have to come from the land surrounding Dobson's Pond. But Powell assured Bethany he would be very delicate to the property and only use the most seasoned timber to build her home.

Scott had left a letter with Gary Powell giving Bethany full power-of-attorney over all the bank accounts in his absence. Her Scotty had handled everything. The blueprints were astonishing. Bethany was in awe at Scott's impeccable taste. The house he was planning to build her was going to be the grandest in all Dobson's Crossroads.

For Bethany, it seemed life was restoring itself at Dobson's Pond. The wildflowers were blooming everywhere, birds sang, and the coolness of the river moved briskly. The day was warm and beautiful, peaceful. But she was missing him miserably.

After Powell and his gang left for the day, Bethany stayed behind to enjoy the place a while longer. She had hoped the new owners would cherish Dobson's Pond as much as she had. But Bethany never in her wildest dreams could have imagined this place would one day become her very own home, a place where she would live with Scott and raise a family of their own.

Bethany heard Martha approaching from the railing and sent her a smile.

"So, I guess the rumors in town are true." Martha smiled. "You really are the luckiest woman in the world."

Bethany beamed in spite of herself.

Martha seemed different to Bethany. Her hair wasn't flashy, but simply pinned up, very light color on her face, with clothes that lacked the usual trashiness. Martha actually looked very lady-like.

Martha laughed and looked down at her simple dress. "I figured dressing the other way didn't get me very far." She looked up at Bethany. "Maybe if I just tried to be me I could meet a great guy like you did."

Bethany sent her a big smile. "You're welcome to try, but they broke the mold when they made my Scotty."

Martha leaned against the railing with her. "Sure never pictured you living in the lap of luxury at Dobson's Pond."

Bethany looked out into the prairie where the contractor had put up red markers outlining the construction of her new house. "I was thinking how very overconfident it is for Scott Jenkins to just assume I would come up here and live with him."

The girls looked at each other and laughed hysterically.

Martha folded her arms and looked into the water, "You and Scott—the two of you belong together. I saw that from the start. Maybe that's why I was so jealous."

Bethany tipped her head at her friend. "You were jealous?"

Martha nodded and looked up at her. "Oh, for years." She sent her a sad smile, "My reputation was the only thing I had going for me, but that was all a lie too."

"I don't understand."

Martha took a deep breath. "Let's just say that when a guy gets rejected the last thing he wants is to admit it to his friends. It doesn't do very well for a girl's reputation. I've never been with a guy, Bethany, not even with David Carson. It all got stopped the minute you walked in the room."

Bethany looked at her in shock.

Martha took a deep breath. "He told me the two of you had broken up, otherwise I wouldn't have even been there." Martha looked at the ground. "Not an easy thing to be on the other end of a rumor. But it was all I had." She looked at Bethany. "At least I thought it was all I had. Scott helped me see a lot about myself, that it's okay to just be me. Perhaps just being me is more attractive than who I pretended to be." A tear sparkled in Martha's eyes. "I hope it's okay if I love him too?"

Bethany wiped her tears and put her arm around her friend. "I may have to set some ground rules, but I'm sure we can come to an agreement." The two dried their eyes and laughed. They started toward the new homestead. "Come on, I'll give you the million-dollar tour."

"So, when do we make wedding plans?" Martha asked excitedly.

"Well, I figure if he can be so bold as to assume I'd say yes, I have every right to start planning without him."

The two laughed.

"He'll be home soon," Martha said reassuringly. "Maybe he'll bring me a man in uniform like Jeffrey did for you."

Bethany laughed. "I'll suggest that in my next letter."

They stopped at the construction site and looked at the area that had been staked off. Bethany picked a beautiful spot overlooking the Roanoke River. Every morning when the sun comes up, it will shine right into their bedroom window. Bethany smiled—*theirs, what a great word*, she thought.

Bethany's heart ached for him.

"So, how big are you planning to make it?"

Bethany wiped a falling tear from cheek, "Big enough to give Scott the family he always wanted—all twelve of them." Bethany leaned her head against Martha's shoulder. "I need him here with me, Martha, so very badly."

Martha put her arm around her friend.

Bethany and Martha spent the early evening at the construction site catching up on lost conversations they deprived each other of growing up. Bethany shared her dreams and hopes of a life with Scott and Martha told stories of growing up as an only child, alone and sad. By the end of the evening, they made a promise to each other that no matter what, through good or bad, they would always be there to support each other.

As the days turned into weeks with no word of Scott's whereabouts, Bethany relied heavy on her friendship with Martha. Bethany was at the starting line of the hardest months she would ever have to face. But her family and friends were there to support her. On days when Bethany felt she just couldn't go on, Scott had left her something to cling to. Each day she would visit their dream home and regenerate her strength to continue another day without him.

Their home was nearly finished on the outside as Independence Day came and went. But, like her heart, the inside was empty and incomplete. It longed for that missing piece that would make everything finally fit together. Bethany didn't know where he was, but held tight to the faith that he was somewhere thinking of her. She believed in the love that had grown between the two of them. Bethany's mama was right, she had found her soul mate in Scott and the love he had so graciously offered her. God has his own perfect timing and one day Scott would come home to her and Bethany would be waiting.

AFTERWORD

Bradley Jenkins looked toward the voice that persistently called his name. The chauffeur held the back door of the town car open for Bradley, waiting patiently for the man to enter.

Jameson Flannery raced up the block. "I'm so glad I caught you!" he hollered up the street.

Bradley shook his head irritably. "What in blue blazes is it now?"

Flannery stopped when he reached Bradley and attempted to catch his breath. "It's Scotland. I found him. A few days ago, a young man called trying to locate you. His name is David Carson. He claims Scotland is in a town called Dobson's Crossroads, North Carolina." Flannery continued to fight for his breath.

Bradley tapped his hat with his cane. "I see. Just how sure are you this Carson fellow can be trusted?"

Flannery nodded. "I spoke with him personally." Flannery sighed. "That's not all. He said that he heard about you from the town sheriff...Grant Masterson."

"Masterson!"

Flannery nodded. "I'm afraid so."

Bradley clenched his teeth. "I see." Bradley took off his hat and tossed it in the back seat along with his cane. He glared at Flannery. "I want you on a plane heading to North Carolina by nightfall."

Flannery raised his brows. "What did you just say?"

Bradley moved himself into the backseat of the car. "I'm not partial to repeating myself. I want Scotland and that father of his taken care of. I have a meeting with Churchill in the morning. By the time I get back into town the end of the week, I expect an update."

Flannery leaned against the car door. "Just what kind of an update are you looking for?" Jameson Flannery asked sternly.

"What do you think, man? If Scotland has been in touch with his no-good father, you can bet he knows about his brother." Bradley glared at him. "You've been pussyfooting around this charade for weeks. It ends now!" The chauffer slammed the door shut, and Bradley rolled down the window. "Find my grandson and find my money!"

Flannery stood alone on the sidewalk as the car pulled away. The man looked down sadly. The harder he tried, the deeper he got. Bradley wasn't going to be happy until he ruined his grandson. Flannery suddenly felt sorry he ever heard the name Sir Bradley Jenkins. He lifted his hand to call upon the taxi.

The driver studied him in the rearview mirror as Flannery slammed the door shut behind him. "Where you headed to, mate?" the driver asked.

Flannery sighed and gazed out the door window. "Take me to the airport. I have a plane to catch. Unfinished business, you could say." Flannery looked out the window angrily. He was so desperately tired of the bureaucratic nonsense. It was time to finish it once and for all. "Step on it," Flannery insisted. "Let's get this over with!"